The Searcher

RAY DACOLIAS

The Searcher

Library of Congress Control Number: 2012911267

ISBN 978-0-9888177-3-9

Contents

Forsaken

The man with the wild black beard walked down the hot, white sidewalk, slowly lifting up his old brown boots and then tentatively setting them down again as though he were not certain he wanted to move at all; sometimes he would stop, simply staring at the faded concrete, as if he were making up his mind whether to continue. His matted black hair hung over his forehead as his fiery eyes stared with a power that seemed to bore a hole clear through the hard cement.

He paid no heed to passersby or to cars or honks or yells or curses, for he was enveloped in his own private cocoon; if people happened to stop next to him and speak to him, the filthy-skinned, heavily clothed man would normally not respond in any way, but if he chanced to look up and show himself to the citizens, they nearly always fell back, at first in revulsion at the ghastly smell that seemed to come with the raising of his head, and then because of their own bewilderment and dread, for what they beheld was a darksome face radiating a raw, scintillating energy that was pulled from the seldom-seen, seldom-visited country of boundless freedoms that was formed without restraint or order, motive or direction; when he looked upon his audience, his handsome visage twitched as if to burst, as if he sought to speak, as if to let loose the swirling storm inside his skull.

And then, just as it seemed that this tremendous powerhouse of violence was about to explode from him, his animated countenance would yield to a pitiful expression of sorrow; his thick black eyebrows would arch, his wet lips would pull down, his eyes, as black as pitch, would bleed agony; his entire body was wrapped in an aura of supplication, as if he sought rescue from his ills; and then he would lean toward the observer, bowed in want, hands out, eyes misty with piety, his hot, stench-filled breath blowing in his victim's face; and when the ritualistic transformation was consummated, his face and body would become flaccid again, his head was bent down again, and he would begin to shuffle along the road once more, a prisoner in his own blown mind.

He bothered no one as he trudged along at his methodical pace up and down the streets and dirt roads of this small town, but there were times when he visited the most public places, walking into the thickest of crowds, stopping in the midst of the most animated conversations, standing quietly and eerily still, seemingly oblivious to the anger he caused in these people.

No knowing police officer ever bothered him, for all of them understood this man's legacy; but if any officer deigned to touch him, dared to verbally harass him, to even respond positively to a citizen's complaint, it meant certain alienation for him on this small police force.

And any police officer who knew the history of this man, and gazed too long at him, secretly wept.

Memories

Rain often fell in heavy, pelting torrents in this small town, driving every sentient creature in Redwood to shelter, but such hard rain did not stop people from executing those chores necessary to sustain their lifestyle, for hard, cool rain was expected, and as Winter was approaching, it was expected often, and often came with flooding and snow and long days and frosty nights orphaned from the wondrously warm sun; but on this particular day it was a blinding rain, so intense in its volume and scope that the landscape was a blur; even outdoor workers had to pause and admire its fierce tenacity—yet one man was not deterred from this downpour. He kept to his ritual of moving along certain paths that eventually led to one area just inside the town borders; and once there, in a small clearing littered with fallen and rotting trees and dense bush and tall, verdant grass, he would come to a standstill outside its exact periphery, standing on the hard ground, peering intensely at a precise spot that was nestled between two dark brown, petrified logs. Sometimes, he stood as immobile as a rusted statue for hours in the boiling sun or long hours in the unrelenting rain, and even cruel hours in the snow; but then he would move methodically toward it, halting often, as if approaching the site gave him over to emotional and physical pain; inevitably, he gained the accursed place and stood in its haunting nucleus, staring at its woody borders, staring at its flattened center of crushed grass and dandelions; then he would kneel down, head held low against his chest, and his chest on his thighs, hands clasped, and he would pray, silently, passionately, mournfully.

"Forgive me for murdering my sweet baby girl, my sweet Maria," he would whisper in his thoughts, and he would sob, "and forgive me, O Great God in Heaven, for murdering my sweet, wonderful wife, my love, my life, my Anna." The utterance of her name would cause sharp spasms in his heart. "I repent before thee, and ask for divine punishment and for revelation."

This day, he lay supine, feeling the rhythmic beating of the heavy raindrops chattering away upon his naked face and brown leather coat and blue jeans and brown leather boots, and he wondered why God allowed him to live; he had not the courage to take his own miserable life, as he had designated God as his executioner. "Punish me, God, humiliate me, I beg you," he thought, seeing the beautiful images of his wife and daughter in his tortured mind, "make me suffer, heap every kind of pain upon my sinful mind and body." He felt himself drifting away, as if a heavy illness was coming, and he smiled. "Finally, death, my good and only friend, but no," he shouted inwardly, for he did not speak aloud, "death is too easy for me; that is my sinful flesh begging for mercy! No easy death for me."

The torrential rains evaporated, leaving a dim black sky that was soon swallowed by the golden rays of a yellow sun; warmth burrowed into the wet body of the man, infusing life into him. If he could not properly gain penitence here, he would gain his usual route into town and mingle amongst those people whom he supposed loathed his presence; he wanted to be trodden upon, spat upon, struck down like a leper, driven to the lowest social rung and humiliated, shamed, and scorned; but he would not, could not purposely place himself in harm's way, for he waited for God to take his worthless life.

Thus armed with such lowly ambitions, he arose and purchased once more his usual walk around the gallery of

Nature, refusing to admire the beauty of any living thing; he took no pleasure in any flower's beauty, nor any azure sky or pretty woman's face; truly, he averted his eyes from all such comely visions, for he sought to fill his life with vile ugliness and to leaden his heart with depression and sorrow and emotional rot; truly, whenever he beheld any natural phenomena of surpassing beauty, he would immediately thrust his face into the abyss of disease—whether it was falling to his knees and smelling animal waste or smothering his face in mud and muck—he would close his eyes to think of the horrors within and drive out these pleasurable images; but if all of these actions failed, he would simply beat upon his head until the gentle image faded.

"I am rotting inside," he would often think; "how dare I cherish beauty." He looked to his right and saw the small, yellow straw basket with food inside, and he felt a gush of glad tidings toward the woman who had brought this; but then he buried his face into the ground and flushed this golden memory into the brown slush.

He had followed the same path around town for the past five years, unmolested by the townsfolk; he always walked slowly, his head held down, his posture stooping, his submissive nature bowing before everyone. The townspeople called him El Buscar, "The Searcher," because he always seemed to be looking for something, but it was something they could not see. Everyone in town knew who he was, but no one spoke to him except for a few officers, and a few citizens who gave him food. Some of the old women would cross themselves as he passed near them.

No one expected anything from him except to one day find him finally and gratefully dead.

It Begins

Then there came a day like most other Winter days, one that was icy cold, where the black clouds had fastened a thick veil over the fading yellow sun. Most of the citizens here lived in homes set far apart from each other, on lots with many acres, with horses and chickens and goats, and some had ranches, while others had small farms.

Juanita Chavez drove into town with her four children on this early November morning, leaving her small farm to do errands in town; her eyes, like misty emeralds, narrowed as she turned around and let her feminine instinct analyze the data coming into her brain. "Hurry up, Carlos," she said to her eldest son; "help your little sister with her seatbelt."

Carlos grunted, as he was losing patience with the role of surrogate father to his younger siblings.

The children were layered in warm clothes as the Chavez family headed toward the bank, where Juanita paused at the entrance. "Carlos, get in line," she said, looking down the wet, gray sidewalk.

"Mom," he whined, and then he too gazed upon the shuffling image coming toward them.

"Go, mijo," she commanded, and after watching her children go inside, she turned her attention to the approaching figure; she felt a deep hurt billow up inside as she pulled her heavy black woolen coat around her slender body. She walked up to the man and spoke to him in a tone that was barely an emotion above weeping.

"Hello, Joaquin."

Joaquin looked up from his stooping posture to behold her beauteous face, and his countenance saddened; she began to touch him, but he pulled away swiftly, for it must be remembered that to him human touch was pleasure, a gift for good men and women, and he must deprive himself of it. "I must be punished for my sins," he thought, and he tried not to think of the woman in front of him, but he could not dissociate her image from the memories of his beloved wife and daughter. He let his head fall down against his damp brown coat as he stared at the wet concrete.

"If you need anything," Juanita said, but she felt as if she were talking to a comatose person. "Joaquin," she murmured, but her words died on her thin lips as she stared at his outward appearance. He was a colony of lost hopes.

She moved through the bank's glass doors, restraining tears.

Joaquin stood still, desperate to erase the memories of Juanita's husband from his mind; sometimes, he would stand like this for an hour as he contemplated his own bleak past, unable to hear anyone or anything, a human monolith fused to the surface below him.

Citizens walked into the bank, ignoring the town madman, the town imbecile, the town embarrassment; it must be known that he was merely a reminder to them of how delicate the human mind is, and from this unsettling thought they gained some secret solace that it was him who had gone mad and not them, and that for every lunatic they viewed, it somehow lessened the chance that they would join them. To them, he was on one side of the weighty balance that tilted and teetered from the growing weight of those who had breached the barrier of insanity, and the people on the other side decided that he alone, by his austere presence amongst them, ensured their sanity, and thus balanced the scales.

The Chavez family walked out of the open glass doors of the bank and headed across the street to the drugstore.

"Mom, I didn't see Jose," Carlos said; "didn't he start today?"

"I thought so, honey," Juanita replied, feeling her breath lift out of herself as she passed the unmoving man.

And then it happened.

Serendipity

Three men of ignoble purposes had crept into the bank, at least one of them unnoticed by Juanita; and if she had seen his arcane assemblage of fleshly features, she would have been chilled to the bone and would have attacked the man; but as it was, these three men were now merely potential patrons standing in line.

And what are the profiles of bank robbers as they stand in a line in a bank? Would you know them by their faces or clothing? There would be many descriptions of what they would have with them, but the one thing they certainly would have is a mind possessed of a single purpose, which is to say, they would be intent on committing mayhem, and their internal machinations would spill onto their grim and desperate masks.

These three men, having sensed the right time to announce their sour presence, did so.

Explosive words rained down upon the heads of the employees and patrons alike, incinerating language promising death to rebels, and in less than two minutes' time, the three robbers had acquired their intended booty and had fled toward the exit.

Bloody carnage exploded in the frigid air.

The first two robbers ran past the motionless figure on the frosted sidewalk, who then lifted his head just as the third robber passed by him.

Joaquin, the man who wandered the streets in the garb of the town mental defective, the town fool, the town shame, glanced at the third robber, expecting nothing more than an ordinary face; but he saw an extraordinary face, and his own swarthy face blanched white as his body became numb with the electric shudder of shock and awe. Disbelief ate him alive, head to foot.

He could not feel his body, nor move any joint or think any logical or even illogical thought, for his mind was hostage to the heaving, fleshy, sneering soul who stood bemused before him.

"Eh?" the third robber exclaimed, as his fellow assailants sped to their hot cars. "You! Ha! Fancy now! Die, then," he yelled, and he aimed his long, steel pistol at his intended victim.

A terrific explosion blew out the glass of the bank door, and its shattered, tiny daggers rained upon the third robber, who was violently pushed toward his retreating crew.

Jose, the man Carlos had sought, he who was the new security guard and who had been in a meeting with the new manager about proper procedures to be observed during a robbery, had fired the shot when he saw the third robber lift his gun.

"Go, go, go," the third robber yelled as he watched his men leap into the stolen black Camaro and the stolen plum-colored Thunderbird.

The owner of the liquor store across the street, upon seeing the masked gunmen fleeing the bank, picked up his shotgun, and once outside, he proceeded to fire without caution at the robbers.

The security guard, dressed in his gray and blue uniform, burst through the open bank doors, firing his black Smith & Wesson Model 13 revolver.

It was then that the third robber, seeing his chances for a successful escape imperiled, decided on a particular kind of action—an action in concert with his past behavior, to wit: he grabbed a citizen, and after depositing the girl's protesting mother to the concrete, he held the female closely to his heavily clothed person, his pistol held tight to her head.

Hesitation is a cruel taskmaster; it breeds weakness the same way filth breeds germs.

Jose paused, gun in hand, surveying the riotous scene, watching the huge third robber cling to the distraught hostage; thus, he did not see the other bank robber, who was hiding in the Camaro, stick his gun out and shoot. Jose was propelled, with great force, against the red-brick wall, and he collapsed to the wet pavement, his black revolver falling and sliding and then hitting an immobile object, namely, a soggy, brown boot.

Joaquin, still unable to function in any capacity, looked down at the weapon.

It was as if he were looking at a part of his physical self.

Manifest Destiny

When Juanita Chavez had exited the pharmacy, her children in close proximity to her, she had scrutinized the street and surrounding businesses; she had breathed in skepticism and breathed out caution. "All right, let's go," she said, her brown hand joined with the hand of her daughter, Sylvia, who had the hand of her little sister, Beatriz; and as Carlos held the hand of his little brother, Juan, all of them crossed the street. Somewhere along the way, Sylvia dropped the small, raggedy doll her father had given her long ago. The doll was more than a gift from her dead father, for it was a bridge to the man she had briefly known but loved, a man she loved more and more because of the growing ache and emptiness in her little heart.

So when all of the family was in the car, and the robbers had just come out of the bank, the family, with Carlos listening to the radio, heard nothing, and because their car was two places down from the two stolen vehicles, and was blocked by a huge truck, they saw nothing.

"My doll," Sylvia screamed, as if her life were in imminent danger, and so she promptly jumped out of the left side of the car despite the protestations of her mother.

"Sylvia, come back here," Juanita cried, unbuckling her seatbelt as the first of the shots rang out; but her instinct, like all mothers, was to protect all of her children, and so she yelled to those still inside the car as she ran to her daughter, "Get down." She clutched Sylvia tightly to her body and turned away from the masked men, only to be grabbed by the third robber, but she would not let go of her child; no earthly force could break her grip now, nothing human, no beast, nothing, could pry her away.

A bullet ripped into the mother's right shoulder, but she would not relinquish her grip; the third robber, accompanied by surges of great strength and aspirations for villainy, hit the woman with the butt of his gun and knocked her down with his fist, but still she would not let go; undaunted, the robber took the small child in the blue coat and brown pants and lifted her up before his antagonists, and he finally kicked the mother away.

It was then that Jose hesitated and was wounded.

Joaquin stared at the metallic weapon, its gleaming surface and lofty configuration sending an articulate message of revival into his dead heart; he saw the third robber gleefully hoist up the crying girl, kick the woman in her head, and then run for the stolen cars. He looked to Jose, who had been a policeman once, and he saw the man, bleeding profusely, nod to him.

And thus equipped with a noble purpose, he bent down, clutched the gun, lifted it up, and aimed.

It was as if he were merely directing his outstretched hand toward the speeding stolen cars as he walked fearlessly out into the street; he fired once, twice, three times at the car that had no hostage in it, and he felt the return fire from the robbers lubricate the air around him with liquid fire; but he cared not, and he continued to fire, each time hitting the fleeing target.

But it was all too late, for though he had perfectly sent bullets into the body and window and tire of the last car, it had managed to limp away. He walked back to the guard, acknowledged him with a nod, and received a nod back. Joaquin then set the gun down in the man's hand and ran over to Juanita, placed his hand upon her forehead, and said, without hesitation, without any doubt, as if he knew he were already there and was done with the whole affair, his voice burning with passion, "I will bring her back to you," and he turned and ran, but stopped suddenly, stooped down, picked up the Winnie the Pooh doll, smelled its unique scent, and then continued running down the road.

Juanita lay upon the black asphalt and watched Joaquin turn the corner of the street and disappear. The noise of sirens came into her ears as Carlos ran to her side.

Her words were soaked in blood and vengeance as she murmured, "I believe you," and then she became unconscious.

Through The Hills

Joaquin Bridger ran and walked along the side of the highway for one hour, observing the contact point between the rim of the worn asphalt and the sloping dirt embankment. Black and white patrol cars sped past him in both directions as they searched for the two stolen cars used during the bank robbery and kidnapping.

He would sometimes stop and examine a black skid mark on the road or trail from a tire, and as he knew the make of tires on cars, he could recognize their tread patterns and so could distinguish them from other tire tracks. When he did find a skid mark on a track or trail, he looked for tires that had been flattened out by his bullet and found them; he saw that this car had stopped and had its tire changed and that it sometimes tore in circles and made numerous false leads down dirt roads, the second car close behind it; sometimes, the two cars would split up and go down side streets and then back to dirt roads and then to the main highway and then back to dirt roads again. And then he found the two abandoned cars deep in the thicket, and he determined that the crew had picked up one new car and then boldly sped off toward the highway. He followed this trail up the main road for a while, and then he abruptly stopped.

There was a spot next to the dirt embankment where a set of tires had gone down its length and onto an off-road path that wound around and through the forest. He bent down and found the tread pattern of the new vehicle and observed how the tire had moved through a small pool of water and violently pushed the water forward, and this told him the car was traveling at a great speed. He thought these tracks could be another false lead so he carefully walked down the road, sometimes crawling along the dirt and examining the small pebbles, seeing how they had been moved forward in the dirt and then kicked back. He followed this sign until this road veered off into another direction.

A dirt road through the dense woods terminated at a pristine lake enveloped by a rising valley.

The surface of the lake was like polished glass, smooth and shining, reflecting the vivid scenery around it, so that it looked like a liquid painting with the plush hues of the forest living in it; further in, the calm lake narrowed to a small cove and gave up its territory to tall, green Noble Firs and Grand Firs and the mighty Redwood trees, all of which towered over their little friends, the pink Rhododendrons and Rocky Mountain Maples and evergreen Huckleberries, and the thick moss and dense green shrubs that were growing up the steep canyon alongside the majestic trees. Freshly powdered snow lay in small patches, painting the sloping mountainside a clean, pure white color. The canyon turned to the east for hundreds of miles of desolate wilderness.

Joaquin gazed at the snow-tipped mountains, nodded to himself, and started off down the tree-lined dirt path at an easy run, his senses sharp for any noise or smell or sight that implied human beings. Occasionally, he would stop and lie upon the hard ground, closely examining the depths and widths and direction of the tire tracks.

There, up ahead, was the abandoned vehicle, and he did not approach it with any caution or worry, knowing that the men would be long gone; but by force of habit he stooped low and looked for the shine that would be evident in any tracks left by his quarry; it was the shine, created when particles of dirt are smashed together to produce a reflective surface, that a tracker might observe at a low angle. He knew the sun was low in the sky and before him, and thus between him and the tracks, and as it was late afternoon, it was an optimal time to scrutinize evidence contained in the tracks; so, he moved cautiously and moved closer and closer until he was nearly atop the multitude of signs, and immediately he fell to the ground next to them. He inhaled deeply and experienced the array of fragrances about him.

He reached out his palm to measure the tracks; first he measured the footprints from the top of the shoe to the back of the heel, and he saw that one of the men had unusually large feet, and measuring a smaller one, confirmed that it belonged to Sylvia. The other two prints were average in size. He measured the strides heel to heel and saw how the two subordinate men had run and hurried, dragging the girl, and he reasoned that their superior had stood for a good while, observing this action, thus allowing the big man's feet to cause a deep impression in the soft soil. Joaquin moved on and saw two new hastily moving tracks that extended from the water's edge, and he knew that these men must have come from a boat. He moved over and saw more small, quick steps, small prints from the girl, as she must have been dragged to the boat and then lifted in. He carefully moved back to follow the big man's casual walk up to the boat, and he measured the loping, confident, even stride, and he burned the image of the man's arrogant scowl into his sharp mind.

He stood up.

He came to the edge of the lustrous lake and stood still, watching the barely susceptible ripples that gave up their wave-like spirit on the midday, pebbled shore; then he walked, with great circumspection, to the water's edge, and placed his hands and head into its shallow, cool body, and closed his coal-black eyes, his bearded face aimed toward the high canyon walls before him.

It was then that the two black and white Redwood patrol cars came up to the lake and stopped abruptly; four men, two from each car, came walking toward the stooping Tracker, stopped behind him and stood quietly, as if they were in the company of someone who had a great skill they did not understand.

This vagrant, this dirty, despised hobo, held the four men at bay for close to one minute as he explored the lake with all his senses, and then he fell to the ground, the right side of his face plowed strongly into the gravel and gray sand; he stood up and pointed behind the men, holding up one finger. The men turned around, expecting to hear or see something, and then turned back, each wearing a disconcerting frown.

The captain of this group spoke. "What is it, Joaquin?"

Joaquin's face was without emotion, his voice without care. "One car is approaching just now on the dirt."

The Captain expelled an incredulous breath, his hands on his hips. "How..."

"It is the hum of the vehicle on dirt versus asphalt." He stared at the Captain as if the officer were nothing to him, nothing at all.

A minute later, a black car, with the words "United States Marshals Service" emblazoned in white on its side, came up, and out stepped two men with the swagger of prevailing authority.

The Captain looked over to them. "What are you doing here, Shipper?"

Supervisory Deputy United States Marshal Jacob Shipper glanced for a moment at the Captain, then cast a longer look at all the men at this scene. "We have reason to believe the kidnapper is a fugitive." He would say nothing more about the fugitive, for now. "We checked the main roads up to the interstate, and one of our men saw your locals come in this way." He looked toward Joaquin with scorn. "Is this one of the men involved? Why is he standing freely?" His white hand rested anxiously atop his black leather gun holster, barely touching the gold butt of his revolver.

Joaquin looked to the police officer from his city. He continued, his dark eyes absent of emotion. "Here," he said, and he turned around and walked a few steps before squatting on the road and pointing to obscure footsteps, "two men arrived and helped carry a struggling passenger," and he walked to the lake and pointed to the north, "and then six passengers took a boat to the old Blackfoot Trail."

"Who is this fool?" the Deputy Marshal demanded, even as the three local officers walked toward the Tracker.

The Captain, Ricardo Montoya, waited, and then he turned toward the U.S. Marshal. "He is Joaquin Bridger." He was careful to say it without an apology as addendum, as was usually the case for those who spoke of Joaquin. This revelation managed to harass the Marshal into a momentary silence.

"How do you know about the boat?" one of the young local officers asked.

"A lake is a body," Joaquin replied, his words cold and lifeless, "and just as a man knows the individual sounds of his own body, and can recognize disturbances within its borders, so it is true with the lake." He began to remove his heavy coat.

"Outrageous," the Deputy Marshal exclaimed, his disciplined mind rebelling at the notion that such a man as Bridger still existed. "We're wasting time here. You," he stated emphatically, pointing at Joaquin, "you are not to be in this; you," and then his voice hardened, "you are a civilian; we will use trackers and dogs."

The Redwood officers ignored the Marshal.

"Joaquin," Captain Montoya said, as he walked toward him and watched him take off his stained, dirty clothes, "how do you get to the Blackfoot Trail?"

Joaquin threw down his shirt. He gestured to the left around the lake. "There are no paths to it around the lake, except trails over the mountains; it would take hours." He undid his shoelaces and pulled off his shoes and pants, leaving only a pair of filthy, tattered gray woolen long johns.

Shipper walked up to the local police offer, leaving his bewildered partner safely behind. "Why are we listening to the ranting of a madman? We need to go after those kidnappers right now; I'm calling in a state chopper to aid in our search." He turned around. "We're going on the main path," he said, and when he turned back, he instinctively reached for his gun as he watched the Tracker run and jump into the cold lake and start swimming for the westerly shore. He cursed. "Madman."

Joaquin halted his swim and turned around. "It was Slaughter. Ricardo, it was him," he said, his voice now rife with passion, and he continued swimming.

"Slaughter," Captain Montoya whispered, and for a brief moment, he forgot the role he played in life as he walked to his patrol car, reached in, took out the mic and radioed his headquarters. "Susan, I need the state chopper to come to Mono Lake, and have them bring Winter clothes for a man about six feet tall, about one hundred and seventy pounds; and Susan, include tracker's equipment, too. Over." He listened to her confirmation and calmly put away the mic and turned to face the U.S. Marshal.

Men in positions of authority, where undiluted molecules of raw power are intravenously seeping into their spongy brains, do not tolerate dissension, for they feel as if the reason they are in power is not that they are greedy for it; no, indeed, it is because they think they are undoubtedly a person with special skills that enable them to make the correct decision about everything and everybody all of the time. Deputy Marshal Shipper was not yet this man, for although he was in the labyrinth of power, he had carefully left small crumbs of logic and Love along the way, just in case he needed to find his way out.

Shipper had charged up to the radio in his car and begun to issue orders to his dispatcher when he experienced something hitherto unknown; he felt a hand violate his royal power and cut off the radio transmission. He looked up, incredulous, only to see the Captain standing in a pose of defiance and disrespect.

The Captain was merely Ricardo Montoya now, sans the title of officer of the law, and his voice was ravaged by the acid memories of horrific acts, wherein his bitterness was a solvent that kept his memories of the past crystal clear. "You will listen to me, mister," he cried, as if his righteous tone was sufficient to protect him from the seemingly inevitable mechanical fate of retribution that occurs after one rebuts a superior officer. "You don't know who Joaquin Bridger is," he continued, ignoring the rookie Deputy Marshal, who was anxiously close by.

"He is a civilian," the Deputy Marshal retorted, his face reddened by wrath, "who needs to be committed—a danger. Look!" he exclaimed, beside himself as he pointed to the swimming figure. "Mad, mad as a hatter! And I don't care what he once was—he broke." He saw the effect his black, tarnished words had on the other three local officers, and he grinned in a menacing manner, a malicious grin that ached to strike out at all things undisciplined and unproven that refused to yield to the staid, cautious mind of an authoritarian lawmaker. He looked directly into the emotional countenance of his antagonist. "He failed, and the penalty for failure," but he moved even closer to the bold face of the officer, his hot breath carrying his volatile words, "in the business of life and death, is death." He moved in so close now that the other man expected a conflagration to erupt between the two burning faces. "Life is for the living, and he is dead; bury your dead, Redwood, bury them in the light and the deep, and walk away and forget them, or they will bury you, too, in their dead grief." But even as he said it, he felt betrayal in his own mind, and he did not know why; yes, he had heard some of the story of the Redwood officer who had committed himself to purgatory on earth, but he could not, would not concern himself with such things now.

The venomous barrage of words from the Deputy Marshal, he of the flat nose and black, arched eyebrows, settled upon the clear brown face of Captain Montoya, but this was the seen part of his flesh, not the unseen, scorched oasis of his heart that cried out for Justice.

"You," Montoya cried, his sharp tone piercing the heavy air, "you don't know who he is; you can't know," but he said it as if he were damaged beyond repair with a guilt that stemmed from his inability to make anyone understand Joaquin's fate. "You can't say that he 'was,' you can't say that," he cried, aiming his words into the man's fortress of apathy. "If you knew him, you would understand that he will always be one of us; to say he is no more, is to say," he paused, and averted his eyes to the frosty ground, "that the planet is dead. No," he spoke emphatically, looking at his nemesis once again, "you cannot separate him from what we all are—that we are soldiers in a war that never ends. He is the good sentinel, ever diligent, the last good man who refuses to yield up his post, his gun, and his life to the enemy; he is the man we can count on when the rest of us cower and run away."

The Deputy Marshal, beginning to feel shame about his attack on Joaquin, said, with less harshness but still wrapped in the battle cloak of authority, "We cannot trust a man whose mind is not stable. He is not to be involved, no matter what you think of him. What are you thinking of, to even allow a mental cripple to join a police hunt?"

Captain Montoya stood still, his brown face placid, his dark eyes bewildered, and then, abruptly, he fell backward, smote his thighs, and laughed heartily. "Is that what you think—that he is just another man, like you and I?"

"I am not interested in what you think. Now let me state this one more time to be perfectly clear, that this is a police matter and he," and he nodded toward the lake, "is not an officer of the law—it really isn't that difficult. Now stand down on this one and let us get on with this investigation," and he turned to take the radio from his patrol car, but in a moment, the radio was ripped from his large hands and pulled clean out of its metal socket.

Ricardo stood firmly, his posture ready for attack.

The other men stayed away, just as bear cubs do when their parents quarrel.

The Deputy Marshal, with the enormous chest and girth, nearly banged heads with his perceived enemy. His voice was a growl, a portent of imminent danger. "You want trouble, is that what you want, Captain? Am I not being patient with you and your ridiculous requests to bring in a civilian," and he shouted it because he knew he was right, "into a crime scene, a homeless, crazed ex-police officer? Have you lost your sense of duty and command?"

"No, I just want you to listen," he replied in a guttural tone.

"Go ahead," the Deputy Marshal returned, his hands gesturing about, "but it doesn't matter what you say; you've broken clearly established protocol, and you'll have to pay for it." All along he had wanted to hear the story of the famous ex-Ranger and police officer who had abruptly left the world of the living but continued to physically walk as one dead in the town of Redwood; in his mind, he knew his other officer was wondering how he would react, but he also wanted to believe in the impossible, and so he let Ricardo begin.

Ricardo turned around and walked away, stopped, drew a deep breath, and proceeded. "Joaquin Bridger was a member of the 110th Infantry Division." Nearly every man and woman in America knew the story of how these gallant men provided the impetus for the battle that eventually broke the spirit of the enemy in the last war, a battle where nearly all of the men died or were wounded, a battle where the men willingly provided a false front so the Allies could attack the enemy from another position; if the men of the 110th Division had not done this, tens of thousands more Allies would have died. It was the last battle of the war, a war the men of the 110th had fought without rest or peace of mind. Ricardo continued, his voice full of passion. "He came here to settle fifteen years ago and became a police officer in Redwood." His voice was drained of hostility, as there was fondness now and affection for times lost. "For ten years he was part of our town, a good officer, a good man, a good friend." He turned around to face the Deputy Marshal, his own visage betraying his weakness, the weakness of remembering emotional pain and being subdued by it. "Five years ago, there was a bank robbery, and as the robbers got away, they took two people as hostages. We chased them till they crashed; the leader of the gang was in the car with the two hostages, but the car had flipped, and was sitting on a set of wet logs, sideways, in a field just outside of town. The two other robbers were unconscious in the backseat while we negotiated with the robber who had the hostages; and all the time we were setting up a spot so Joaquin could get a good shot." The memory of it made him physically impotent.

"Joaquin," he continued, murmuring now as he walked toward the Deputy Marshal, his eyes staring into the wilderness beyond, "was a champion marksman, a professional shooter who could shoot out the eye of a rabid dog at a thousand yards. That day, he set himself up for a shot." He turned to watch the distant figure, who was still swimming in the sparkling lake. "The robber was threatening to kill one of the hostages if we didn't give in to his demands. Joaquin was ready, and our chief, who never negotiated with criminals, gave him the command. The criminal held the two hostages underneath and in front of himself with a coat over his and their bodies, and we couldn't see their faces, but sometimes, through the scope, we could see a speck of his face; the robber held a gun to the head of one of the hostages and threatened to kill the hostages if we didn't comply immediately. Joaquin had to take the shot, he had to, you see; to save the hostage's life, he had to take the shot." He murmured to himself, "He had to shoot.

"But then the criminal shot; he shot a hostage; I mean, you could hear the explosion; I can still hear it now, the terrible bang of the gun." His face was drained of life. "And blood seeping through the blanket; Joaquin had to shoot." His voice was pleading now. "He had to take the shot. Don't you see, he had to…"

He nearly wept. "He took the shot when he caught a glimpse of the robber's face, but the car moved," he said and had to stop because his breast swelled with a great pain of remorse and sorrow. "It moved because it was resting on these wet, slippery logs, and Joaquin's aim was off now; but how were we to know?" His head was shaking as he turned round, his dark face flushed with pain, wet with pious tears. "He killed the other hostage, a little girl instead of that human monster, he knew it instantly because the girl…" But he could not finish his words as he choked on his sobs. "Joaquin came up running like a howling madman toward the car, the kidnapper all the while throwing out his gun and surrendering."

The Deputy Marshal could see the horror that came to the eyes of his narrator; and yes, he had heard that a police officer in Redwood long ago had accidentally killed a hostage, but he had not realized it was Joaquin. He felt an unexplainable dread engulf him.

"Joaquin ran up to the car, crazed out of his mind," the Captain said, and he had to pause again, swallowing and lifting up his head. "And when he came to the car and tore open the doors and threw off the blanket, he fell down as if one dead upon the two bodies." He could not speak for a moment, weeping now as only a father could. "O, God, while he lay there with them, kissing them and crying over them, he wailed and screamed and howled just like a wounded animal." He turned around and stared at the figure near the distant shore. The birds of the forest were singing their mournful song; the sky was sooty dark and cloudy gray overhead.

"And do you know," his voice became eerily calm, and it frightened the Deputy Marshal, "who they were?" He could not speak for a full minute as he sobbed quietly, and then he turned around again and gazed at the Marshal, his face wrought by a profound empathy, and he shouted, from deep within shared suffering, "The first hostage was his wife—that's right, you heard me—and the one he killed was his own daughter; he had killed his own daughter, and let his own wife…" The Deputy

Marshal, with the stone countenance, felt his body shaking as he fought to abstain from weeping. "Do you know," Ricardo continued, his face imploring, his voice soft, "that he would not let anyone near them? That he screamed and spat at us when we tried to approach them? And after they were buried, that he, Joaquin, that man who had survived the great war and its suffering, and who had found solace and a miracle with his family, began to wander the streets, a destroyed man, a deserted man, a dead man, until today; don't you see, Shipper, that if he can rescue this girl he can live, maybe not like you and I live, but maybe he can look at the world and not see…" His face was revelation and awe. "But I didn't tell you who the robber was that day, did I? It was John Slaughter; that's right, the same one," and he turned around and forcefully pointed to the faraway man who was nearing the other shore, "who took the hostage and now has a man on his trail who just won't give up until it's over, and this Slaughter is no ordinary man; no, he most definitely is not—you mark my words, he will outwit the other trackers and their dog teams; he needs someone on him who will not rest. Don't you see that Joaquin will never quit, cannot quit until he finds the girl, because he can't quit, and that there is nothing on earth that will stop him from doing what he knows he must do; oh," and he shook his head and raised it proudly, "and can Joaquin track! Why, he can track a spider through a wheat field, an ant across bare stone, a bird through the air; yes, he can track and find anything, and he won't stop; no, he won't stop until he does what his heart and body and soul command him to do, and he won't rest until victory comes, and no," he shook his head, "I do not believe there is anything wrong with his mind, except guilt." He walked right up to the Deputy Marshal with the black leather hat. "Now you know it all; so call if you like," and he walked over to the radio and its black plastic cord, which he had thrown down, and he picked it up, walked over to the U.S. Marshal's squad car, and connected it. "Do with me what you will. I will contest none of it."

The Deputy Marshal pursed his lips and shook his round head clean of maudlin ideas as he grabbed the radio. "We cannot," he said harshly, "let sentiment cloud our official judgment. There are reasons for protocol, for rules, for…" He pushed the black button and spoke in a voice devoid of emotion. "This is Deputy Marshal Shipper," he said and paused as he gazed across the calm lake, watching the esoteric man disappear into the dense thicket, and he thought of his family, though he desperately sought to obstruct their image; and as he looked down, he saw some of the shiny crumbs he had left in the labyrinth of power, and he looked from whence they had come, and he saw a reflection of who he once was. "This is Shipper," he repeated, his voice fading away into a kind of melancholy reverie, where it resided for a short while, his mind listening to the hum and rhythm of this timeless pastoral country, and his tone changed. "Captain Montoya of Redwood Police radioed in," he began, and the immaculate image of his own daughter spread its golden wings and slew his hardened heart, "about specific instructions for warm clothes and tracking equipment," and he sighed, inhaling the perfumed air as if for the first time. "Help them with that order. Over." He placed the radio down and looked at Ricardo Montoya, his shout encased in a residue of wrath. "I'm trusting you." And even then he began to shrink away from his rash decision, but he knew he could not rescind the order.

"No," Ricardo said, putting his hands upon the broad shoulders of the Deputy Marshal, and then he turned around to face the vast, verdant wilderness, "we are trusting him."

Making Amends

Joaquin rose up out of the icy lake, his balled-up clothes in tow, and he immediately fell to the muddy shore and inspected the deep striations in its surface. "The boat," he whispered, and then he inspected the human prints, and he deduced that the men had exchanged shoes, and then he rose up to follow the tracks into the forest. There, under a pile of freshly torn tree limbs and leaves and uprooted brush, was the black speedboat. He bent down and found tire tracks of a smaller truck that led up a serpentine path into the slumbering white mountains. "He won't travel long this way," he reasoned, and then the psychological intrusion of his emotionally scarred past burst finally forth because of this new revelation. He was the walking dead once more, sitting absolutely still, thinking of his dead family, oblivious to the approaching helicopter.

He felt as if his mind were encased in a monolith of thawing ice, where occasionally a sliver of ice crystal trickled down its sides to reveal a picture of the outside world to him; but too many ice crystals, too often, too soon, sliding down its frozen embankments blurred the view of the world he had missed for five years.

No man, once thawed, ever wishes to be frozen again.

He would have sat, if he had been alone, in his long woolen underwear until he froze to death; he would have sat there, his mind buried in a swamp, regardless of the presence of anyone, had his mind not seen clearly for a brief second, but just as a man goes into coma after a trauma, and may suddenly come out of it, Joaquin came out of his.

Captain Montoya and Deputy Marshal Shipper stepped out of the helicopter and found Joaquin sitting next to the speedboat.

"I owe you an apology," Shipper said, hand extended. "I want you to know I was wrong back there."

Joaquin looked to Montoya for confirmation, received it, shook Shipper's hand, and thus put their animosity away. Such is the way of hard-thinking, hardworking, dangerous men that they can resolve to forget with a signature gesture.

Even as he stood, his bearded face stolid, his posture erect, Joaquin directed his deep emotional wounds around his emerging and lucid, intelligible mindset.

Within two hours, three more state helicopters, forty state and local police officers, and four teams of bloodhounds had been called in to scour the woods.

Despite Deputy Marshal Shipper's belief in Joaquin's singular ability to track, he still insisted upon accepted protocol; thus, Joaquin shaved, was given warm clothes and tracking equipment, and had his picture taken to be sent to authorities across the country.

"We can't have you killed accidentally," Shipper said, watching Joaquin putting the last of the tracking devices into his backpack.

And all the while, Joaquin watched as the police trackers and eager bloodhounds arrived and commenced, with great enthusiasm, to attack the trail of the kidnappers. He knew that soon any good sign would be muddied or erased. He was not interested.

"Now, I go," Joaquin said to Montoya and Shipper, and he bent down and picked up some mossy fibers of the forest floor and then inspected and measured the shoes of the five police trackers who had gone before him. He rose up. "Now, I go," he said, with great certitude.

"Now, we go," Montoya said, his face steadfast, his clothes changed for the hunt.

Joaquin looked up at Ricardo, stood up, nodded, walked over to his wet bundle of clothes, picked up the wrinkled, wet Winnie the Pooh doll, tucked it into the front part of his leather belt, and turned and began to run up the steep mountain. Montoya followed.

Thus, it all began.

The Hunt

His body had been dormant for five years, comfortable in its waxy malaise, the magnificent muscles leaning toward atrophy, the joints and tendons becoming stiff, his bones growing soft; and now that he ran, now that he pushed and dug and lifted and pulled and heaved, his body was in exquisite agony. As he was the warrior, he would evince no pain, issue no excuses, paint no picture of weakness to those around him. "How can any around me have confidence in me if they think me ordinary?" he thought, grimacing, turning his face from Ricardo as the two of them trotted up the main trail that wound up the steep mountain. He would not even glance at the crush of human and dog tracks littered beneath him.

The narrow path meandered through a hundred miles of thick, hilly terrain, with red and brown leaves scattered on its sloping sides. A bubbling stream trickled on the forest floor on their left side, and on their right was a dense thicket of green and brown foliage. Soon, though, the trail terminated, deferring to a towering waterfall replete with great boulders up and down its height. There sat the abandoned truck at its base; he carefully inspected the tracks of the police and all of the kidnappers that danced around it. After ascending the rocks, they stood quietly, hemmed in by a vast, rugged territory. Joaquin felt himself come alive as he surveyed the virgin swath of fertile plant life. "Here, I am free from constraints," he mused, and he fell to the cool, damp surface, smelling the pungent aroma of the rich, black soil and hearty, verdant grasses. He said nothing to Ricardo, who knew to stand still, and then he began to crawl carefully in small circular motions, taking mental notes as his eyes took in the minute breaks in the soil and leaves, the subtle impressions in the soft dirt, the cluster of grass springing back to full height. "Six of them still," he said, entranced, and then smelled the doll again; "five adults and Sylvia." He refused to say "hostage" for Sylvia, for it was important to him to speak her mother-breathed, father-given name, and to draw an inviolate image of her in his mind at all times. He stood up. "They're still going north." He looked to Ricardo. "We need to eat."

"But they will gain distance on us," Ricardo protested, frowning.

Joaquin took off his backpack, sat down, crossed his legs, and began to search the black nylon pack for food. "A soldier is only as good as his last meal." He spoke it thusly, not to impress, but to state an undeniable fact. He pulled out some dehydrated beef and looked up at Ricardo. "Eat."

Ricardo reluctantly sat down, pulled out his cellular phone, and checked in with all the teams involved in the hunt. "No one has heard a thing," he said, despondently, "but we will find them."

"No, they won't," Joaquin returned, casually, eating a dry biscuit with almonds.

"Joaquin," Ricardo said, gently pushing Joaquin's shoulder, "Joaquin…"

Joaquin shook his head and looked up, his dark eyes narrow, his black eyebrows knit in bewilderment.

"You were gone for nearly twenty minutes," Ricardo said. "I couldn't rouse you."

Joaquin's skin was flushed with cold sweat, his face numb with shame; he sought to turn away, but instead he looked directly at Ricardo, and his voice was sullen. "I must go alone."

"If you go on alone, you'll die, Joaquin, and Slaughter will win again, because your pride prevailed. No, I go with you."

Joaquin, feeling stiff and cold, and too old, slowly stood up. "We have to go," he said, and he moved on, silent, plodding, determined.

The rain came, hard and unceasing, and its fierce brother, the cold wind, came on the fluttering wings of ice.

The two men trekked silently for hours, slowly, filtering through each section of the forest. Joaquin stopped often to separate the tracks of the trackers and kidnappers. He plainly saw where the two teams of trackers had split up, and he scrutinized the area for signs, looking left to right, up and down, but the rain had cleared away most of the clues.

Joaquin, studying the broken twig of a birch tree, and then examining the crushed leaves and impressions on the soil about him, expelled a weighty breath, nodding his head. "Every mile they sanitize the area," he said, lifting up the brown tip of the twig that had dried white pulp on its tip. "This pulp is about five hours dry," and he moved to a small, green, prickly plant that sat a few meters away, "but this plant's juices are three hours dry." He looked at Ricardo.

"Doubling back? Why would they lose so much valuable time?"

Joaquin's dark eyes narrowed as he looked about the thicket, and then, closing them, his lips pursed in wrath, he said, "He knows the police," and he pointed, "expect him to flee straight up, just as if he were a hunted, dumb animal, but he isn't so dumb, no," he whispered, and he opened his eyes. "He is an animal, yes, but crafty, and he knows how to lose himself." He sprang onto a giant Sequoia tree and began to climb it, just as if he were a panther; he reached the top, fifty feet high, and felt the powerful ache of his weak muscles. "He will camouflage himself," he said in a hoarse whisper. "He will be the green shrub our patrols walk past, yes," he whispered again. "He is smart, like the bear, and ruthless, like the lion."

"I can barely hear you." Ricardo said, keeping his voice low.

Joaquin raised his voice a decibel while he lifted the mini-binoculars to his eyes. "Now, he is wearing a dark green serape, so if he needs to fall down, curled up like a bush or plant, or be absorbed into the shadows, he disappears." He climbed down the tree and stood before Ricardo. "All of the plants, here in the woods," and he gesticulated about himself, "have a uniform texture, which gives off a certain light or darkness." He knelt to the ground and ran his hand along the blades of thin grass and small brown shrubs. "There is little light here because these plants cast shadows. But as a man walks on them, he creates a distinct pattern of light, a pattern easily seem from high above." He looked west now. "He knows this; he will walk under protective barriers." He seemed entranced again, as if he were analyzing past events. "He will wear colors of varying contrast because he knows it is difficult to separate them at a great distance. He will eliminate the contrasts between his camouflage colors and his background; in effect, he will become invisible. He will be able to move from area to area, and even a man watching from a helicopter would see nothing. He is like the chameleon, climbing tree to tree, blending in, undetected by his hunters and his prey." He paused, his face animated with passion. "He will travel along the crest line, avoiding the skyline, and change his camouflage from time to time." He looked at Ricardo as if he was in a fury, but his visage quickly lost its wrath. "But he is the hunted." A faint smile appeared, and Ricardo saw Joaquin clutch the Winnie the Pooh doll. "Let's move out."

Fade Out

It was the beginning of Winter that surrounded the combatants in the forest, the birth of a cold Winter, a smooth, frozen, translucent toddler already capable of expelling a snowy, frigid breath that encapsulated all living things in a white, icy tissue of agony.

Darkness, a black, inky, vaporlike fuel spread over the sky, feeding into every patch of light and saturating it with its morbid self.

"We need to radio in for a pick-up," Ricardo said, confident that Joaquin would not gainsay him. "Have I not lasted this long without requesting the toys of civilization for assistance?"

"No," Joaquin said, staring at him, "you need it," and he moved up a steep embankment.

Ricardo stood, shivering from the encroaching cold weather. "You," he began, but censored himself, for he knew that there was no talking to this man who lived outside of the boundaries of society. In his own mind, he had expected to search for the girl till nightfall, go home, rest up and eat and sleep, come back the next day, and resume the hunt; all of this was now evanescent, dull vapors carried away by the powerful force of Joaquin's dedication to Justice for any and all creatures. "But I am not him," he mused, attempting to justify his position as he took out the radio; "no one is." He called in for retrieval.

"I need more equipment if you're going to go," Joaquin said, and he delineated each item with precision.

"Done," Ricardo said, relieved that Joaquin was not outwardly angry at his apparent treachery of desertion.

In an hour, the pair shook hands, and after Ricardo had stepped into the police helicopter, he and the pilot observed in awe as the lone figure moved out into the heart of the bleak, black, cold forest, knowing that in twenty minutes' time they would be back in the warm embers of modern civilization.

Joaquin was utterly exhausted, and he collapsed upon a mound of Sycamore leaves, and he lay there for some length, feeling muscles that seemed to be torn, feeling a body pounding with an unnatural ache and fever; he felt dead, paralyzed, a pathetic vessel worn out by boundless inner grief. His tissues were clogged with regret and despair, his blood flooded with tiny specks of self-flagellation from the dirty iceberg of haunting nightmares that had sat like a dagger in his brain. "It would be better had I died then," he said as he lay outside of himself, as he thought outside of himself. "I am so ashamed, a failure, a ruin, a bad man, a bad father, a bad…" But he could not say what he wanted to say, needed to say, and so he lay there, wanting to die a miserable death. "Here I am again in town," he thought, seeing himself now as the man who filled a void wherein the failures of society dwelled, as the social leper who frightened people to cling to normalcy. "I'm a disgrace," he whispered, "a failure to everyone, to myself." He didn't know how he had physically moved today, how he had communicated today, how he had stood up to the Deputy Marshal, today. "But it doesn't matter, for today, sleep, the brother of death, will come, and I will think no more." Thus, he felt absolved of any duty to live beyond the immediate present. But it was at this precise moment that his cold right hand touched the Winnie the Pooh doll, and his hand seemed to fondle it as if it were indeed a foreign object; but then his eyes, opened now as his hand lifted the object toward his face, widened, then closed as he wept. He tucked the raggedy doll back inside his belt. "Now I remember," he cried, and he lifted his hands to his face, but behold, he felt not his warm flesh, but cold, hard skin. "How long have I lain here?" he wondered. "Have I been here too long? How selfish I have become!" And he coerced himself to sit up and look about himself.

He expected to see a snow-covered, frostbitten body, stiffening with the chuckling hello of scornful death, but in its stead, he saw, reflected in the dim moonlight, a body covered in sprinkles of falling white flakes and a light, misty rain. "I live yet," he said and rejoiced, "and I must work fast."

Snow had not yet evacuated the last foundlings of fading Autumn. Joaquin set to labor on an evergreen bough bed; first, he took out his serrated hunting knife and cut two long branches, each about three feet long and nine inches in diameter, and he set them, six feet apart, on the cold ground. He then collected clusters of evergreen boughs and placed them between the two logs. He assiduously piled the thick, prickly green boughs into a smooth, long bed, heaping more upon the end where his head would rest. He then laid his thermal blanket atop the evergreen cot, which now added more insulation for warmth from the frosty ground. But he would have been too cold even in this device, so he set to building a temporary wind wall made from fallen branches and twigs, one stuffed with leaves and debris. Soon, he had a three-foot wall surrounding his soft bed and now satisfied, he crawled inside his specially designed polar sleeping bag; and as he drifted off to sleep, he nearly smiled. "Ricardo was right to go, for I had intended..." But he chose not to complete his macabre sentiment, and as he pondered this, he fell to rest.

He dreamt that while he slept, John Slaughter and his fellow criminal conspirators were standing over him, mocking his timid form, taunting him, laughing that the forest would be a better assassin than they.

And then he awoke.

"Morning, Joaquin," Ricardo said, standing next to the wind wall with a black thermal canister filled with hot coffee in one hand and a white cup of coffee in the other. "I know you don't drink the brown cocoa seed, but I brought you some herbal green tea."

Joaquin released his grip on the pearl handle of his parang knife. "You found me because of the GPS tracking device in my backpack."

"Yes," Ricardo said, as he reversed the two-part canister to pour out the green tea into another cup; he handed the simmering herbal drink, seasoned with a dash of lemon and honey, to Joaquin.

"This will never happen again," Joaquin mused; "letting a man get the best of me." A singular thought occurred to him then. "I have wasted my..." But though he knew what word would finish his thought, he could not say it, for he reasoned it would be a betrayal to his family. "My life must be as one dead because they are dead," he thought. "But I must find the girl, and in order to do this, I must come alive." He no longer wished to think about the contradiction, and he removed his stiff, wounded, aching, and feeble body out of the warm, green thermal bag. "I feel a hundred years old," he raged in his mind as he remembered what he had once been. He had to question his present condition. "I must get into shape now," he vowed, "for the girl," and he again felt the cloth doll, and he concentrated upon the unifying theme for rescue.

He could not hide his horrible physical condition from Ricardo; and as no honest, lifelong, dedicated warrior would ever dare to reveal a physical flaw in another warrior, Ricardo merely watched, silently, as Joaquin struggled to break down the wind wall, roll up his sleeping bag, dispose of the natural cot, eat, and begin the hunt again.

"We have found nothing," Ricardo said, as they slowly walked up a trail that was littered with green moss and gray pebbles. "And Juanita is doing well."

Joaquin wanted to say something, to acknowledge his pleasure that Juanita, who had always been kind to him and his family, was healthy, but he did not know what to say or how to say it, or he worried that perhaps his words would seem insincere or superficial, and so he said nothing and merely kept on walking up the steep hill, plodding ever so slowly, but ever upward, onward, destitute of even marginal strength, ever aware of the faint trail left by his cunning quarry.

Fade In

A week hence, no trace of the Slaughter Gang could be found, and the local authorities scaled back their intensive search soon thereafter, until one week later, the hunt was called off in this wilderness theater.

Joaquin stood before Ricardo, fifty miles from the spot in the forest wherein their search had begun, his body slowly healing of its internal wounds, his strength slowly returning. Ricardo put his hand toward his friend, but found no hand in kind to shake.

Joaquin's voice was hard, like the cold, bitter wind. "We haven't succeeded." His intense black and luminous eyes bore into Ricardo's face. "When it is over…" His gaze turned toward the high mountains.

"You know I have been ordered to return," Ricardo said, ardently. "They no longer want me to help you."

Joaquin looked at him, his visage resolute. "I will call," he said with great certitude, "and you will do as your Christian conscience tells you." He placed his hand upon the officer's shoulder, nodded, turned, and began to run up the sloping banks of a shallow creek.

Away from the contrarian personality of Man, far from the chattering, blithering, disruptive nature of Man, separated from the foolish ideas and customs and worships of Man, Joaquin began to feel the natural heartbeat of the earth beneath his feet. There were times when he found it necessary to lie down and place his bare hands and feet into the rich, fertile, wet mulch of the forest floor, to bury his nostrils into the living blood and tissue of the planet, and smell its pungent, vibrant odor.

It was as if he were an infant in the womb of his mother.

Perhaps it was more liken to a toddler in his mother's caressing arms.

He would close his eyes as he lay upon his heavily clothed back and let his mind sink into the electromagnetic pulse of Nature that hummed at decimals normally reserved for the lower life-forms who needed this spiritual milk, this constant current of trilling rhapsodic song being fed into their life's hot blood, and it was their private pleasure, their special secret and impenetrable glory, shared by no two-legged beast.

Yet, there were a few human creatures who understood the esoteric discourse of Nature, a select few who had transgressed beyond the inherent boundaries set up against them like a high prison wall.

Joaquin gave himself to the living breath of Nature, asking for nothing, expecting nothing, and in return, he found the very marrow of its essence; here, he heard the voluptuous beat of its blossoming heat, felt its fiery, molten blood pumping to every vital part of the inner chamber of the earth.

Once the veil of confusion was removed from his human feelings, he experienced the thrilling hum of Nature's nerve fibers, which connected all living things to its central core; he heard the blessed hymn of its warm pulse, the chime and chorus of its birth pangs and death throes, the heaving frame of its massive bulwark and rocky bone and meaty sinew. He felt the great ripples of destruction caused by black hearts who disobeyed the inviolate laws of the Universe, and he wept, as would a child who sees its loving mother wounded.

He felt not the cold when he was in the blessed crib of Nature's love; and when he felt full of piety and good of heart, and when he had ascended to a nobler temple wherein dwelled gentle souls, he recovered his senses to the reality of his flawed world. Sorrow and desolation slew him then, but he understood this as his humanity drained back into him.

The trail of his elusive quarry had grown cold as Winter had set upon the forest. He would tramp through the tangled underbrush and over the frozen streams and through the narrow valleys, finding no sign of human life.

Snow had begun to cover the land, and the conifers began to accumulate layers of the white powder upon their boughs and branches; soon, the Pine trees, the green sentinels of the forest, would be desperate to conserve water, for their root systems were incapable of retrieving it from the frozen ice about them. Animals competed for the seeds of cones, hibernated, and ate each other, while others headed south for warmth; but in this particular stretch of the forest, a lone man deliberately moved north, into the heart of the increasingly harsh Winter.

When the deep snow came, and the forest was sleeping peacefully in its thick bed of crystalline flakes, Joaquin ventured onward and upward, searching still on foot for any clue of the kidnappers. He wore caribou skin now, in several layers, over his entire body; he knew that several thin layers were better than a single one because they have air space between them, providing more insulation. He wore thick fleece gloves inside beaver mitts. He wore knee-high boots, consisting of two layers of white fur: the first layer facing the skin, and the second layer on the outside; he wore a parka of caribou skin, with a white fringe on the bottom, and a sunburst ruff made of wolverine fur; his sleeping bag was lined with down feathers. He rarely felt the icy chill of Winter that attempted to stab all about his body.

Every day he moved on, walking with a deliberately slow gait calculated at a rate to enable his keen eyes to scrutinize the forest for the disturbing signs of intrusive Man. It was easy for him to see the violent trail of Man in Nature, for Man alone alters his environment for greed, scarring and destroying its fragile equilibrium.

When the snow was dry and powdery, and the wind hard and harsh, he would bend down and inspect what he thought were faded footprints, and sometimes he would find the little bits of piled-up snow that a boot had dragged just beyond the footprint. If he found suspected footprints during the day, he would shade them with his body and use a mirror to direct sunlight at them at the proper angle to create a shadow, so he might better identify the shape of the imprint.

But most of the time, he found nothing, and he simply moved on toward where he determined, by logic and reasoning, his quarry was headed.

It was early January, and the snowflakes, unique and beautiful, only weeks before denied permanent residency on the leaves of firs and sloping green hills and tender green shoots of grass, now fell to the soil and kept their fine Winter shape.

"It is cold," Joaquin stated, staring at the side of the hill that was three feet thick with snow; "time to build the fan shelter." He sat his backpack down and took out a lightweight ax with a titanium blade, and he set to chopping away at the limbs of a fir tree. After procuring five sturdy, fat limbs, he proceeded to place one of them vertically into the deep snow.

He reached into the backpack and took out a long, thick roll of brown reindeer skin and placed it over the five-feet-high limb and spread out its ends and then drove the limbs into holes already made in the tough hide. He knew this reindeer tent would afford him great warmth, but it would not last in a snowstorm. He looked up again at the icy blue, clear sky. "No," he decided, "no snow tonight."

But then, he had to be sure, and so he took out his compact computer and checked the weather reports for the area. "I am a natural man," he said and smiled, "but not using such devices today is unnatural."

He crept into the tent that had the two thick branches on the ground, and he went outside and gathered enough tree boughs to once more make the bed; he unrolled the thermal sleeping bad and crouched inside its cozy womb, and then he began to search databases of websites concerned with embedded sensor networks or ESN. The ESN system had been developed years earlier as a method of measuring the goings-on in the woods around the country.

Microprocessors were implanted into various sensing devices in certain sections of woods like these, and the very movement and sound of life there—of the fall of a mature leaf, the crawl of a gray lizard over the black mulch, the merry chirping of a boasting Blue Jay, the graceful flight of the Monarch butterfly—were all measured, and algorithms devised by scientists were used to check for singular patterns. In the beginning of the experiment, no logical sequence of events could be derived from the data; then, slowly, when the element of Man was introduced into the small patch of woods, and his blundering ways interrupted the Harmony of the woods, things were made clear. Soon, large chunks of woods were covered by ESN systems, and it became apparent that the scientist observing the seemingly infinite stream of data could tell if a human being had entered the zone of sensors. When the intelligence community entered the picture, the program changed.

As it was, only certain individuals with expert knowledge in forensic and computer science could access the data, and as Joaquin was one of them, he now checked the sites for the area he had just entered, but found nothing.

The hunt continued.

First Contact

He had been on the trail for nigh three months, and neither he nor state authorities had found a trace of the kidnappers. He knew that a case thus far unresolved had little priority for officers of the law. "They do not know where to begin, nor do they have the manpower," he mused, sipping hot herbal tea as he sat on a frozen log. "I have purpose," he said, thinking of his wife and daughter, but then his mind began to fade as it had for so long, into a dark cavern where he could repose in peace and shield himself from woe. "No," he cried, "I will not," and he stood up and began to walk up a steep hill, hearing the crisp, hard crunches of ice breaking beneath his feet.

To care for any other living thing since the death of his family had been to him an act of heresy, especially for one who should have died with them; searching for the female child was an act so unselfish that no one could condemn him, not even himself.

He could never have said, not even in a furtive whisper, "I want to live and be happy," for such an act would have buried him in shame and grief.

A heavy storm was coming, and so he took out a shovel and built a snow cave on the side of a small hill. He cut an entrance in the form of a large T, three square ice blocks across, three blocks of compacted snow down; once this was completed, he dug five feet into the side of the hill, into the dry, cold dirt, making an oval-shaped cave shelter. Once inside, he resealed the entrance, which created an air vent atop the shelter, and he lay down to rest in his sleeping bag. The temperature inside was now five degrees below zero, and that was thirty-seven degrees below freezing, but his body heat alone raised the temperature significantly inside the snow cave, and the downy bag provided him with extra insulation and warmth. He would not have to burn wood chips for heat, he thought, and he could survive the night.

His dreams were of those things he no longer had possession of.

In the morning he awoke with a start, and quickly he recognized the reason for his abrupt awakening. "Voices," he murmured to himself, and he instinctively reached into his backpack to take out his Accuracy International 7.62 mm sniper rifle. He carefully attached the black stainless-steel barrel to the green stock. This was his rifle of choice now, which he carried in a beige-colored sheath that hung down his back or hung over his shoulder by a slender rope, because of its ability to withstand all weather conditions, and because he could make repairs on it with a mere screwdriver and a set of three Allen keys.

He took out his videophone and placed it into his pocket even as he carefully pushed out the entrance block of ice. With his other hand, he slipped the ten-round box clip, with the 7.62 mm caliber bullets in them, into the icy green, steel magazine; he crept out as surely as if he were a hibernating bear coming out for some Winter fuel, still adjusting the artificial lung that was slung over his shoulder.

He saw two men ascending a tall, steep mountain that was covered with freshly fallen, powdery snow, and he stood, contemplating their identity. "I have to be sure," he whispered, oblivious to the morning chill as adrenaline surged throughout his body.

"Good day for hunting," Joaquin cried to the men, as he stood with his rifle held to his leather-covered right side, the gleaming black barrel sticking up sideways in the frosty air. His left hand carefully posited the ultrafocus lens of the videophone on the faces of the men as they turned, and in a moment, he had sent their images to the authorities.

The two men, dressed conventionally in thick woolen jackets, each holding a rifle, turned, their faces betraying their surprise.

"What's that, Chief?" the quicker-witted one shot back as he gripped the butt of his rifle.

Joaquin had a relaxed smile now. "I say, any good game in these parts of the woods? I'm looking for White-tailed Jackrabbit." The extreme cold had already turned his face crimson red; dazzling white frost hung everywhere, on the outstretched limbs of tall evergreen trees, dripping in a frozen ballet, covering the bouquet of ground plants, sparkling on the snow; between the three men was a luminous white harvest of freshly fallen snow, a blinding white color spotted by few patches of rich, luxuriant green.

The sky was vivid, icy blue, deep with a rich luster and a polished sheen, as blue as the bluest sapphire.

The two men looked at each other, and the smarter one said, warily, "Haven't seen much."

Joaquin felt his warrior sense surging throughout his body, and he thought of his wife and daughter, and he found he could not differentiate between what was and what is, and he forgot, despite the terrible cold, where he was; he could not erase what he had been these long, insufferable years, which now seemed to him as if they had no beginning nor end, as if those mindless, aimless, colorless, agonizing days had always been his life, as if his beloved wife and daughter had been a blur in a rain-soaked hurricane that resided in his rusty mind. He had then wanted with all of his mind and heart and soul to be unknown, to suffer, to be tormented and punished in mind and body; to be otherwise seemed now impossible and terribly wrong.

He had been like a soldier who, in combat, adapts to a way of living that will help him to survive, but upon returning home, he expects simply to disregard the other nature that he has developed; it is not to be for him, and it is too late, for what was done in the brain, and how every tissue and cell was modified with the bleak character of survival, cannot be undone.

So it was with Joaquin, and so he stood there, entranced, looking at the men and seeing not their faraway images but the dead images of his family, and he was content, because now he was secure; he was triumphant, he was obedient, and therefore he was under the yoke of his own tyranny of remorse. It gave him great solace to be subservient to his penitence again.

He was a man paralyzed by conscience, and he stood absolutely still, a testament to Man's inner region of self-persecution.

Consequently, the two men, their curiosity assuaged, turned and moved on, albeit cautiously.

A signal came then to Joaquin, a voice, raspy and loud, accompanied by a sharp buzz.

"Joaquin, these men are part of Slaughter's Gang. Joaquin…"

It was the malevolent name of his adversary that beckoned him to the now of his life, so he reached in and clicked the black button on talk; his voice was eerily peaceful, as if it belonged to a man who had just found what he had been desperately looking for. "It's a good day for an avalanche," he whispered, and he set the videophone, still on, deep inside his coat pockets. He looked to the men, who were still ascending the hill, and he raised his voice in a brooding, chilling shout. "I'm going to give you a chance."

The men whirled around in response to this threat, for they too had developed a sense of survival, but one without empathy. His words had foreboding in them, spiked with tiny thorns, minted by an author who had no fear of death.

"You have families," he said, his voice calmer now, softer now, so much so that the men had to strain to hear as they gripped their rifles tighter. "You must choose life with family or a living death in the grave; choose now, and tell me where your Master is."

The men had already raised their rifles toward him, but their hesitation to fire was prudent, and one of them said carefully, "You're bluffing, mister; you won't fire, and besides, we don't know what you're getting at."

"Death is not life with family," Joaquin said, frowning with furrowed brow, speaking as if he were not replying to them, as if he were merely finishing his commentary; "a slow death alive is not life." But then he cried, "Choose life with the living or death with the cold grave."

"You're a liar," the slower-witted one replied, rifle still in hand and pointed at Joaquin.

"You'll bring down the whole mountain," the other shouted; "then you'll be dead."

"No," Joaquin replied, emphatically, almost incredulously, and he reached behind himself and pulled an orange string. "You will die; now decide, and be swift. If you love life and family, you will decide correctly." It was a mistake to do what he did, activating the orange avalanche airbags that were filled with nitrogen, but he did it to show the men that he would survive, that he was not insane but careful, calculating and precise in his cold sanity. "Count to five," he said calmly, as if he were playing a game of hide-and-seek. "One," he said easily, but the men stood absolutely still, bewildered. "Two, three," he continued on, not even pausing in between the frightening numbers, but enunciating them as if he were speaking into a tape recorder for a test. "Four, five." There, it was done, and the men, incredulous still, rifles aimed at him, waited.

Joaquin had been resting his hand on another small, black, metallic box, and he pressed the button in its midsection as his other hand held the Accuracy International rifle on high, as if it was his last signal to the men for their redemption. He hesitated, then fired two shots high up into the crest of the mountain.

It had snowed heavily for days, and depth hoar crystals had begun to form at ground level, forming a zone of weakness, where it would act as a lubricant between itself and the upper layer of snow, where these layers of white powder clung precipitously to the mountainside, waiting like a macabre headstone to be placed upon an icy grave; and so when the shots came, when the 7.62 mm bullet dug deep into the fragile core of the loose snow blanket, it disturbed the equilibrium of the tender ecosystem. It takes only a small amount of resistance to create a tidal wave out of flowing energy.

The giant heap of lovely, dazzling white snow, activated now, awakened from its ephemeral sleep, overcame the frictional resistance of its steep bed, and thus began its consuming ride. It was a wet avalanche, the snow having a heavy texture and weight, and apt to solidify after its maddening run abated. Rock debris hopped onto the joy sled as the roiling thunder poured its fluid self upon the first two humans.

It must be stated for the record that the two men, loyal members of the Slaughter Gang, had been educated to the highest level by their fierce mentor, so much so that if their education had degrees, theirs would be doctorates in blind obedience and unnecessary self-sacrifice; such is the way when men worships Man. Both of the men, as the white beast of a thousand tons roared down upon them, had the presence of mind to shoot at Joaquin; they missed him, but managed to puncture one of his orange inflatable airbags, and then the sea of plunging snow swallowed them whole.

Joaquin, having activated his distress beacon in his backpack—a signal never to be received by authorities—was running for the cover of the trees when the towering cloud of Winter wings engulfed him.

It is the same when one is torn under the turbulent water by a crushing wave as it is when one is caught in an avalanche; one loses all sense of direction and is enveloped by the awesome magnitude of the swirling flood. In a few seconds, the mouth of the ice monster had ceased yawning, and Joaquin was buried five feet deep in frozen flakes of crystalline perfection.

Back in Redwood

In the beginning, after the kidnappers had fled and Juanita had been released from the hospital, the townspeople met nightly in the town hall to discuss ways to aid the trackers and the local dog teams and how to use the internet and related technology to coordinate efforts around the state and neighboring provinces to help with the search.

In the beginning, the energy and optimism of the townspeople to achieve success in this quest to find Sylvia was high, as it always is and must be when all quests based on altruism and Goodness exist. The Chavez family was fawned over and hugged and watched over and their every need met by seemingly every citizen; every citizen reassured them that everything would be all right, and everyone was sure that the authorities would quickly find the kidnappers.

In the very beginning, in the midst of a sparkling diamond dawn of hope set in the crown jewel of an azure sky, everyone in town was exceedingly optimistic and determined to ride this journey to the end. It is always this way when the fervor of optimism is the engine that drives a quest; it is always, in the beginning, that the pearls of success appear in every briefing and information log and sliver of news, where everyone involved in the search for an Innocent yearns to do what is so obviously right and good. Every day for a week no one in town talked about or read about anything else except helping to find the child, for everyone in town knew that they must do this, had to do this, wanted to do this. They could not live within the small parameters of their own minds if they refused to help.

And then came the second week, and no good news arrived, no news from the state trackers or the dog teams or other county agencies, and then people began to talk of things normally hidden in the far recesses of their hearts, of that unacceptable but inevitable word: failure. Those who were adults knew the timeline on kidnapped children, and they knew that pessimism was quietly leaking into the thinning cloak of hope that was still hanging over the town.

And then came the third and fourth week, and then another week, and another and still another aggravating and insulting week of dismal news, and people decided that they had to do what they had to do, which was to work and take care of their own; and slowly they fell behind in their attempt to rescue the girl, and soon they began to trail so far behind the work of the authorities that the dust of their fellows covered their solemn retreat back to their own homes. But would they mention this desertion to the Chavez family if they ever were to see them? Would they still offer encouragement to the family later by proffering that this tragedy was an unhappy, unresolved affair? Most of them decided it was best to leave things as they were, and offer condolences when the time was right.

It was Springtime now, and the stirring hope of an early rescue of the child from the grips of the three kidnappers had slowly faded with the slowly melting Winter snow. The town had thrown a black funeral wreath over the tragic affair, and people had resumed their lives to the utmost. It is true that an entire nation cannot live the sorrow of another for too long, not even a state, nor a town; for in the end, sorrow to a family is the sorrow just of that family, and no one else. It is the family who must endure.

Juanita refused to capitulate to defeat. She still worked the internet sites and placed advertisements in the newspapers across the country and kept up the phone bank and put up posters and sent out flyers to nearby city officials and called police stations and hired and fired detectives and dreamt and hoped and prayed every day. She would not bend like a reed in a gentle breeze, she would not be moved by false leads, she would not be swayed by gainsayers or crime statistics—no, she would continue the fight until she held her darling Sylvia in her arms again.

It was Fall and the anniversary of the kidnapping, and everyone in town was strangely silent to Juanita as she went about doing her errands; they cast furtive glances at her and looked away when she looked at them, and some of them smiled, and some of them nodded their heads in understanding, but most of them wore expressions of pained grief upon their faces. A few of them came up to her with tears in their eyes and hugged her and then walked away. No one said a word because it had been a year, and there was not a bit of news from state agencies or private firms or of any lead, anywhere, and nearly all of them assumed the worst and did not want to say it to her or even imagine that such an awful tragedy could happen to them. They were still a close town, but there was nothing any of them could do but act accordingly in such situations.

Juanita came home that day and checked her messages and her internet sites and made a dozen phone calls and then went to her room and picked up the Bible and read it; and then she knelt on her knees in front of her bed and then leaned her beautiful head with the long black hair against it, and she wept. She wept as does the woman who secretly has lost hope for the return of a loved one but who must not overtly show that loss; she wept as does the mother who listens to logic and reason that insists her child is dead but will not yield to it; she wept as does the mother who still loves her child and always will but fears and knows that she will never see her child again. She wept now and wept often in the confines of her room, her pious tears flowing in private, away from her children, away from the townspeople, weeping only in the divine embrace of God. And this day, she wept past the point of her own woes, for she felt as if her own faith was dwindling. She would pray and pray and listen and pray and implore and pray and ask and plead, and nothing, nothing would come from God, and she felt just like the woman who gives birth to a baby that is not strong enough to survive. She felt helpless and frustrated that her prayers were not working, that somehow she was to blame or that God had deemed her little girl to die, and that was simply the cruel way of the world; and who was she, after all, but simply a woman, no better or worse than any other? She knew that children all around the world died and often died for no apparent reason in utter chaos, and sometimes in circumstances utterly preventable, and she wept for them too. She did not understand any of it or why her child had been taken or why she had not been returned; she would think about these matters every day, and she prayed that God would reveal His divine will to her so that she might understand; she always found time now to read her Bible and pray more and think about why the world is the way it is. For many months she put her great energies into thinking about such things, and she finally decided that her faith must not waver, or all would be lost, and that the world was the way it was because of many things, but mainly because people allowed terrible things that were easily preventable, and that she would not be one of those who stood by in the comfortable and cool shadows and complained and whined about the world, but who went boldly out into the bright sunshine and was identified as one who makes a proud declaration to engage an ominous tide. She decided her only hope was in God, and that God could bring about a miracle. She joined associations that helped look for lost children, donated more to charities, and helped the poor more often. "I must do this," she thought, "not just for now, but for all times, for this is how I should have been and must always be. All of us learn from life, and this I have learned, that we are here to help one another."

And she thought of her dead husband, who had served with distinction on the police force but had died courageously in the line of duty, and of the man who had tracked down his killers and brought them to Justice, the man she had helped over the last few years with small, yellow straw baskets of food on the spot of his own tragedy; and she would feel a deep hurt that she had not done more for him. And as she lay there in the dark, and her warm tears streamed down her dark face, she thought of his vow to come back with her beloved daughter, and she felt as if God had brought all of them together. "We are all connected, despite our best intentions," she whispered.

And still, time went on, and she heard nothing, but her faith was established, and she moved on toward the mark, unimpeded by pessimists and gainsayers and by those who quoted statistics and logic and reasoning, for she now knew that God was above all of them, and she was with God.

Andrea

They were marching at a steady pace, as they had for the longest time, as they had for many months, too many months for the little girls to remember; they had lost track of time and dates and birthdays and special occasions, and they now only kept time of the world as the ancients had, and that was through the coming and going of the four distinct seasons. Some of the girls had been on this endless march for nearly two years, others a year, a few less than six months, and a few more, a month or so. Many girls had come but had not stayed due to the prevailing philosophy of the thinning of the herd, and these girls had simply disappeared. The girls knew that some of the older ones were sometimes dropped off at certain cabins that were deeply embedded in the most remote places, wood cabins that the marching crew would sometimes stay at for a brief interlude and then depart again to resume the eternal long march. They were always on the move, never near a city or town or farm, as they ventured exclusively into the inner recesses of the dense thicket.

On this day there were four girls on this particular trek, a huge number for this fast-moving caravan. One of the girls had just joined them because one previous girl had failed at a task and had been expelled from the dark troupe.

This was a difficult march because the weather was exceedingly humid and the sun exceedingly hot in its mastery of penetrating deep into the tissues of the girls and withdrawing as much precious liquid and salt reserves from their tiring bodies; nay, but the sun was blameless in this affair, and it must be said that the true culprit was, again, the philosophy of thinning the herd. The girls knew this and lived this and breathed this and ached this and spoke of it and dreamt of it and cried over it, and as much as they did and as much as they wished it away and wished themselves home and prayed themselves anywhere but here, it was their one and only true reality. The weak, they knew, the weakest among them, weakest in body and mind and spirit and emotion, would perish like a tiny drop of water in the boiling noonday sun.

The rules on the march were always the same, that the girls and the adjutants must stay within shouting distance of the Master or perish through any number of unpleasant actions; and that they must never speak unless spoken to or risk immediate physical retribution.

His burly form was swaying to and fro as he reared up his square head with the thick black hair, and he looked up at the green canopy above him, his large, protruding eyes glowing with the insolence of unchecked power. He looked at no one but the earth and sky and trees as he spoke, knowing his subordinates were rapt in attention at his every word. He lifted his arms up and out and high and wide and breathed in and out heavily and nodded his head. "I can smell the stench of Man from here," he growled, as if dislodging some rancid piece of food from his throat. "Are they any better than a clot in a corroded artery, waiting to kill the body? If they were of but one mind and body, I would gladly plunge the wetted knife through their flabby heart; I would do it, through the very feeble atom that stays their existence on earth, so help me I would," and he turned around and looked back at his eager biographer and faithful adjutants and the now-immobile girls, and he raised his large right fist as his different-colored eyes turned down to see far beyond the ordinary dimensions and limitations of the time-space continuum and into the eternal fires. "Had I another ancient Rome to burn, I would do it gladly, I surely would; I am only sad I was not alive to do it, then; had I another Europe to invade, gladly would I do it, and do it famously; had I another city into which I might render a nuclear holocaust, gladly would I have done it, and done it well, and to more cities; yes," he paused, his mind reaching for conclusion, "for my duty and conscience would shame me until I did it, for no sooner can I behold infirmity in peoples and nations than I want their imminent destruction." He turned around, nodding his head. "Wars, we don't have enough of them." He asked the biographer to read his words back, and once satisfied, he moved on. "And now my thesis on the female of the species," he said and cleared his throat as he continued the march. "They are nearer to their cousin, the common cat, than anything else, but like anything else, they can be changed, and ought to be more like that perfect soldier, the ant, who from birth has but one goal, and that is to serve the queen and her eggs, and in their faithful service, gather food and fight to the death so that the colony lives; but in this affair, I would want these accursed females to serve me and my armies. Ah, but what do I hear myself say? I want nearly all people dressed in such strict disciplines, a race of human-ants to serve a race of superhumans." He nodded his head in accordance with his inner philosophies, and then proceeded, thusly, "And confound it all if I have met a woman who is my equal in mind or body or spirit. Are women nothing more than children, only bigger? Do they not hem and haw and wax and wane—like our friend, the black crow—at every turn and tumble? How can any man suffer to live with such a genetic mutation?" He glanced to see if his troopers were listening, who knew that if they did not give him back adequate answers to his query, he would surely punish them. "And on the topic of altruism, it too must be bred out of them—no, sucked out of the very red marrow of people—in order to have the perfect soldier. Yes," he said and paused, looking this way and that, as if to interconnect diverse notions flying about in his wildly illustrated brain, "and the perfect soldier has no feelings for fallen comrades, only a notion for the mission, like an army of loyal ants! Give me an army of men who will fight without fear or hesitation and with their eye on the treasure, and I will give you the world in a golden handbasket! Ho!"

Two of his adjutants had waited eagerly for him to stop and consider his next soliloquy, and when this happened, as it did often, they whispered, as was permitted, in hushed tones.

"Earl, have you checked your account as of late?" the first one asked excitedly.

"Yes," the second one responded, glancing ahead at the Master, and he grinned a grin of diamonds and pearls. "Festus, if I had not looked once but twice, I would not have believed the figures," and his head dropped at the recollection of it, and then he said slowly, as if he was still incredulous, "Ten million..."

"Dollars..." the other whispered, nearly giggling, "unbelievable." He looked ahead to reassure himself that the Master was still formulating his thoughts. "It is a dream, I tell you, and only the beginning of one." He looked ahead. "Shh."

The Master had turned around to glare at those trailing behind him, but he did not see just those physically behind him, but the assembled nations of the entire human race. "And if it is one thing I cannot stand," he bellowed, beginning to jog, "it is a lazy, good-for-nothing, sagging bag of flesh and soft bones," and he began to run faster, saying, "that the establishment calls the obese, the corpulent, the oversized," and he accelerated his pace, and then turning his head, shouted, "but whom I affectionately call a great weight on society who should be boiled and skinned and fed to the cows and chickens—fat people, do you hear me, fat people against whom I claim a legitimate self-defense if I want to save us from being eaten alive by their gargantuan appetite! Do you hear me, they will devour us all, and then by their vulgar proportions tilt our planet out into the frozen sea of space!" He was running full bore now and shouting and laughing. "Run, run now, you mad dogs, run for your scandalous lives or be eaten by the eager ant this very night!" They were running madly now, and he was boasting, and his head was turning this way and that, and his adjutants were trailing closely and sucking down his human exhaust, and the girls were straining and moving their legs and arms with all of their might.

And when this brief run was over, he stood before his tired slaves, and he let his words build a fortress of steel around them with his barbed tongue. "And I would that Heaven and earth," he grunted, his face flush with perspiration and arrogance, "be consumed by fire and that I might fashion a new world in my own image."

He stood before them, his adjutants worshipping him just as if he were a newborn Titan, a newborn man-into-god.

That night, they bedded down in a makeshift camp. The icy wind and icy cold could penetrate the tents that housed the girls. The girls lay in a close huddle, speaking in hushed tones. The latest addition to this collection of children was sobbing in her green and brown sleeping bag. Her body ached from the run and ached from carrying this sleeping bag and other provisions, and she cried because she was tired, and she cried because she was afraid and alone and away from her family for the first time in her young life.

"Hey," one of the other girls said to her in a whisper, "are you all right?" There was no talking permitted once the girls were in their beds, and any infraction of this law meant a severe physical beating. "My name is Andrea." She heard no response and then kept quiet as one of the men walked by on his perimeter check; she waited until the man was gone and then spoke again. "Are you all right?"

The crying abated, and the little girl with the swarthy face nodded her head. "Yes," she whispered.

Andrea smiled. "That is good. So what is your name? How old are you?"

"Sylvia," the little girl barely whispered, anxiously looking around, "and I am nearly nine."

"How long have you been with him?"

She sniffed. "Two weeks, I think, two weeks, and then I came here with you."

"Where were you before you joined us?"

Sylvia told her about the kidnapping and the subsequent escape into the mountains and the flight to a cabin and the ride in the helicopter and finally the landing here. "I want to go home," she sobbed, and then, in her budding maturity, she said, "How long have you been here?"

"One year."

Her face sobered quickly. "I am sorry," she said, and she sought to say something else. "How old are you?"

"Twelve."

"How long does he keep us? Why are we here?"

Andrea was not so quick to answer this query; she would answer the first, and not the second. "I am not sure, but some of the girls say by age thirteen…"

But the man came back, and the conversation died for good.

The next day the girls were on the march again, and Andrea and Sylvia walked together.

"Can you get these off?" Sylvia asked her, looking at the electronic bracelets on her ankles, her long black hair falling on her bare shoulders.

"No," Andrea said, wearily, knowing only small and scattered whispers were allowed during marches, "and anyone who tries to is beat, and anyone who runs away is caught because the bracelets have sensors and a tracking..." She stopped short when Slaughter came back to inspect the girls.

"I hope you are plotting against me as usual, ladies," he said, his voice jolly. "It just wouldn't seem right if little girls weren't up to something; isn't that right, Andrea?" He surveyed her lithe form with the distinct mockery of the slave owner. "Today, we will see how well we run—loser leaves town." He then turned around and walked back to the top of the line and continued his casual walk and philosophical talk, his biographer writing down every line.

"What did he mean?" Sylvia asked.

Andrea was staring at her captor with loathing. "He means to thin the herd," she whispered, and explained the theory to her young friend; and then, to turn Sylvia's attention away from the morbid topic, she said, "You have run pretty good so far. How come?"

"Oh," she responded, smiling, "I used to run with my brother, Carlos—he is on the cross-country team; he used to let me beat him sometimes..." She became melancholy, and her eyes instinctively looked toward the south. "I want to go home, Andrea..."

One of the girls begged them to quiet themselves, and they obeyed, for two of the adjutants had come back, wooden cane in hand, inspecting the girls.

In one hour, it all began again. The pace began to quicken, and the shouts of the Master began to grow louder, and the visages of his loyal crew became hard. The girls were once again caught up in the swirling tempest of the swiftly moving march, and they assumed the mindset of the warrior.

He moved in long, fast runs and slow jogs and long, sustained runs and long jogs and teasing fast spurts, and then back and forth and slower and faster runs again, but no walking, no resting, no drinking of water or sipping of tea or any other auxiliary device, just the human body pushed to the outer limits of its capabilities; and then he turned around and shouted, "The last girl to the finish line is sausage for the centipede," and with a roar of laughter, he shot ahead in a furious run, closely followed by his own men and women, and trailing them were the four girls. The adults were fine, and there was never any doubt as to their outcome, for all of them were magnificent athletic specimens, but the girls were running with fear and dread, running out of their heads, drenched in perspiration, running in pain and agony and with leaden legs and weary arms; and then came the finish line, and the girls were looking around, and three of them knew they too were fine, because the last girl to join them was lagging behind, and it was logical, too, that she was back from the pack, logical because she was so small and appeared so fragile and had so much less experience, but it all seemed so wrong that she would lose but it simply had to be; it was over for her, and the three girls in front knew they would live another day, knew that self-preservation was their only compass now, knew that the game on these marches was survival of the fittest.

Their captor turned around and jumped up and signaled the finish line and eagerly awaited the results as his adjutants easily ran up to him.

And then an extraordinary event occurred that baffled the big man. As he watched the first three girls easily outdistance the fading fourth girl, one of the frontrunners turned around and ran back to the girl and ran alongside her and shouted words of encouragement to her and kept on running with her as both of them purposely crossed the goal at the exact time. Slaughter stood in awe, and he did not move or speak for several minutes, and when he did, he spoke, and only to his adjutants, his hands intertwined and pressed against his jutting jaw. "If I believe what I just saw, it was altruism, but upon further inspection, it was loyalty to a fallen comrade, a fallen soldier; yes, she broke the rules, but she saved the one to risk death for herself. I may have been wrong about the ants; yes, a great man must admit error if it is to mean even greater deeds; I have seen ants, as of late, stop and try to assist a fallen comrade, yes," and he rubbed his chin, "I must deliberate upon this quandary, and then render a decision." He would not tell the girls, yet.

The girls stood in horror, waiting for their captor to release one or both of the girls, but when he did not, there was much celebration, and the girls spoke of nothing else in line that day and the next.

Sylvia thanked Andrea for what she had done. The two girls embraced. The long march continued on.

Months passed, and there were times when Slaughter announced competitions, and there were times when the girls deliberately held back to finish together and were amazed when their captor did not kill any of them or punish any of them; they felt, for now, that they had figured out how to please him, and that was by evincing loyalty to each other in the field. But six months hence, and it was no longer necessary for any of the girls to drop back to help each other, for they were all fit now and ready to run without falling or suffering utter exhaustion.

Sometimes the girls would lie in their sleeping bags and gaze up through the patches of sky that poured through the canopy of treetops above them; they would talk of their homes and of their hope for rescue, and they wondered if the world had changed at all.

"I wonder sometimes," Andrea said to Sylvia as they lay next to each other in the warm cuddle of Spring, "I wonder if the world has forgotten us, or even if they still care."

Sylvia pondered this notion the best she could, and then said, thoughtfully, "How did he take you?"

Andrea sighed and shook her head so that her soft, long hair fell off her bare brown shoulders. "I was at an academy for girls, and he and his men took me when I was outside in the yard, near the gate." She lay silent for a long while, and when she spoke again, her voice was melancholy. "I sometimes wonder if there are cities, anymore; I don't remember cities, anymore; I don't remember my family, any..." But she could not speak anymore, so great was her sorrow.

Sylvia listened, and when her friend looked at her and nodded her head, she spoke. "I know they have not forgotten us," and she closed her emerald-colored eyes; "I am with them now, and I know they still love me and wait for me." But all of this longing for the seemingly impossible caused them to weep. It was the same every night, after listening to their captor's rants, after every day of running and studying and learning how to cook and clean and sew.

And then one day Slaughter announced another competition, only the fourth in eight months. Slaughter stood before the girls and announced that they were going to a cabin and then to a helicopter and that there was room only for three girls on the ride. He then turned around and took off running, and all of the girls and the adjutants sped off behind him. The girls were running well in a tight bunch, and the cabin soon came into view; they had already decided to finish together when Andrea stepped into a hole, and they all heard a loud pop, and then she fell. The two frontrunners continued on, albeit slowly, while Sylvia slowed down and turned around and came back to Andrea.

"No, no, you must go on; it won't work this time," Andrea protested, but Sylvia would have none of it, and she helped her friend up and put her arms around her and helped her hobble to the finish line, purposely finishing with her. Slaughter merely stood there and said nothing as they did so, and then he turned and went into the cabin. The girls waited in terror, but when he did not react to this violation, they once more assumed that he would allow it. They then watched as the adjutants walked the perimeter and dug in the ground along the way, planting something the girls could not identify. Nightfall had come.

Soon, the helicopter came with its whirring blades and loud spotlights, and Slaughter got into the black metallic monster with the adjutants, and then the girls began to go in. "Andrea," Slaughter said, pointing to a can of rations on the ground beside her, "pick that up, will you?" And as he watched the girl, the last girl still on the ground, limp back to retrieve the box, he signaled for the pilot to fly. The girls sat in shock as they saw Andrea standing there, alone and trembling.

The helicopter hovered just out of the reach of the girl as Slaughter spoke to his crew and her. "It was admirable to help fallen comrades on the field of battle, but to continue this kind of help does so at the risk of the army, for it perpetuates a cripple," and then he pointed to Andrea. "She has given this perverted thing a soul, and so with her dies its memory. Yes, it is good for her to go," and he reached in and pushed a red button that sat atop an electronic box, and the girls were stricken with terror as the perimeter of the place burst up into flames. "The authorities were getting too close—time to erase all markings of our past," he yelled, signaling for the pilot to ascend. He looked to Andrea and said, "And time for you to die." Sylvia, when her brain processed the dire situation of her friend, tried to leap out of the helicopter, but her captor caught her by her legs and held her fast. "You little fool," he yelled.

Sylvia was screaming and crying as she held out her hands to Andrea, who stood, forlorn and dejected, staring up at the departing machine. And then Slaughter, staring at the face of the girl he held fast, nodded his head, and then signaled to the pilot to lower the helicopter; but the pilot balked at this and pointed to the swirling, engulfing flames, so Slaughter pointed to his adjutants' holstered guns, and the pilot carefully lowered the chopper. "Go ahead, talk to her," he said, amused, looking at Sylvia's pained countenance.

And Sylvia, straining to reach her friend with her outstretched arms, cried in a loud voice that was full of pathos and Love, "Pray, Andrea, like we talked about, pray to God," and she sought to speak more, but her captor had already motioned for the pilot to swiftly take the helicopter out of the path of the encroaching flames.

And as the helicopter cleared the tops of the trees, and the flames swept toward the girl on the ground, Sylvia watched, weeping, praying, suffering just as if she were with her; she watched Andrea kneel to the ground and clasp her hands and bow her head as the hot, smoky flames converged on her. Sylvia wept as deeply as if she had lost her own sister.

Slaughter, his face aglow with fascination at the entire affair, turned to his adjutants. "Did you witness that, you miserly weasels? She was willing to sacrifice herself to bring solace for one moment to a fallen comrade. Outstanding! Now, is it altruism that I abhor?" And upon witnessing their nervous assent, he scowled. "No, you broken-brain donors, it is fanaticism, fanaticism of the highest order, a soldier willing to sacrifice for the common good of the mission!" His eyes—one dark black and the other brown—lit up like red-hot coals in a fire. "This is what I desire—zealots, prepared to die for the cause, yes; oh, but I must admit," and he looked to the grieving girl he still held tight, "she thinks it is something else—like friendship, like sisterhood, some ridiculous virtue synthesized in books and television shows—but she is young and can be cleansed." And then he nodded his head as if his thoughts had taken a new course. "But then again, if I am wrong," he said and hunched his shoulders, and gesturing with his hands toward the open door, "out she will go just as if she were the morning garbage," and he nodded his giant head, and then said, thoughtfully, "I will render my decision on that one day." He sniffed, pleased with his pronouncement on the matter. And then he looked to the still-struggling little girl, and then to his men and women, and winked, and then back to the child. "So tell me, child, why did you watch your friend being burned alive, while all the other good little white chickens averted their eyes, eh?"

Sylvia looked up at him with wrath emblazoned on her tear-stained face. "I wanted to remember," she whispered, her voice bleeding Love, "her," and then she gulped and lost her words, but pressed on again, and this time her tone was trimmed of every nuance of childhood and innocence and immaturity, instead filled with a decree of sacred vows and savage oaths. "Because every time I look at your ugly face I will see her dying, and I will hate you." And she wept, so great was her sorrow.

Slaughter hesitated and then laughed uproariously. He pointed to her, the same way a hunter points to a dead animal as trophy. "See, see what I mean! Remarkable, and in someone so young!"

Yes, there was much laughter and gaiety in the cockpit from the adults as the helicopter flew away into the midnight sky.

The next day a man walked through the burn zone and came upon the kneeling, dead body of the girl. He stood and stared for a while, his mind taking in the massacre of an Innocent. It was not the first time he had found discarded bodies or deliberately-set forest fires that were attributed to his nemesis, but it was the first dead child he had found.

He knew it was not Sylvia, for the body was too big. He knelt down beside the dead girl and stared into her charred remains and shook his head, and then he looked on high. "I have to find him, I must," he whispered, and sorrow plowed his head into the hot ash. "I must find him, nothing must stop me," and he pounded his right fist into the hot soil. "I vow it, I must do this, I must vow it or die; I must be the one, I will do what I must to find him, for there is no other like me." And at this realization, his head rose up, and his fists opened up, and he reached his arms into the air. "I will pursue him to the ends of the earth and the four corners of the world and across the seas and into the deserts and mountains, and nothing, nothing, nothing evil will be able to stop me as long as I go to sleep with Righteousness and wake up with Justice."

The Accursed Huntsmen

The crushing symphony of noise evaporated as the ice cocoon absorbed him. He lay perfectly still, perfectly wedged inside his frozen womb; lying in a curled-up position, he placed the tube of the artificial lung into his mouth, and after pressing the red button on this device he instantly felt the intoxicating rush of oxygen pouring into his body; he then reached, albeit a few inches, for the videophone but could not find it, for it was buried elsewhere, having been knocked out of his pocket during the crushing swarm. "Where am I?" he said, and he spat, to see where the spittle would flow. "Well, now I know."

He cursed himself for his conspicuous errors. "Who am I now?" he raged within. "I have compassion for murderers?" He shut his eyes tight and recalled past days when a mere thought in battle was manifest into action; it was as if his inner warrior sense had been stripped from him and replaced with a man who could not easily pass the barrier between an orderly, law-abiding territory and one ruled by the laws of survival. "Have I lost my instinct?" he cried, punching the compacted snow about him, and then he thought of his family, and he disappeared.

Twenty minutes later, he awoke from his fantasy sleep, roused from it by the icy chill in his bones. "It's cold," he whispered, shaking horribly. "Have I lived to die so ignominiously?" He felt a chill straight from his human heart. "Do I want life?" He did not want to admit that he yearned to live simply to live, but to live to rescue the child; this was acceptable, for only this thought appeased his guilt. "I will die," he mused, analyzing his situation. "Ricardo is too far away." Regret seeped into his mind, the regret of five years wasted as a living testament to what once was but could never be again. "Weakness of heart, of mind, of soul," he whispered to himself as he felt the burgeoning cold sear into the very molten marrow of his bones. "Failure, failure, you could have done something, anything," echoed wretchedly, hauntingly. "Anything, anything, anything except self-pity and shame, shame, shame; weak, weak, weak of mind and of heart and soul," resounded in his sleepy brain, and no longer could he suppress what had once slammed incessantly against his inborn partition of resistance. Hypothermia wedged into his slipping consciousness. "God forgive me," he murmured, and even as he mouthed such contrition, he felt a distant, curling, daggerlike vapor lick upon his dying thoughts, and in its gray, burnished coat of steel it asked for forgiveness too. "No, not you," he argued. "Only for me; live by the sword, die by the sword." He closed his weary, heavy eyes. "Justice, at least, Justice always; Justice, Justice now and forever," and as he fell into a deep, luxurious, and satisfying slumber, failure was written in black ash upon his shrinking heart.

He dreamt in his serene sepulcher, a blissful, peaceful dream that brought him to his beloved family, through which all things, to him, existed.

"Darling," his wife said to him in the dazzling white ice palace wherein she and their daughter resided in their brilliant white gossamer dresses, "live not for yourself, but for others."

He lay in her lap, his black-haired head resting upon her gentle bosom. "My love, I live for you," he said, looking up at her exquisite beauty.

"No, not for us, but for the whole of humanity; in that way you serve every family and Justice."

He sought to weep, but then a great clamor arose about him.

He awoke, and he beheld a giant of a man, dressed in animal skins, who had a wild visage, peering down at him.

"Nobody dies on my mountain unless I allow it, and that is a natural fact, pilgrim! Up, up, you rascal," he cried, and after lending a huge hand to a bewildered Joaquin, he hoisted him up and over his huge shoulders as if, indeed, Joaquin was a mere pittance of weight. "My cabin is yonder," he said.

Joaquin felt the gliding attack of unconsciousness creeping over him, but still he managed to say, "The law is coming..."

"The law, you say; why, those meddlers! Well, sir, they'll sooner find a wedding ring in the frozen scat of a one-eyed bear that belonged to a girl named Doris than find my cabin! Ha! And that's the wedding ring that belonged to Doris, not the scat! By thunder, one must watch those dangling modifiers!"

Joaquin felt a total blackness sweep over him, and he fought it, shaking his head and breathing sharply, but it was too late; his body had submerged into the icy fathoms of hypothermia.

He awoke some five hours later, wrapped head to foot in bear skins, lying next to a large hearth, in which blazed a flickering yellow fire. Pain had awoken him; an uncomfortable, weak, stabbing ache that inhabited his muscle and bone now pulsated throughout his dulled senses. He gazed, his eyes vacuous and unmoving, at the crackling, brilliant sparks that flared out and danced and flipped atop the spiked flames inside the blood-red-brick hearth.

"Well, O man, how do you feel? Ready for a simmering cup of yarrow and chamomile tea?" The voice was boisterous and unkempt, crumpled, as it were, in rough, unrefined social skills. Joaquin lifted his head to see a huge, bearded man, dressed in brown leather deerskin and boots, walking up to him. "By the grace of God, I declare you fit for living, youngster!" he bellowed, smiting his enormous thighs with hands that were as big as a bear's claw. He carefully unwrapped the skins from Joaquin, lifted him upon a couch made of bearskin and Sycamore tree trunks, and offered him hot tea that was sweetened with wild honey and honeycomb.

"Thank you," Joaquin whispered diffidently; "I am grateful." He was musing on the deep snow grave of his enemies.

"Grateful, eh?" the big man said as he sat on a light brown wooden rocking chair, "for what, O man?"

Joaquin knit his brows as he looked up at his rescuer, his hands still clutched loosely about the porcelain cup. "You saved my life."

"'Grateful' is a relative term, youngster, and sometimes it means one thing one day, and another, another day, and applied one way in one circumstance, and in another way, something altogether different." He nodded his head—like a lion's head it was, too, magnificent in proportion to his great girth and resplendent in its wild, thick mane—and then he slapped his knees. "Better to illustrate than to explain," he said, and he arose and walked to the door. "Did you think I saved you, alone, O man? Why, I'll pull the hungry wolf and fleeing rabbit from a trap and set them both free; it isn't up to me to decide who is to live or die; by the grace of God, I merely live; I don't have the divine credentials to determine fates of living creatures I do not eat or must not defend myself against." He opened the heavy wooden door to reveal the two men from the mountain, now asleep near another roaring yellow fire.

Joaquin leapt up and promptly fell to the hard wooden floor, breathing heavily, crawling on all fours toward his prey.

"The power of hate is strong in you, O man," the Giant observed, shutting the door; and then, walking over to Joaquin, he picked him up gently and placed him back on the bearskin sofa.

The heart of Joaquin was brooding dark-cold rage, his face smoldering dark-fiery crimson vengeance, his eyes like boiling pools of blood set in a milky-white lake; and then he spoke, the injustice of life forming each flaming syllable and tone and inflection. "They have earned death." He was as certain about this as he was that the azure sky was above him and the good green earth below him.

The Giant sat down in his wooden rocker before Joaquin, his face frowning, his bushy, brown eyebrows knit in despair as he stroked his long, brown beard. "Isn't it amazing how a man can be so absolutely certain about something and be so absolutely wrong? It does amuse me, on the one hand, but on the other, my heart grieves. God knows the mind of the sinner."

Here lay Joaquin, a man who had deliberately avoided the comforts of civilization and who had forged an ancient hatred rooted deep in the unwashed snake pit of blood feuds; in here there existed no sweet milk of mercy, as he had displayed upon the hill. Freed now, he would surely have crushed the necks of both villains as they lay asleep.

Self-righteous men do not think they need the blessing or wisdom of outside forces as they journey on their sacred mission, nor do they feel the need of explication for their actions; it is their inner sense of Justice that compels them to cast judgment upon a world they deem emotionally unfit for their profound and singular revelation. Joaquin knew he was right, felt it, lived it, breathed its savory fragrance, and he would not issue reasons for condemnation of his enemy.

"You've been captured, no doubt, by the machinations of living every day unnaturally, putting your mind on those things not leading to Salvation of your immortal soul; be you heathen or Christian, you need internal Harmony, brother," and he leaned closer to Joaquin and whispered, "I am partial to God, but that is my honest opinion." He sat erect once more, pulling his hands through his long brown hair. "I, myself, gave up on Man and his machines, Man and his obsessions with luxury and wealth and running from suffering as if it were the sixth plague of Egypt. A hard life is hard, and you spend much time laboring—but brother, you know who you are and where you are going, and you feel good about what you've done at the end of the day because it's a clean harvest." He issued a hearty grunt of inner satisfaction. "No man ought to subjugate another. It isn't natural, friend, and it only perverts the soul; personally, I don't like taking orders from some snake-charmer-peasant in a plastic suit, but," and then said loudly, "truth be told, I don't like giving orders, either; one must be consistent when one philosophizes about Nature." The big man sat still for a fair amount of time, stroking his long beard, his eyes feasting on his past, but then he looked at Joaquin. "Little Brother, you'll blow a hole in your heart just as surely as any bullet would if you brood like a caged tiger all the day long; come now, give, youngster," he said, and as he laughed, his luminous black eyes twinkled.

Joaquin, his wrath somewhat lessened, uttered in a guttural, nasty voice, "Those men bring danger to this gentle place."

"A prophet! Ha! The stone oracle speaks! Pray tell, little brother, tell thy story, and give me no little amusement." His eyes sparkled as he slapped his thighs, and his head rocked back and forth, as his wide-open mouth delivered a hearty laugh; but anticipation soon weakened into disappointment as he realized Joaquin had neither the proclivity nor the joy to tell his own story. He shook his head as he frowned. "Youngster, hatred has you in an amorphous chrysalis; why, you think hate has transformed you, as if it's some magical antidote to life's misgivings; well, child, it's only scar tissue, and it will never heal as long as you need it. Well, aha!" he shouted, abruptly standing up. "Of course, you can't explain Man into blissful change; it has to come through doing, and citizens, talking ain't doing, as they say; and, truth be known, I tend to favor that proverb." He moved his fleshy, animated face closer to Joaquin. "But I will tell you something that you can muse your brooding brain upon, and it is this," he whispered, his face sobered, lacquered now with solicitude and worry, "you can't live righteously until you forgive sins against you; O man, you can't fight the world," and he leaned closer, his voice darker. "I see it in the dark fury of your black eyes. You will live in chains until you let yourself be free from hate, and that is forgiveness toward others." He sat erect again, his tone now one of ease. "You can stay on as long as you like."

"Men will come," Joaquin said gravely, "looking for their own." He never took his intense eyes off the Giant. "Release them now; they kill anything that touches them. It is who they are; they hate living things, even themselves."

The big man squinted as he looked at his guest. "An animal in the woods is not very different from a spider in a silky web—both feel the vibrations of their environs; so too do I, as does Man who lives in Nature, but not while in the filthy ruin of city and sin." But there was a puny residue of bitterness in his hot words. "God forgive me," he whispered. "I sometimes forget." He nodded his head. "Man is a perfectly sinful creature, perfectly created to sin all the day long—it is a struggle not to; sin is so convenient. Ha!" And then he stood up abruptly. "I'm preaching! Music is what savage souls need," and he walked away and returned with a fair-looking, chocolate-colored violin and bow, and he began to play it, tapping his feet upon the wooden floor in rhythm.

That night, as Joaquin and the Giant feasted upon the fruits of the big man's labor, in particular, roast bear and wild sweet yams and fresh, plump cranberries and thick, crisp orange carrots, and after he had served the other two men their supper, he narrated his life story to Joaquin.

"He is me, but not me," Joaquin thought as he listened to this story of pain and suffering.

The big man had no name for Joaquin to call him, as he had renounced the name that the mutable and fleeting laws of society had given him. The burly man before him, dressed in bearskin and sitting in his wooden rocker while he sipped milk thistle tea, had once been a university professor of history, had once had a wife and two children, had once lived in a fine, upscale house in Pennsylvania. He had been a man well respected in society, a man who had carefully crafted out a good and serene life, a life without much risk or melodramatic expression or sorrow, a life without great strife or woe, an existence void of obstacles, controlled and fated to simplicity, order, and conservatism; he had risen up through the ranks of the elite class without comprehending life beneath him or around him or how his luxurious lifestyle came to be, his nobleman's life built on the bleached bones of bygone civilizations; thus, he had no foundation for his easily secured success, a sweet and savory success constructed on the gray sand of the aristocratic notion.

He had been driving home one fine day, a freshly minted sweet-smelling day when the bright flowers come into full bloom, and their vibrant, silky petals of yellow and white and red decorate the landscapes of houses, a day that now seemed part of a parallel history; but as he was driving home, he turned the corner of his comfortable street to see a mass of black and white police cars. There was no mistake about it. All of it had occurred, no matter how often he tried to wish it all away; his life had abated that day; his former self died, his earlier life vanished, his entire history was gone, his filtered vision of the world was evanescent, every concept of what was Truth and Justice and Virtue sank into the great chasm that his heart fell into that day, burying him forever.

He had rushed to the four huddled officers in their black uniforms as they stood behind the barricade of cars in front of his house. One of them had explained to him what was going on—the Giant no longer remembered which one or exactly what he said—but the words, like tiny cinders, blanketed him with a bizarre story about five prisoners escaping from a maximum-security prison some sixty miles away, and how they had broken into the house of the Professor.

The Professor no longer listened to the man, for the idea that a maximum-security prison existed in reality was undeniable, but the idea that the inhabitants therein might escape and infect the lives of freedom-loving people was unacceptable; he instinctively watched the body language of the officers, which stated that he must not let these men—who had no real interest in sacrificing their very lives for the women and two children inside—stay and decide their fate. He was now a savage in the wilderness, having shed his cloak and fine veneer of civilization all too quickly; the impulse to save his family at all costs became supreme, and it was a primal instinct he could not disobey.

His life no longer had meaning, and thus, he would do anything, including gladly sacrificing his own life to preserve the lives of his family; his heart was pounding and directing his captive mind to look for weapons, terrible, efficient, and reliable weapons to combat terrible, awful, desperate criminals.

He stood absolutely still; his big arms, covered by his white long-sleeve dress shirt, hung listlessly at his sides; his brown necktie flapped against his navy blue dress coat; his blanched face was distinguished by an extraordinarily dark, fomenting cast.

And then he spied the black, shiny steel revolvers in the shiny black leather holsters of the officers.

There is no hesitation when the spinning wheel of fate steps on your chiseled number and opens her slender white arms for a beckoning embrace. He lunged for two of the revolvers.

One moment he was upon his unsuspecting prey, and in the next instant, seemingly in between the profane still frame of this stark tragedy, he was charging his home, both guns pointed at the terracotta-draped windows.

To shout at the wildly running man would surely have insured his death from within, so the officers of the law merely crouched low, guns drawn, their combat-ready senses on high alert.

He did not slam into the beige wooden door, but slid uneasily against the white stucco wall as he pulled out his house key and then carefully and slowly inserted the silver steel into the brass door lock; in a moment, he was in, creeping like a panther through the hallways.

He would have murdered an unlimited amount of creatures, human or otherwise, who stood in his way to secure the safety of his family; all adversaries had to die, be they young or old, unarmed, asleep, armed, awake, aggressive, or compliant, for none of it mattered except that those three people held captive, his own warm flesh and red blood, must live.

Already incised into his chaotic brain was the idea that anything moving and not exactly fitting the description of his family would be promptly executed.

A man, holding a gun in one hand and a baloney sandwich in the other, came around the corner from the kitchen—the Professor's kitchen, the splendidly white-tiled kitchen recently remodeled with new brown wooden cabinets. The Professor shot him dead as easily and simply as if the man had been a filthy cockroach in the flour jar.

The Professor announced to his intruders his name and association to the family held hostage. "To kill them is folly, I assure you," he cried, frozen still in the hallway next to the dead man. Acrid, poisonous perspiration soaked his clothes, but his lucid, taut, and powerful voice spoke of a terrible vision; his body, crouched low, was ready to spring forward; he was a hunter now, a predator, a merciless savage, a brutal, unwavering warrior yearning to cover his hot skin with the thick, red, salty blood of his enemies. “I will kill,” he said again in earnest, and the meaty grit, the terrible resonance of it rang true, spitting flaming daggers into the steely air, “all who come up against me.”

An electric, stench-filled shudder stiffened the rarefied air inside the house, gruesome legislation from an avenging angel rattling the walls; black horror painted the steaming tension as he crept forward.

A gunman appeared and fired a fearsome bullet into the Professor, who quickly fired a round into his assailant, killing him. “I will not die,” the Professor shouted, not arrogantly, not boasting. “I am coming for you; hear me, you monsters!” His voice boomed sparks as its eerie cargo fled around sharp corners into each room of the house.

Another gunman appeared and fired a fearsome bullet into the approaching Professor, before he too was felled by a bullet to his chest. “I yet live,” he shouted, bleeding now from two wounds, “I live!”

Two more men appeared and shot two rounds into the hulking Professor before they too were downed by bullets into their puny chests. “I yet live,” he screamed, a war cry that vouchsafed nothing to human antagonists, and then he turned the corner, bleeding profusely, to see the surviving convict from the prison break.

The Professor, blood accumulating from the four bullet wounds about his white shirt and charcoal-blue pants, walked in, two police standard-issue black steel 9 mm guns pointed at the greatest threat to the stability of his known world.

"Fancy the entrance," the lone convict said casually, crouched low behind the trembling wife and daughter and boy. Peering with amusement at his challenger, he said, "Finally, some variety in all this trite drama."

The Professor stood, immobile, in shock at the sight of his family in peril, his face steaming with anguish and thick sweat; his deep voice shook with righteous judgment. "I will kill your history if you harm them; it is the eternal law of Justice."

The convict laughed uproariously. "And I have no doubt you will; but man, I do believe you when you say won't die yet; why, you must be held together by adrenaline and an inborn brute strength. Behold," he said abruptly, holding out his hand toward the object of his derision, "the fifth force of Nature."

"Free them," the Professor cried, his guns pointed at the small slit created between his standing wife and daughter.

"But I do need them as hostages, you see; surely, being an educated man, you can appreciate the difficult position I am in." He laughed. "Oh, you don't think I kept them alive these last few seconds based on your silly threats! Don't flatter yourself!"

The Professor no longer allowed the reality of the outside world into his private realm, where everything was part of a whole, where any part of the outside world was inseparable by its relation to other parts and to the rest of the real world, where no individual can exist alone. He stood alone now, an island of resistance to ancient law and customs and proper procedures, where he had become his own order of things.

He spoke with an erudite, eclipsing authority, something primeval now awakened. "Harm them," he began, in a mighty bear's roar, in a cunning wolf's howl, in the savage war cry of ancient warriors, "and I will surely dry up your seed forever, all who have begotten you; your mother, I will kill," his black eyes gleamed like twin stars bursting into life; "your father, I will kill, and likewise your brothers and sisters; your children, I will kill; yea, all of your ethos will I slay so that your history is wiped from the records of humanity; yea, but you I will let live." His crooked scowl was fastened on with a sanguinary mask as he dripped streams of hot sweat. "You shall see it all and rue this day, and then will I kill you as I would kill a virulent germ." He bled so that the floor beneath him was covered in dark-red blood.

The convict, couched down low between his hostages, roared with laughter. "How absolutely charming! No one has ever cared so much about me to threaten me thusly, and believe me, I've done some very naughty deeds to provoke a wide variety of peoples; well, you do live and learn. Big man," he said, winking playfully, "I must thank you; this whole prison escape was about to become so dull, and there you have it—threatened with the destruction of my history by a dead man. Live and learn." He snickered as does the child who steals with impunity. He suddenly cupped his ear with one hand. "Hear that, big man? It is the sound of bullets that keep the wicked policemen in their place." He smiled wickedly and said, "My people come for me."

"Release my family," the Professor demanded.

"Or what, Giant?" the convict replied, bemused. "What will you do? Rush me? Come now, Professor, use that educated brain of yours; I could kill you any moment I desire it; and oh, make no mistake, I do, I really do desire it, but you're just such good company, the witty banter," and he laughed uproariously. "I do apologize, really, but the real reason I now keep you around is for insurance against those nasty policemen outside," and his face grew grim, and his tone defiant, "who want to incarcerate me again; I won't have it, do you hear me!"

When all was right with this convict, all was right with the world, and woe be it to those who were near him when it was not.

The Professor, transfixed by the horror of his past and present and future life, where every memory and emotion, where his very essence and identity and life force were in peril, no longer felt his body or heard anything other than the frightened breathing of his family.

A strange cackle of noises pierced the air from the backyard. The convict sneered like the snake that finds the bird's nest. "Behold, my rescuers!"

A horrific clamor dug holes of fire into the room. Glass shattered, people screamed, and the Professor, now with two more bullets lodged in his massive bulwark, fell; two bullets had passed through his wife and daughter and into him, and then a third bullet cut a sharp path through his son and then spent its metallic self in the white wall behind him. There was noise, great clusters of panicking noise and gunshots and shouts as he crawled to the three fallen bodies, to his life, his loves, his dream and hope and future, to hear them crying in agony and pleading to him for succor.

"I love you," he whispered, weeping, struggling to grasp them. "I love you, I love you," he said over and over, as if the very saying of it, the very meaning of the inviolate words, would envelop them and heal their mortal wounds. He said it as they lay dying and the police offers in their tactical gear rushed in and swept the place; he said it as hot, pious tears flooded his bloody cheeks, as the police officers found seven of their own, who had been strategically positioned behind the house, dead; yes, he said it with all of his heart and soul and mind, praying to God for their lives and the destruction of his as atonement, and he said it as the paramedics came and set to work upon the fallen.

But his family died that day, and he too died, at least all that he had been, up to that chapter in his history.

Revelation

Joaquin had not averted his passionate gaze from the melancholy, dark face of his host, a once-robust, rosy-colored, meaty face now seemingly haggard, drooping, lifeless, its life juices drained from it, leaving it a dry oasis of forlorn emptiness. "Man cannot refrain from the ravages of life," he thought. "All are susceptible, and all are victims of pain; life is tragedy, life is so…"

But the big man before him began to speak again, and his ardent narration captured Joaquin's thoughts and laid them to rest.

He sat slumped in his wooden rocking chair, diffident, fragile to the ravages of the world; his voice was sullen, pitiful, destitute. "I lay in the hospital, dead to those creatures around me who called themselves people, for I could think of only one resolve—only one—only one weighty vow, and that was to kill all those things that shared the same DNA of his wicked seed, and no earthly force could dissuade me from my bloody mission."

The intense gaze of the Giant, which often veered off into the flickering yellow flames of the roaring fire, would sometimes freeze, as if the inner thoughts of the man could not extricate themselves from horror, thus abandoning his face to drift into a desert wasteland. Joaquin felt an uncomfortable chill strangle his thoughts as he saw his own history the last five years. "But we are kin to tragedy," he mused.

Several quiet minutes elapsed, and the big man silently wept, his hulking form still, his sad daze swept into the crackling fire. His story continued. "I befriended several nurses, and they saved the very bullets shot into me through my..." But he could not utter it. "Bullets that had lodged in my shoulder; later, one of the policemen who admired what I had done gave me the bullet that had passed through my little..." But once more he faltered, and his mind sealed off any more attempts to speak of that which was unspeakable. "...That was the bullet that had passed into the wall behind me, and so I took three spent bullets and married them into one avenging sword." He pulled out a braided, wooden chain of thorns and thistles, at the base of which rested the newly fashioned bullet. "This one I saved for him." His thick lips began to tremble. "Thus, once I recovered, I set out to keep my blood oath." He turned to look at Joaquin, who shrank away in fear at the manifest wrath on the face of the gentle man. "Human beings are capable of anything given the circumstances; how did I know I could murder so many just to scorn one wicked soul? I hated him with all my heart and soul and mind and body, so that I felt no remorse every time I thrust home the fatal dagger into his wicked tribe; hatred was the fuel that fed my conscience."

Joaquin gasped, and his eyes widened as he listened to the incredible story of retribution.

The Professor lay in bed with vengeance for six bitter months; the laws of humanity eroded from his heart and mind, and thus resolved, he set off from the hospital one foggy night to begin his quest. He spent six months researching the malignant past of his nemesis, all of which he related to Joaquin, but he did so without ever mentioning the name of his foe. A week later, he struck down the first relative of the man he referred to as the Wicked One.

He murdered the parents of the Wicked One, an elderly couple who lived deep in the backwoods of Tennessee, two irascible people who had a criminal history of violent deeds, and the Professor killed them casually with a bullet to each of their hydralike heads. He kept a list of names on a faded yellow scroll, and after this deed, he crossed off the names of the progenitors. "Thirty-one left," he spat, staring at the bloody corpses at his feet.

A month later, and he had killed ten more of the Wicked One's family, including three brothers, two sisters, and five children, and he had done it all as easily as if he were wringing the necks of scrawny, diseased chickens. He felt stronger after each kill, cleansed to his very red marrow, as if with every murder he was reaching closer to the high state of Nirvana; but he also felt as if he were filling up his empty vessel, and he thirsted for more. In every one of his victims, he had seen some remnant of evil that he conceded needed destroying; indeed, the twelve he had killed were, in a traditional portrait of a citizen, people of little merit: con artists, thieves, defrauders, grifters, and degenerates of all species and variations. He saw all of their innate sins worthy of the pit of eternal damnation.

The police were slow to act on the murders; but the Wicked One, incensed beyond rage, sought out the killer, whom he knew to be the Professor, but in vain; and as there were no relatives of the Professor for him to kill, he fairly went mad with frustration.

There came a night, a sultry, choking, humid, black-as-soot night, with air acrid and dead, deep in the gnarled woods of Tennessee, and the Professor was standing over the sleeping seven-year-old son of the Wicked One, a white pearl-handled dagger gleaming silver in the beams of moonlight as he held it above the chest of the small boy. Five bodyguards lay dead outside the small cabin that was ensconced in the tangled thicket. "Tonight," he thought, "I kill the last of his own evil seed, and free the world from the tyranny of his progeny." But as he let the heavy knife descend toward his sleeping prey, he halted, for a great horror had seized him. "The boy looks like my son," he cried, and he stood, transfixed.

He saw his antagonist, his nemesis, his hated foe, poised above his own son, his dead son; he saw the Wicked One smiling merrily, whispering, chanting, taunting the Professor. "I won! You are me, fool, butcher, and braggart; we're brothers!"

All of the doubts he had sequestered, every anxious dread of his own while he carried out the executions, came to fruition, swarming upon him like locusts in a black fog; but he would not relent, and he raised the dagger again, but his hand quivered, and his face bled the perspiration of torment; and he dropped the curved dagger as he cried, "I am not him," and he felt his mind implode, blinding his eyes to the outside world, and so he crashed through the wooden door and slammed into the darkened woods. "I shall destroy my history," he cried, running wildly like a madman, tearing off all of his clothes and socks and shoes and then depositing them in a great fissure in the rich, black, fertile soil. "Who I was, is no more," he declared, weeping, and he ran naked and free into an unnamed destiny.

As fate decreed it, he was found by an old hermit who lived in a secluded quarter of the mountains; it was the long-bearded hermit who taught him how to make clothing from animal skins, how to hunt and set traps, how to live exclusively off the land, how to respect Nature, how to smell again like an animal, like ancient man, how to navigate around the woods with one's nose and ears and eyes wide open. The old hermit died two years later, and the Professor wandered across the vast wilderness, eventually catching a freighter to Europe, where he explored its great breadth for three years, until he reached Israel, and he broke bread and prayed with the Jews and the Palestinians, and from there he crossed the Red Sea to Sudan, where he met the Nubas, and lived there as one of them.

He traversed the African continent, laboring with the poor, aiding the sickly, protecting the innocent, but always refusing to participate in warfare; he took a merchant ship from Sierra Leone and landed in Brazil and hiked and worked across its great breadth until he reached Peru, embraced its culture and then lived and worked with the Andean peasants, where he learned their ancient customs and ways. He traveled up the South American continent, through Central America, and stopped for a year in the state of Chiapas and lived with the Tzeltal Indians. Two years later he arrived in California, but he hesitated once he stepped within its wealthy border. "I am no better or worse if I am the same man I was when I left."

He walked through the ornate splendor of the rich cities, and their opulence repulsed him. It was liken to this, he reasoned: that it was as if he had been, these past years, in a high castle, where he had gone from room to room, where every room was unique from the other, each room representing a unique culture. "And now I am in the room of a spoilt child who has never seen any other room," he reflected mournfully, and it was then that he decided to dwell in the heart of the woods, a hermit.

The tale was over.

"That was twelve years ago," he said, his voice low and despondent. "I do not favor the track of time, but I am condemned to remember that date, alone."

Morning had erased the black-velvet encasement of night, and the indigenous wildlife sang their melodic salutations. Joaquin lay still, intuitively knowing that silence served him best right now.

The Giant closed his tear-stained, swollen eyes. "My friends awaken; do you hear them singing to each other? Is that how you, O man, awaken in the day? You, O man, who has the gift of thought, do you choose to christen the day with hope and Love?" He closed his eyes, and a faint smile sailed across his dark visage. "Do you hear our friend the Douglas Squirrel creeping about for a morning meal of crunchy seeds, or the Magpie hopping from branch to branch, looking for his morning grub? To Man in the city, he merely hears a cacophony of noise, just as a woodsman would not hear the intricacies of the city. Wait! Did you hear the soft bounce of the White-tailed Jackrabbit? And there, the scurrying movement of the sly brown snake, slipping through the dung and compost. Listen to my brothers and sisters of the forest, they who keep me alive!" He smiled and laughed heartily as he opened his eyes, and then he swept his big arms about the place. "How could any living and breathing creature not know this is paradise, eh?" And then he nodded his head as his face became somber. "Well, youngster, in the end, I must say that life is indeed suffering, and the more we desire the more we suffer."

Joaquin, marveling all the while, said nothing. And then, just for a moment, he thought he heard the rustling of the brown-and-white-spotted deer trekking delicately through the rich foliage.

In the Green Forest

Three days passed, and Joaquin was then able to walk about, albeit with weak and sore muscles, on his own accord. In that brief time, he had come to admire the person of the Giant, and in doing so, he honored the big man's palpable doctrine of aiding all injured life. "I will not ask about the two criminals," Joaquin thought. "I must honor his kindness; after all, without him, I would have died."

The next day, upon awakening, his strength now having returned, he announced to the Giant that he would be leaving. "I will take the two prisoners with me."

The Giant, his eyes merry as he stroked his thick black and gray beard, stood next to the yellow blazing fire, checking the heavy black iron pot that hung from a charred steel chain. He laughed. "That would be a mite difficult, citizen." He opened the iron lid, mittens on his hands, and put in a wooden ladle to taste his stew of vegetables and venison.

Joaquin, disturbed now, stood up from his cot. "Why?"

"I let them go—wolves in a steel trap I set free, boy! Let them hunt other game!"

"When?" he cried.

"Two days ago, if that will appease your curiosity." He carefully placed the heavy iron lid back on the large, round pot.

"You didn't listen to me when I told you how dangerous they were!"

"Did you, child?" the Giant replied, smiting his thighs. "You're a traveler in the woods with a story you won't tell; they're no different," he said, pointing behind himself to where they were. "Let Man deal with them, and let God finish it. I don't intercede in the affairs of Providence; that was my old self, who is now dead to that civilized sin." He walked to the door and opened it to inhale the fragrant bouquet of Nature. "This is me, O man," he said, and he closed his eyes and felt the yellow sun warm his face. "Nature does not lie or cheat or steal or blaspheme, it simply is; no quarreling with Her, because you cannot win! Nature is my faithful friend, wise counselor, my healer, virgin birthplace, and by my own will, my woody grave." He turned to face Joaquin, and his face was solemn. "Here I cannot hate, because I know who I am, and I know what She is; the equation changed. Humph." And he assumed the position of Professor as he lifted his big, round head on high. "Wash a dog, comb a dog, still a dog remains a dog."

None of this profound worship of the innocent world of Nature meant anything to Joaquin. "I have to go," he said, urgently, gathering his belongings. "I may be able to find their tracks."

"No, son, the snow has begun to melt; those two boys are long gone without a trace."

"Well, we shall see," he said, his attitude encased in a block of bitter ice as he packed his gear into his backpack. "I will call the authorities to alert them about these two being here; you need protection."

"No," the Giant returned, his thick eyebrows knitted; "you must not invite interlopers here! I need nothing but the sentinels of Nature, which defend and sustain me! Honor my request!"

"I have to go," Joaquin said, his head down as he finished securing his backpack. He stopped. "I will do as you wish," he said, with an imperceptible shake of his head, and in a moment, he was at the door, shaking the Giant's hand. "Thank you," he said with great intensity of honesty, and he felt the grip of a human being who could easily crush him, but in that hand, he also felt a quiet peace and gentleness and kindness; it was the hand that planted the red rose and nourished the brown bunny to life, the hand that stayed death and ushered in life. He departed.

He had to flush the image of the Giant out of his mind, or his journey would be severely slowed. "I feel good again," he said to himself, scrutinizing the thinning snow pack. "To be outside..." But his heart sank when he thought of the future. "I must forsake all others to continue my mission," he mused. "Who is he to me? Did I not thank him for his kindness? He lives as he chooses; I am not my brother's keeper; have I not promised her mother to bring her back alive? I must move on." He stepped boldly and sought to harden his heart. "May he be punished for interfering! Better that all of us died on the mountain than this uncertainty; O, curse it all, ambiguity is a millstone around the neck of Man."

He squatted upon a barren rock that was covered with frost and smatterings of dirt, and he contemplated the failures of Justice, searching through the registry of social injustices from history; he desired an impetus to abandon the big man, so he tried to gather up the Giant's character and drop it ignominiously into a rubbish heap of queerness, feeblemindedness, and villainy; he thrust his gloved hands onto his cold face and massaged his dark skin and scalp. "I cannot serve him up to be ignoble, no matter his past; I only know him, now." He felt petty and loathsome, attempting to judge a man who professed Love for all Mankind. "Who am I but a miserable sinner who..." He thought of himself as a decaying, ugly, homeless drifter. "Am I not a man inside?" He leapt up and stood, looking back toward the wooden cabin. "They will come for him; to this end I have no doubt, but if I stay with him, yes!" He grew animated. "I can recapture them, or better yet, we can hide, and I can follow them back to their lair; yes, perhaps that is the answer…" But a gunshot interrupted his reverie and sent him running quickly up the hill, all the while assembling his rifle; upon reaching the cabin, he surveyed the scene from a deep thick of bushes and espied the Giant holding up a dead pheasant.

"Hello," Joaquin yelled, coming into view and wanting to give the Giant news of his approach. "I heard the shot." He was standing now at the foot of the small hill upon which the home stood.

"Boy, you're much too city," the Giant said, grinning; "every loud noise doesn't have to mean something terrible; noises simply are…"

Joaquin, with his rifle laid on his bent right knee, looked about, not certain what to do.

"Well, come in if you want breakfast," the Giant said, beckoning him onward, his large hands resting on his hips, the pheasant dangling from his right hand. Joaquin assented.

Three weeks elapsed, Winter receded, Spring bloomed, and every day Joaquin grew more restless, hoping for his quarry to return. He slept little, keeping guard often, walking around the small wooden home at night, rifle in hand as he checked the perimeter.

"Youngster," the Giant said one day, a month after he had saved the man from death, "listen to the song of the wind," and he cupped his hands to his ears as he peered out of the open door and into the dark forest. "She brings the smell of Creation and its sublime symphony; listen! Do you hear the cunning cricket chirp? She sings of the subtleties of temperature fluxion; listen! Do you hear the ripe rustle of the great Black Cottonwood branch? Our friend, the brown-spotted deer, rubs his musky scent onto it to announce his claim to territory."

"Shut the door," Joaquin complained, checking the ENS website on his small computer screen, scanning his location for human movement, but finding nothing. "I should have left." He cursed his own stupidity. "And why can't I move this abominable cot?"

"Citizen, the way in and the way out are not barred; all are welcome who come in Peace and Love. If you forgive your enemies, the Peace in your heart breaks down all barriers and opens all doors."

Joaquin leapt up from his white cot. "And what of those who bring the sword?"

The Giant looked grim as he thought of his own wicked past, and he did what he had never done; he remained silent to Joaquin's query, but in a moment, he was outdoors, checking on his steel traps.

"I don't like this," Joaquin said to himself, feeling very much the warrior. "How can I count on him in a fight? Forgiveness and kindness have their place, but in battle," he grumbled, shaking his head, "enemies are to be vanquished, not accommodated. The strong rule in war, and the weak die; men need to be warriors in battle as well as in life. To tame a warrior is a tragedy. Life is war." He brooded over his reinvigorated philosophy, and he decided he was indeed correct. "It is when men are no longer vigilant that they fail; but I will not fail; vengeance is my sustenance, feeding my heart—it is my oxygen when the air is full of death and treachery." He scowled as he thought of his accursed foe. "I will not rest easy until I am standing over his bloody corpse."

That night, as Joaquin scanned the ENS site, the Giant walked in, carrying a small female fawn tucked tenderly under his arms.

"Dinner," Joaquin said, bemused.

"Vegetarian tonight," the Giant said tenderly and, setting the deer upon a pile of brown bearskin blankets, he tended to its wounds.

"You help it so you can eat it later," Joaquin said, who had begun the sentence in jest and finished it in earnest.

The Giant, with a deep frown, looked up at Joaquin and murmured, "Revenge poisons the spirit and blinds men to the Truth," and he set back to work on the deer's injured, bloody legs.

"I am glad I did not tell him anything," Joaquin thought, irritated. "He would not understand, and he should understand, of all people; but he groans against my quest, and what if I do seek revenge? Am I not righting a wrong? When a man is right, he is right with the world." At that very moment, he could see himself, feel himself, and hear himself draining the lifeblood out of John Slaughter, and as his inner spirit brightened like a star exploding in the great cosmos, it lit up his entire soul with its nefarious creamy, frosty, colored light.

Weeks melted by, and Spring sucked the last ice crystals from the forest, bringing to life the slumbering wild fauna; warmth oozed into the soft fur and hides and feathers and skin of the animals, bathing the creatures in its fertile yellow light, encouraging them to feed and procreate and explore and frolic in the deep mysteries of the wild thicket.

Joaquin sulked; he swaggered, he swore, and he grew melancholy as he watched the Giant tend to the forest inhabitants as if they were human. "The man is beyond redemption," he often thought. "He has no more fight; his past sins have rendered him impotent; why, the man can't even bring himself to kill a spider; he captures it and places it outside! He kills only what he eats. God save him if he meets an angry bear." He smiled at the very thought of it.

The next day the Giant, and Joaquin, who was not sulking for the moment, were walking the perimeter of the cabin.

"No movement," Joaquin said, checking the ENS system.

The Giant laughed. "Technology can't beat the human nose, youngster; here," and he held out a ripe onion, "drag this anywhere through the brush and leave it at a good distance from here," and he closed his eyes and began to inhale deeply, waiting patiently until Joaquin gave the all clear to commence the game. Then, he abruptly dropped to the forest floor and began to sniff the plush vegetation, pushing his nostrils deep into the rich flora and rich black soil; presently, he began to snake his way through the tall grasses, muttering, sniffing loudly, and crawling like a passionate bloodhound. He quickly found the onion, smiling broadly as he held it in his hand, laughing merrily as he took a generous bite out of its juicy, spicy core. He walked back to Joaquin. His voice now was like the invisible colors of the rainbow, and each time he spoke on a particular topic, that color was shown; and so, with his eyes shut, his voice was indigo and steeped in the innocent marvels of Creation. "I smell the sweet scent of the Evening Primrose, the pungent fragrance of the Scrub Oak, the..." But his great lionlike head, with the flowing, curly, brown locks of thick, matted hair, tilted slightly. "I hear," he whispered, "the scurry of Merriam's Chipmunk as he glides over fallen green Huckleberry leaves, and there," his head turned toward the east, "the rhythmic hip hop of the Brush Rabbit as he forages for food—eh? What's this? It is the marked squeal of Anna's Hummingbird; why, that squeak is an admonition to others of her species in her territory to stay away from her newborn. My my, isn't she just like her cousin—that eternal rascal, the human being—as he leans on his horn on the road, or shoots out of his front door at burglars! O, the darling, feathered,

red-throated jewels." He opened his eyes in childlike wonder, and he winked at Joaquin. "And I don't mean the humans, by thunder! Ha! Well, youngster, let us go and eavesdrop on the wee family and see if we can receive an invitation for a viewing!" He tiptoed, as if possessed by mischief, frolicking toward a group of green Pines, a sly smile planted upon his merry face. "Eureka," he whispered, turning to Joaquin, "we have found it!" And he looked down carefully as he stepped toward the small, round twig-leaf-twine nest; but as he reached up to grab a limb, he frowned, gazed at his feet, and lifted up his right leather boot; and lo, there was revealed a tiny, feathered ball of dead flesh, its feathers awash in radiant chartreuse, its head the color of a translucent and vivid sapphire, its breast wine-red, its little neck having been twisted under the massive weight of its unintended killer, its body crushed in its brief death throes.

Joaquin sighed a little, and then looked to the Giant, but he was not prepared for what he saw.

It was as if the Giant had just killed his own son, so remorseful, so ashen white was his face, so complete was the lacerating shock reverberating throughout his slumped body; the big man fell to the clump of Pine needles and decaying brown leaves and stared at the dead infant hummingbird for a long time; and then, as if he were indeed lifting up one of his own fallen children, delicately, and with great solicitude, he picked up the bird and placed it in his right hand, cupped his left hand over the creature, turned around in grave silence, and headed back to the cabin.

Joaquin stood, incredulous. He remembered a long ago time when he was on a Special Forces mission in the arctic region, and he had come upon a small, pale white insect that had dwelled its entire life in extremely low temperatures, and he had removed his glove and picked it up with his bare hand, and he had watched the innocent insect succumb to the simple presence of Joaquin's body heat. "He," thinking of the Giant, "is like that, so fragile..." He shook his head, checked the perimeter once more with his keen visual senses, and headed back, rifle at the ready, toward the cabin.

The Giant spoke nothing more that night, and he buried the fallen creature in the cold, black, soft soil.

For three days, stricken with alarm at the vulnerability of his host, Joaquin slept little, sitting next to the fire on his white cot, rifle in hand, frequently checking the ENS system.

On the fourth day of his vigil, just before rosy dawn expelled the last wisps of an icy, smoky night from the starry sky, he fell into a deep, exhausting slumber upon his fine cotton bed.

The Giant too slept upon his cot, near the fire, disquiet prancing over his beard as he dreamt of past sins; but present friends subdued his furrowed brow—those residents of Nature smoothed his anxious countenance; it was the metered chirping, the sweet song, the melodic chant of the chorus of the forest that cuddled him and swaddled him in its familiar rhythm and dance and special language; but one mere tone or octave off, just one interloper in—a snap or rustle out of sequence or just one song out, a call or shriek or whistle or warble—would be like gall in his mouth, and thus would disturb his mind and heart and soul, which were in utter concert with the land.

And then it happened that very moment, exactly ten minutes before the pouting orange ball of flame ascended to its temporary throne, where too much unrecognizable clutter sank like a virus into his brain.

He awoke with a start, wide awake as an animal, his ears pricked for the slightest aberration, and then his face grew melancholy. "My time has come," he whispered, and he looked to his friend; "live, youngster," he said with Love and devotion; he nearly wept as his hand swept quickly to the hidden wooden lever behind a jutting red brick on the side of the warm hearth. He looked at Joaquin. "Live and forgive," he said as if he prayed these very words into the heart of the sleeping man, and then he pulled the lever.

The wooden rectangular area around Joaquin, having been sprung, headed downward four feet and rotated to the left, while another slab of the precise size and shape, resting neatly and securely under the cabin floor, rotated in from the right and was lifted up until it came to rest in the floor, seamless in its fit.

It was then that the three intruders broke in, all of them armed with weapons designed primarily by Man to destroy Man.

The Giant sat still, facing them; he shuddered to his very core when he beheld the lead executioner. "It is you," he whispered, resigned to death. He was like a man in rusty chains, limited by the poverty of his resolve to forgive himself for past sins; he bowed his massive head, and the great flow of brown hair fell forward as he knelt before the invaders.

"Get up, you big ol' mule," the youngest of the men exclaimed, and he struck the Giant on the back of his head with the heavy butt of his rifle.

"No talking during tasks," one of the other men complained, frowning, and he too received a rifle butt–whipping upon his bony head.

"Ain't I the last of my kin?" the youth who had administered the blows boasted. "My word is law when my pa ain't around," and he turned his attention to his victim. "Up, you old goat," he said, and he battered the defenseless man with his wooden rifle butt until the man bled profusely about his cut face. "Shoot, ain't nothing better than torturing a soul, 'specially when he don't have the guts to fight back; cain't tell you boys how it feels to beat a yellow coward," he said, and he clenched his teeth as he smacked the Giant, with his small fisted hand, upon his forehead. "Ouch," he cried. "Uriah Heep! That hurt!" And he laughed as he kicked the Giant with his steel-toed, black leather boots. "There, that makes up for it; well, I am my father's son, after all; cain't stand to be aggravated. Now," he shouted at his men, "go at him like two lions on a sick sheep." He watched in glee as his two silent comrades pushed the Giant outside and onto the green, silky, smooth blades of sweet rye grass. His sweaty, salty face assumed the frightening black mask of the executioner. "Now, you will understand why the strong were meant to rule this mangy world," he shouted, chunks of his wet saliva blanketing the leaves of green plants, and he signaled his comrades to commence the beating of their prey.

It was at this crucial juncture that Joaquin finally realized where he was and exactly what was happening.

The Green Pastures of God

He awoke in what he perceived to be the tight black box of his omnipresent mental frailty, and he nearly lost consciousness. His thoughts were jumbled and chopped into fragments and placed in a gooey dispenser that shaped them into nonsensical curves and jutting crevices, upon which his wilting sanity lay; he had no memory of where he was or where he had been or what Age he was in or if his family was alive or if what he had done recently was dream or reality or a spoiled mixture of warped landscape upon which his grieving spirit roamed.

His eyes seemed to be open, yet he beheld pitch-black darkness—solid, creamy, smoky fog curling in and around him like the cold breath of night; he could feel far around himself, and his senses were muted; but then the violent words from the outside rained down upon him, greasing the clogged mechanisms of his mind. He halted his panic and listened with great intensity.

"Beat the old hermit to death," the heinous voice taunted; "break all of his bones so he's like one of them jellyfish washed up on the beach." The voice spat in disgust. "He won't tell us where that scum is, and he needs to die anyway, so beat him double hard, boys."

He felt his personal essence, that which defined him as man and human being, grow cold and numb. He remembered, and the name "Slaughter" echoed like a brass ringing bell in his thoughts.

A loud bang against the bottom of the cabin logs released a fragment of dried mud and delivered him from his sentence of a total eclipse of light. He espied a sliver of the gruesome scene outside as the three executioners pulled the badly beaten body away from the house.

Joaquin instinctively began to dig forward.

"Fight back," he screamed in his mind as he pulled at the mounds of tightly packed dirt that had been built up over the years from squirrel and gopher and rabbit holes, dirt that was muddy and chunky and squishy as he tore frantically at it with his hands. "Fight back," he screamed again in his tormented mind as he heard the sickening physical blows falling upon his friend.

It was like a constant beating upon a tight drum, this savage mauling against the prostrate man who neither protected himself nor cried out in pain; every second was measured in terms of damage done against the outraged flesh and bone, for every second more tender flesh was torn and ripped and stabbed, and bone was fractured and cracked and broken and splintered. Thirty seconds was a full term of events, where one minute was on another plane, in a different dimension of wanton destruction, where the wide scope of damage done was another species; but a full five minutes of undisturbed, undeterred, uninterrupted full-force body strikes by heavy wooden clubs and hard rifle butts and steel-tipped boots had created, in this prey, a creature unknown to the huddled, terrified life-forms in the black forest.

And every second Joaquin heard the horrible beatings, he grew quite mad in his desire to murder those responsible for the physical disintegration of the Giant; a rant was resurrected in his boiling brain, a fanatical rant, seething with blood vengeance: "Kill them all, every last one of them." In such a heightened state of frenzy, he would have burned down the entire forest to kill a single tree he loathed.

He wanted to cry out, to shout down the monsters wreaking unfettered violence upon his friend, but he knew he could not; yes, yes, of course he wanted to cry out and say, "Here I am and I am not afraid. I will kill you when I free myself!" His body burned with the shame of guilt that he had to dig in a silent fury.

And then he heard a revelation that chilled his hot flesh.

The killers, the trio of predators, had fairly exploded their victim into tattered flesh and bits of bone and spilled red blood, and as the Giant lay in his death throes, his body quivering, convulsing near death, he abruptly and impossibly rose up, and the purple, blotched, swollen, bloody meat pulp of a face turned toward the luminous zeal of the azure sky, and the split and cut lips of his mouth opened wide as he shouted, "O Father, forgive them, for they know not what they do," and he stood there, frozen, his arms held up in a supplicating gesture toward the great high vault of Celestial Heaven.

The butchers stood, stunned and incredulous, with awe written upon their weary faces; but then, as they turned to gaze upon the face of their fellow murderers, a gleeful tiding came to them, and a broad, toothy, gay grin broke out upon each of their peachy clean faces, just like a colorful rainbow does after a spry and crisp hailstorm. Thus, laughing all the while, they picked up their weapons of terror and commenced to whaling upon their erect game, beating him with renewed vigor and aroused joy. They thudded and whacked and plowed all of their human spirit and mind and body into the Giant, and as they laughed and spat and swore, they reckoned they were defeating Heaven itself.

The Giant crumbled, slowly, until he lay on the blood-soaked soil, his breath barely audible. The killers continued to beat upon him until they were arm weary and teary eyed from sheer exhaustion.

"Let his God resurrect him now," the leader of the Assassins declared, spitting upon the dying man. "Who knew that the baby this fool did not kill would come back for him? I reckon that's irony, boys." The other two attempted to speak, but he silenced them with a whack upon their arms. "Yes, I know, you fools, the two men he let go came back to kill him; that's irony, too," and he whacked them again. "Do you think I is a fool?" He threw his wooden club upon the Giant, held his face on high, and let out a whoop that echoed eerily into a dark, empty forest. He signaled his fellows to leave, and they walked slowly away, rubbing their aching muscles.

Victory uncontested builds a false sense of invincibility, corrupts the soul, injects the heart with the venom of false Righteousness, inflates the ego; these three men felt as if they could not, would not know defeat or death or pain for their actions, as if the decaying tissue of time and the sirens of fate that ride with it could never touch them.

A minute later, Joaquin, his hands bloodied from the horrific digging through the small wooden cavity, his hands decorated with splinters and cuts, strained as he pulled free, his body smeared in dark brown mud paste and yellow grass and bits and pieces of pebbles and twigs.

He leapt to the Giant, crawling on all fours like a man unbound by insanity, hoping and praying the Assassins would come back, for he felt invincible inside the hallowed cradle of self-righteousness. "My friend," he cried, pious tears streaming down his dirty cheeks. "My friend," he screamed, hugging the Giant. But something in him, something living and breathing, weighted his face down with a numbing violence, and he lifted his eyes to stare into the kindly face of his friend. He saw the swollen lips move, and he lent his ear to the bloodied, cracked, and broken face.

"Forgive…I forgive them…" The voice was hardened with abstract pain, as if talking was like swallowing jagged bits of glass. "You must forgive them. God forgives, and you must love them in order to know God…" And then he died.

An arcane, illustrious phantasmagoria occurred in Joaquin's tumultuous brain as he arose; his body was airy, his mind lucid, his seething thoughts focused on a clear mission. There was no remonstrance in his heart, no pleading, no argument in his mind for the law or contemplation of plans to bury the dead. His mind and heart and soul were merged in the exquisite goal of swift vengeance, and no earthly doctrine or power could stop him.

He ran into the cabin, retrieved his rifle and cartridges, ran back to his friend and mentor, and knelt before him, his brooding, hot, black eyes transfixed on the image of the corpse. "Remember," he banged the iron words about in his raging mind. "Remember this, this," he shouted. "Slaughter did all of this," and he closed his eyes as he knelt down respectfully on both knees, his rifle in his right hand laid across his filthy brown leather shirt, his left arm crossed over the Accuracy International rifle. He was at ease. "I am a warrior." He stated it in irrevocable terms, opened his eyes, bent down, and kissed his fallen brother upon his crushed, bloody forehead; he gently took the bullet from around the Giant's neck, and then from this position, he immediately sprang up and ran in the direction of the open road.

He had memorized the geographical layout of the surrounding forest and hills and roads throughout many excursions these past five months, and he knew that his quarry would have to take the highway that wound lazily down the mountain to the smoggy valley below. His path would be to the south, through dense forest and over several steep, sloping, rock-laden, tangled, brush-covered hills.

He was undeterred by the leafy, mossy, winding, up and down, jagged, and slippery terrain, as he moved like a sleek cougar that was born to this vast wilderness; he was missing no steps, stumbling nowhere, losing no speed. For ten minutes he ran as if inside him were a precision engine and compass and gyroscope that held him in the proper vertical position. The fresh, ebullient air poured like a diamond elixir over his cool face and into his powerful lungs.

With every pounding step he could feel himself, see himself killing his prey, tasting their merciless deaths, feeling their bloodied deaths, seeing their bodies jerk up in spasms after sending a 7.62 mm bullet through each of their wicked heads. Good, warm sweat soaked his dirty clothes, and he felt very much the savage who is rent from the laws of settled civilization; here, he felt as if he were the law, obeying an ancient text that was obscured and perverted and restrained by clownish Man in his polyester blue suede suit.

The first hill he came to overlooked the initial strand of the serpentine highway, and he did not refrain from leaping straight down its steep body. The hill was broken into five distinct small valleys, whose walls protruded up at sharp edges and were covered with dense brown shrubs and green trees and yellow and purple flowering plants; he journeyed along the top protuberance of a valley, dashing about the Elm trees and through the tangled roots of the plants as he managed his path to the black asphalt below. A quick glance to his right revealed no cars, and so when he landed upon the dirt shoulder of the road, he leapt up and ran across it and onto the summit of another hill. He flung himself, without hesitation, down the steep incline, and halfway down he realized that there was an abrupt cutoff from the overhanging hill to the road, perhaps some twenty feet; but he could not stop now, and from the remote territory of his right peripheral vision he beheld a white semitruck that had slowed to navigate a sharp turn. In a moment, he leapt off the dirt and rock balcony of the sloping hill, throwing his rifle far out before him.

He landed not on the road, but across the width of the top of the drowsy truck, letting his foot hit first on the edge of the polished white metal roof, then letting his knees collapse; and then he rolled over on his shoulder, took another step, then another, and then leapt far out to land on a clump of dense brush. He cut and bruised his body and strained his right shoulder, but his forward momentum could not be dulled as he leapt up, retrieved his rifle, and ran onto another small jutting plateau.

He saw the Assassins, driving lazily along the curving roads in a dark car, two levels below him. He did not care about witnesses or discretion or covert actions, for vengeance coursed through his boiling veins as he raised his rifle to shoot, but then the car disappeared below another looming hill. He ran across the level dirt plateau, crossed the narrow two-lane road, and came to another steep hill, upon which he froze in horror as he saw a concrete tunnel just ahead of his prey, which once entered, would take them beyond his reach.

He had no time to shoot all of the men who were draining aluminum cans of alcohol and victory down their parched throats as they sat in the black sedan, for there were two fast-approaching cars on the left of the target, covering them now, preventing a shot at the tires; in the instant between seeing their car and identifying them, he let his focus wander to the huge flatbed truck directly ahead of them, which carried six monstrous concrete pillars; and in between thought and action he raised the rifle and peered through the scope, targeted two of the steel cables that fastened the cargo onto the delivery truck and squeezed the trigger, and then moved the gun sight a fraction to the right, found the second cable, and again squeezed the trigger. The trucker smashed his brakes, and the truck skidded. Joaquin pulled the powerful scope back to the car to watch the reaction of his prey as they witnessed the rolling, crushing death that was coming for them.

He was panting heavily as he eagerly espied his victims' faces. They screamed blanched terror as they beheld their fate, but then his gaze shifted to what he should have seen or might have seen earlier but cared not to see, which was a small figure silhouetted in the backseat on the far right side of the two men in the back, the two men who had leaned forward in terror. It was the undeniable outline, the exact proportions, of a small girl.

Joaquin reached out his hands as if to retrieve the bullets; his face contorted in a grotesque mask of horror and agony, his mouth agape, his black-bearded face crimson with violent regret, his black eyes wide with shock—yet no sound echoed from his frozen posture. He was like the man who had seen the face of Medusa, like the woman who had looked back and was turned into a pillar of salt; he was dead, yet alive.

The gigantic white pillars crushed the small sedan just as easily as a dropped iron wrecking ball on a red, ripe tomato.

Variation on a Theme

The great man, for he was great in his ambitions for the world and in his actions for realizing his grand goals, stood at the black phone as if he were listening to an importunate electronic recording; yet there was a core part of his bold, dark face that suggested he was outside of himself, intently observing the environment about him; indeed, his right hand was drawing a remarkably accurate portrait of Rembrandt, while his left hand was computing complex physics equations. He said to himself, bemused, "Irony is the wit of fate," and then said aloud, "well," smacking his thick, aristocratic lips together as he gently slipped the earphones off, "I may have to adopt; it seems my late son was only genetically related, and no intellect crossed over in the DNA shuttle. I need to be more selective in my future sperm donations; that young fellow way back when did me an enormous favor by thinning out the infected crop in my family tree," and he cupped his right hand to his mouth, feigning a furtive aside. "O my, can you imagine the trouble I would have been in with my parents if they knew I had not stopped someone from murdering all of their kin—can you imagine the verbal tongue-lashing at the holiday barbecues?" He chuckled at his improvisation, nodding his head as he acknowledged the smile of his subordinates. "Well, it's that fine fellow I need to thank for the stimulation of my master thesis." He paused, frowning. "Who am I speaking to here, orange quarks? Where is my faithful chorus?" He gesticulated wildly, smiling, his head tilted to his stoned audience.

"Yes," one of his loyal troops responded quickly, but it was a drawn-out, fearfully lazy affirmative response, as if he were searching for answers. "Yes," he repeated, his fat face screwed up in a perplexing mask. "According to recent genetic research, especially that of Levy and Nguyen, intellectual capacity does not necessarily transcend cellular boundaries; witness peasants giving birth to authentic geniuses. Recessive intellectualism, yes, that's it, sir." He rested, seemingly pleased with himself.

There was a distressing silence, punctuated by a desperate sweat forming in tiny beads on the big man's face, as he anxiously awaited the reply.

"That's old data," the voice of the Master said from the room down the hallway. "Ten points, in the negative." He paused for a moment. "And by the way, you mutant strain of Cro-Magnon man, all people are peasants, except for me, of course."

The red corpuscles on the fat face of the man tinged brightly as they flushed with terror. "Ten points," the man thought; "that's only fifty points from the pit." He trembled in every stout limb.

The man who had so casually issued such a declaratory statement walked into the room, where his associates, sitting around a glass table, shrank away from him. "What is the code of great men?" he demanded to no one in particular, raising his brown eyebrows as his heavy face sat in a gesture of indifference.

"Ordinary human beings are fodder for the production and salvation of a truly great man," said one of the female attendants.

"Such as you, Mr. Slaughter," added a slender youth, and after sensing a vague, nodding approval from the Master, he continued on, bolder now. "If the Western democracies failed just so that they could produce one Great Man, then so be it."

Slaughter let his arrogant countenance absorb this idea as he looked above the heads of his adjutants. "Precisely," he replied, full of himself. He walked around the table, knowing every trembling head turned toward him, just as if he were the movable center of a merry-go-round. He never sat in front of his people except on a rare occasion, preferring instead to stand and tower over them; but when he did sit, he sat high upon a velvet-cushioned throne, while his subjects sat on the hard wooden floor before him. "Tell me more about such a man." Of course, he yearned to see his obtuse biography paraded before them all; it was required listening for all of them, and they were tested weekly. A score of less than ninety percent correct was frowned upon.

"Such a man," a young, pretty female interjected between the opening mouths of her male counterparts, "would possess a will of iron forged through the trials and tribulations set before him by the great unwashed hordes, who persecute him because they recognize and fear his innate Greatness."

"Quite correct," Slaughter opined, in earnest. "And how would such a man react to the news that his only son, his remaining heir, had just been killed—nay, murdered? Yes, crushed like a lowly, insignificant potato bug caught in the steel teeth of the farm harvester."

The beautiful woman sought to read his face for the signals from his extraordinary brain, but she had learned long ago that he veiled his emotions when he was at rest. "He would," she continued with a guarded, searching tone, "steel his will even more against those who seek to destroy him." She noticed a hint, a passing grade or rosy satisfaction upon his dark visage, and thus encouraged, she continued. "His will would be strengthened, and his resolve to find an heir worthy of his name would increase exponentially."

Slaughter moved his great bulk of sinewy flesh closer to his prey. "Minus three points." He exhaled it so forcefully and slowly from the hot furnace of his mouth that his wet words collected in little droplets upon the trembling white face of the woman; she could feel his sinister proclamation burning into her clammy flesh, and she sought escape, but was transfixed by his scalding stare. "A great man would merely cheer the death of his relative, or any weakling, who could not defend himself; I celebrate the death of anyone who is incompetent and unable to execute his opponent. My young seed failed," he said, and he tossed his square head to an oblique angle, "and he needed to be eliminated. His death means as much to me as does," his hand was cupped to his ears, his face screwed up in concentration, "a fly swatted." One of his men swatted the fly, and Slaughter stood erect again, his hand held out, his sausagelike fingers spread wide apart, his coal-black eyes burning bright with passion. "Judgment," he whispered, ardently, and he looked at his historian, a middle-aged man who never spoke in the Master's presence, and who wrote down every word of his exulted leader; "let the whole world be annihilated until there are only those who are strong enough, only then…" His gaze wandered off into a future only he could envision.

Two men took the woman who had failed, and they held her fast before their lord and Master. "You are in abeyance; there is no redemption. You will be given to my citizens for their sensual pleasures before you are terminated." The woman cried as the smiling men took her limp form away. Slaughter turned to his adjutant. "I have always believed in killing two birds with one stone, but I still seek three." He smiled mischievously. "Maybe she can fertilize a crop of golden poppies, hence bringing joy to the poppy farmer, who sells his innocent weed to the narcotics dealer, who delivers his purified product to the addict, who is slowly whittling away his life. Perfect!" He looked to those members who composed his inner circle of confidants and advisors. "We must find another economics professor," he said, rubbing his hands together as he turned his attention to the appetizing cuisine set before him. "Shall we eat, my children?"

The impediments on the road to his consummate glorification of self were large and foreboding, and as he consumed his delightful meal of pheasant under glass, and the finest wines, and pasta with fresh broccoli and wild strawberry sauce, he outlined some importunate characteristics of Man. He emitted words for several reasons, chiefly to scour the eager faces of his disciples, words that clung like rotting meat on faces remade every time he spoke. "If you feel the tiniest molecule," he began, pinching the right thumb and index finger of his hand together, "of compassion for our," he checked his watch, "soon-to-be-departed economics professor, I counsel you now, citizens, drive such an effeminate emotion out of your intellectual house," and he pointed to his large, shiny forehead, "as you would if you found a Death Adder in your own bed," and then he said as an aside, his large mouth cupped, "that is, after you speculated on its journey to our lovely little continent, and found out who put it there, and then make sure the gift-giver became the gift-taker," he smiled, amused with himself, and then continued on; "this world is brimming with an abundance of soft, burdensome, inbred flesh," and he took a small bite of savory and tender pheasant and sipped some sweet wine. "They are like crickets, really; no, like locusts, moving like a mindless horde without design or intelligence. What we need are wars—and not simple wars between weak nations—but mighty wars that obliterate those who otherwise would suffer us to feed their idiot, gaping mouths." He dipped a luscious deep green stalk of broccoli into the wine sauce and fed his gaping mouth. "Thinning the herd," he exploded, raising his crystal glass, an action instantly met by his associates with a clanging of jewel-encrusted golden goblets. "Bring in the children," he said, not looking directly at his adjutant, who immediately obeyed.

A healthy group of six children, all of whom possessed superior intellects, came sheepishly into the room, coming to rest in front of their jailer. They stood still in an uncomfortable hush, engulfed by a miserable pain that restrained them in this artificial, fearful stance.

Slaughter patted his mouth with the cherry-red silk cloth, stood up, ignoring his small captives, and walked away without a word on their fate.

Two hours hence he returned to find four of them sitting upon the plush white carpet and amusing themselves with various childish activities. One of them, a little girl with long, curly brown hair, looked up at him and said in a plaintive voice, "My mommy and I used to go down to the beach to collect shells, sometimes; sometimes we would find—"

"Shut up, you little imbecile," Slaughter interjected, highly agitated, and then looking away, said casually, "Note to the biologist, sterilize that child." He shook his head as his men took the bewildered girl away. "If it's one thing I can't stand, it's a rambler, and a bore." He looked to the two children still upon their feet, a small girl, and a girl nearly twelve years old. "Last one standing, eh?" he said, and then mockingly, "Well, the last one to fall gets a prize."

The older girl stared at him with a mature loathing. "I won't fall; you will, you wicked old man."

He was taken aback for a moment, then hilarity robbed him of his senses, and he laughed heartily as he looked at his adjutants. "This girl has ideas! And why," he said, looking back to her, "do you say that?"

Her sapphire-colored eyes burned bright with the passion of youth and promise. "I challenge you to stand here, old man," and she held her head on high, as her face became arrogant and defiant. "Unless you are afraid to compete," and then she screamed with scorn, "against a little girl!"

He smiled warmly, his eyebrows arched on an amused, placid face. "My dear, I am many things, but tasting fear is not one of them; we are sociopaths," and he waved about his people, "and I freely admit to scraping out a wholesale definition of that particular psychological condition." He leaned closer to her and whispered, "Everyone ought to be in, you know. It clears the system of nasty toxins." He leaned back and stood erect. "Behold, child, your lord and Master," and he sneered a generous, white-toothed grin, his large arms open to signal acceptance of her amusing challenge. "Let the games begin."

The unmasked ire of the girl, trimmed of its eccentricities, loaded with ample venom, radiated from her austere, red gaze to her captor, and this brought no little amusement to him as he concurrently narrated past histories to his historian. "And then there was the epoch of my first capture, where that hallucinatory marksman slipped and killed his own wife and child—irony from the gods, irony from every pagan god, such irony I could not have planned," and he cupped his right hand to his large mouth, "and believe me, I sincerely wish I had," and then he removed his hand and stood fully erect once more. "O," he said, rife with hilarity, "the amusement humans offer is without physical and mental limits," and he chuckled, throwing up his hands. "But can you really blame me? I," and he pointed to his own massive chest, "I who am a lion," he suddenly shouted, "a prowling lion amongst the fat, lazy sheep! Should I lie down with them?" He mimicked and mocked the lover of Peace, and wiped the impression away with a vicious snarl and a swipe in the air with his fist. "Never let it be said! People are damaged goods, best cleansed from the earth in great wars of conquest!" He held his head on high, and pointed to his barrel-like chest. "Wars led by me, of course, as I struggle to subdue those of my kind," and he gestured to his adjutants; "and please note, 'subdue,'" which he said carefully, looking askance at his biographer, "for I wish them to serve me, as I do not wish to rule with blockheads and popinjays." He looked at his followers, and he frowned, then he looked to his youthful competitor, and his face became luminous with a fervent hope. "Our future," he shouted, as was his want, to display outbursts on a whim.

He then proceeded, as he stood affixed to one spot and his six adjutants stood on the ready, to expound on economics, philosophy, religion, history, science, and mathematics; he first spoke on each branch of knowledge in a general sense, and then moved to a particular idea for each one, to wit: for economics, he spoke of the burgeoning markets around the world; for philosophy, he spoke of his admiration of Hobbs, Machiavelli and Nietzsche regarding their views on evil; for religion, he spoke of the contrast amongst the faiths; for history, he spoke of the great conquerors; for science, he spoke of the accelerating growth of technology; and for mathematics, he spoke of its divine expression throughout the world; but he did not merely exhaust himself of one topic and then move to the next—no; instead, he would utter a few sentences about economics, and then talk for perhaps a minute on philosophy, and then a few words on religion, and much on history and more on science and then barely start on mathematics, and then back to economics again; this he would do, minute after minute and hour after hour until his six adjutants had filled many pages with their exact notes.

Three hours later, the hard stance of the older girl had faded, and pain had rooted its vile self into the very blood marrow of her being, and soon she collapsed, sobbing bitterly.

Slaughter stood over her, arrogance skipping merrily across his face like tiny kittens chasing a ball of white string. "You should not weep, my darling girl, for you have already eclipsed the endurance record of any past competitor, and your intelligence and drive is a tier above the common Titan; you are surely one of us, so have no fear." She cursed him, and he nodded. "Yes, I was once like you. I had no direction; well," he said and paused, looking upward, "I was never like you, or anyone else, for that matter; but in the end, I found my destiny." Satiated with his glaring victory and palpable talent as massaging the human spirit toward what he considered its undeniable fate, he stepped away to rejoin his studies. "Isn't that first step just so refreshing?" he said to his biographer, as he was in a jolly mood.

"You lose," a small, earnest voice said, its volatile content spilling upon Slaughter's curly brown hair and broad shoulders like burning coals.

"What!" he cried, turning around in a fright, only to behold the quiet, unassuming girl who had held her fortitude while in the clutches of dark shadows that were colored violet by the spray of diffuse blue light. "You," he exclaimed, his face stiffened by utter shock, but then he laughed, uproariously, bending over in merriment as he pointed at the victor. "It's always the quiet ones," he cried, smiting his thighs, and he then punched one of his men high up on the shoulder. "Reminds me of myself when I realized who I really was." He walked up to her and let out a contented "Humph" in admiration, something he rarely issued. "You're the Redwood girl—the girl from the helicopter; oh, I haven't forgotten about you, no, not at all, missy," he said, attempting to crouch to his knees, but prevented by his tired legs. His fierce eyes sparkled as he nodded to the girl who was still crying upon the white carpet. "Third place isn't a medal winner when there are only three; it's last place, but you'll be a fine soldier yet."

The small girl's gentle demeanor transformed into a glittering zenith of ardor as she stood erect, her head held high. "He is coming for me."

Slaughter, waxing wroth, began to rip and tear everything he could find into bits and pieces and shambles, to be specific, those things easily smashed and broken and shattered; he did so for a terrible duration, during which time his staff were not allowed—never allowed during what he called "cleansing moments"—to move. At the termination of his tantrum, he stood in the midst of the rubble, panting and wiping the prickly, tingling, burning hot flashes off his flushing red face. A minute passed, and slowly he regained his composure, at which time he turned to face his childish tormentor, and he said in a restrained, bitter voice, "Let him come."

It Becomes

The Thing that was, and yet is but sought not to be, did not stir in any way so as to signal to even the most adroit observer that it was alive; indeed, the Thing sought to bury its physical and spiritual essence in the rotting debris, in the cluttered spoilage of the forest floor, to dive under and around crumbling leaves and insect remains and the fine particles of black soil and feel the gnarled roots of the hearty Redwood trees so they might hold the Thing fast under this canopy of brown and yellow filthy sewage. The putrid, acrid scent of the earth's garbage spilled into its dirty nostrils, and it felt great solace as it sought to fuse its burning senses with the pungent cycle of fertilization. It was only here that it felt safety and belonging, with the wastes and the corpses and the lowest life-forms in its close proximity. The refuse was its mounting shame and humiliation, the social environment in which it sought the company of its peers; yet, still it felt guilt at courting life, at wanting breath free from oozing mounds of humus flesh that was flush against its flaring nostrils; something in it, some idea begged for death, and something in it, upon that idea, riding it like a parasite, wanted wonderful, joyous life. Cogitating about what the Thing recently had done brought it great bouts of physical and emotional torment, driving the Thing to dig, much like a five-star mole, with its slender fingers down into the hard, cold belly of the earth, pulling its misdeeds up and over it. "Here I shall die, in this moldy and melancholy grave," the Thing thought. "I shall burden no one ever again." And sometimes when the Thing happened to think about its latest sin, it began to hum and shake, as if to die.

Rain came upon the forest that night, and precious droplets of hydrogen and oxygen molecules slipped into its mouth, and much to its chagrin, revived its sinking consciousness. It had not the exact perimeters in which courage lived, but it had faint superior knowledge of its close and silent neighbor, self-condemnation, and so therein did it romp.

And when the Thing happened to think on the subject of its latest catastrophic folly, the crashing weight of its burly shame sent it to shiver and quake, whereupon it took to digging deeper into the fresh, moist tissues and fibrous muscles and black blood of the earth.

The next day, in the early foggy dawn, after the heavy dew had settled in foamy wisps upon the ground, and life-forms in the velvet forest began to usher in the resplendent golden rays of morning, the Thing lay entrenched in its still-shallow, albeit well-concealed grave. It rejoiced at the slithery creatures that crept along its bare skin. "A snake, eh?" the Thing thought, feeling the soft, treading truck of many legs over its back. "Maybe it is poisonous, and it will deliver its pleasant cargo to me..." But the Thing groaned when the small creature left. "I have become one of them, maybe more like the rock and soil." It sighed deeply. "And here I shall stay until I die." It waited for its breath to expire, and it listened to its strong heartbeat, anxiously awaiting its cessation; but alas, nothing happened of the sort, and time, it seemed, continued its oath to keep the despicable Thing alive.

Then a sound of a curious nature came unto the Thing's muffled ears: the clamor of much movement, heavy movement, ordered movement, deliberate and approaching its geographical location. "How perfectly rude," it thought. "O, how the earth puts up with such vulgar noise the whole day through—what colossal patience." The Thing was very much like a creature upon its deathbed, feeling empathy for all good things great and small, animate and inanimate, living and dead. "Perhaps," the creature thought, eager now, "it is a troop of bears, and they would please eat me like a meat sandwich." Human voices sifted down to its subterranean level, and it grew more despondent once again, and it sighed deeply. "Here I lie." It could, in its mind's eye, discern which direction the human creatures were coming from, and where they were going to.

As the voices became clearer, it desired to hear their content, for it felt a bonding with human beings, as if it owed them a great debt it could not recompense; if at least it heard their words, it could, if the words were grievous, evince unsurpassed sympathy with them. "But I am far too wicked for even that," it decided, but as the voices grew nearer, it had no choice but to allow the passage of their brief history to seep into its dirty ears.

"You should," came in scattered bursts, like words with wings flitting about on a strong wind. "Prepared… better accommodations, hindsight, sir… is twenty…" Fragments sat atop fragments, timid voices clung to timid themes, and aggressive voices forced timid ones to shrink in terror. "The role of adjutant," the Master's voice declared, which was followed by mumbling the Thing could not decipher, and then as the troops moved nearer and stopped nearly atop its resting place, it heard it all.

"You, being a buffoon, are allowed one task, and that is to provide appropriate dwellings for me. I ought to kill you now and bury your diseased intellect right here and now, you stumbling idiot." The man whom the voice addressed, a man of surpassing intellect, a professor of political science, winced, but he could not, in his mind, condemn the Master for such deprecating remarks, for he actually thought himself guilty of all such charges. He had been drawn to the Master the same way a wide-eyed child is drawn to a sports hero, with awe and a willingness to listen and learn and obey. "Do you know that murder is distinguished from killing only by the situation?" the voice declared in a wide, arching shout. "And if I killed this half-wit, I would consider it self-defense against his far-reaching, far-flung stupidity."

"But it is the girl's fault, sir," said one of the bolder adjutants.

"Bah! The girl chased my primal rage out of the jungle! I was expressing myself just like any great artist! Antimatter meets antimatter—ha!" There was a distant calm upon the surface of the forest floor, but when the voice paraded its great girth of personality into the crispy air, it caused its attendants to tremble, and this sent ripples vibrating down into the shallow depths of the soil. It was just as if a poisonous snake had crawled through a plush green meadow full of baby white rabbits. "Well, let's not dawdle all day," bellowed the owner of the voice, and he walked away.

The Thing listened with curiosity, for though it could hear the muffled words of the speaker, it could not register intonation or tone in its ears; thus, it could not, even if the owner had been its dear friend, have recognized him.

It could, however, distinguish an adult voice from a child's voice. "I have heard the other men talk about him," one of the small voices began, sprinkled with ringlets of hope and humanity, "when I pretend to be asleep."

"But we thought he was dead," the other tiny voice replied.

There was a deliberate, dramatic pause, and then a strident shout from the Master ordered them to expedite their walk; but the first child remained undaunted in her ardent and precise elocution. "I remember seeing him bending down, helping my mother as she lay in the street..." But the terrible voice of the Master cleft her speech in twain, and the owners of the small voices reluctantly moved on.

The Thing lay drenched in a clammy sweat, frowning in disbelief, its gritty face stone silent as it began to hum and shake; but then it abruptly abated this disturbing humming and shaking, for its mind had seized upon the impossible. Of course, when the woeful tragedy had happened, the Thing had sought ways out of the seemingly unforgivable sin, to look for other inconceivable and utterly unattainable escapes, but there had been none. The Thing was guilt personified, once before and now again, original sin founded in haste. "Is it yet possible?" it mumbled into the clumps of rotting vegetation around its mouth, and then it abruptly shouted, as if it truly expected an answer, "Is it possible? Is it? Am I mad? Did I not hear the words from her very lips, or were they what I wanted to hear? Well?" it screamed, its mind seizing this stupendous epiphany. "Answer, you fool," and it began to quake, but not to tremble, but to free itself. "Up, up, you fool!" And it began to dig and kick about itself like a mad Thing.

It thrashed through the soft clumps of soil with renewed strength, sufficient to free itself from its temporary shelter, so that in only a minute, it was crawling atop ground. "I will return if I must," it gasped, lying for a few seconds on a bed of leaves, its chest heaving as its mouth gathered in fresh, cool air in great gulps. "But I must move," it spoke, beating itself with a scolding. "Up, up, you fool," it shouted, and it managed to crawl toward the dying voices.

Covered with green moss and moist clumps of soil and crushed leaves and broken twigs, it staggered northward, hopping over thick brush, falling over decaying logs, but it pressed on, pausing occasionally to listen for human voices, all the while vigorously rubbing its legs through its thick green- and brown-speckled and striped woolen pants.

A mile into its tumbling, anxious journey through the tangled thicket, it heard a distant whirring of mechanical origin. "A chopper," it whispered, and it urged its weary, lactic acid–laced body forward, its muscles straining as it pushed mere physical pain clear of its immediate goal to free its emotional pain from bondage.

Panic preened the Thing's feathers for flight, and soon it was soaring over shrubs and ducking in between overhanging branches; panic gave fuel to the birth of a new idea that if it failed now, it would be in emotional limbo, chasing nebulous figures from a distance, a new idea it wanted stillborn. "I have to know now," it demanded in its mind as the whirring roar of the helicopters grew stronger.

It came upon the scene, seeing through the dense network of tree limbs the swiftly rotating blades of the helicopters as they ascended into the deep blue pitch of clear sky. Its legs were leaded, but its will to know what was, and what was not, drove it faster toward the departing aircraft; and as the Thing burst from the thicket and came to the spot where the leaves were still swirling up from the wind of the blades, it looked up to see a fleeting image of the last helicopter as it cleared the treetops and flew away. And just then, at the precise moment that the Thing took in the full field of the chaotic scene, a girl in one of the seats looked back toward the forest and saw Joaquin standing there. He stood in numbed elation as his heart commanded his paralyzed mouth to speak. "Sylvia," he shouted and clenched his raised fist tightly, "live."

Her face evinced affirmation that she had seen him and understood, a radiant face full of hope and Fidelity, and she gave him a little nod of affection, and then her golden image disappeared into the obscure horizon of green forest and icy blue sky.

Everything around him transformed because everything inside him, from his dying cells to his mottled blood and soft bones, to his sagging heart and boiling brain, transformed at the exact moment he had spoken her name.

It was a transfiguration of mind, body, and soul, a resurgence of the shallow sea of humanity in him, a rekindling of his natural desire for life, an erosion of self-inflicted walls suddenly permeable and allowing fresh, warm white rays of sunlight to sift into his starving heart. He was light and free, and his mind was flooded with exhilaration that drove him to his muddy knees, whereupon he wept for untold minutes, rolling rapturously in the sweet aroma of the forest floor. But then he abruptly sat up, his face seized by a solemn, darkening mask of certitude. "But I must find her," he said, and he leapt up and called Captain Montoya and United States Marshal Jacob Shipper, and one other person; he then ordered some special equipment and clothes, and went back to the cabin of his friend before continuing with his quest.

To Those Who Wait

It is said that the death of a child is so grievous to a parent that such a pain is indefinable and without equal; however, there is a pain that approaches the mind of a parent from another point of the diabolical compass, a yellow, poisonous pain that just dips under the agonizing grasp of the mourner, digging deep into a shallow grave and festering there day after day, its noxious fumes robbing the lamenting soul of sense and calm and reason. This is the pain of a parent when they do not know if a missing child is dead or alive.

Juanita Chavez sat in the room of her daughter—a room like a holy shrine now—contemplating what had been and what is and what must be. "O God," she murmured, kneeling on the brown woolen rug that lay before the small bed with the pink blankets. Her knees felt the hardwood floors press against them, and she was not displeased. "Without you, we are as dust in the wind," she prayed, as she had every day for two years, but she prayed in privacy, as she wanted, not in the open places, where she knew sinners sought the approval of haughty judges within society. Her humble home lay nestled in the midst of a green pasture of shrubs and wild Oaks, barely inside the city boundaries of Redwood, in a place she and her husband had carefully selected to avoid the encroachment of civilization.

When she felt the burden of her guilt lifted, Juanita removed herself from the room and returned to a family who understood that to disturb her when she was in Sylvia's room meant severe emotional trauma for the offender. There was a tacit agreement in the Chavez house that the room was a sanctuary for anyone who entered, for Juanita knew that every practicing human being had to have a special place for solace.

Carlos, the eldest, understood this better than his younger brother, Juan, and his younger sister, Beatriz, and so he had always, like a loyal and protective son, made sure his mother was never disturbed when she visited the room of his absent sister.

"Mama, what do you do in Sylvia's room?" Juan asked this warm Spring night, as he lay sprawled on the family room floor amidst his toys.

"Juan," Carlos cried, casting a stern glance at his little brother.

Juan, although only eight years living on this green and blue planet, comprehended the social error he had committed, and thus hung his head low to his chest. "Sorry, Mama."

His mother held out her gentle hand and massaged his black hair, calming him; such is the power of a mother's touch, to swiftly absolve the past sins of her children against her. She smiled reassuringly at her little mijo, issued a knowing look at Carlos that spoke of a special bond between a parent and her eldest, adult child, and then she headed for the kitchen to prepare dinner. Carlos, buoyed by the ever-present protective sphere he drew over his mother, followed her.

"Mama," he began, as if he dared speak to her as an adult, "I need to talk to you." He looked down, searching the hardwood floors with his dark brown eyes, his heart heavy with the burden of his dilemma.

"Go ahead, Carlos, speak freely," she replied, pulling silver pots and pans from the brown cupboards, and she turned to face him. "A man does not hesitate when he has something important to say; say it, Carlos."

But his voice was the baying of the sheep, not the roar of the golden-haired lion. "It's about Sylvia."

"So," his mother replied, raising her right hand on high, "what about your sister?"

Mounds of firm, crisp eggshells and their respective fragments previously distributed everywhere about the house began to fade, first into thick-veined versions, and then into tiny, soft specks.

Carlos spoke again, fear dripping from every consonant, pain from every vowel; his face was drained of all color and warmth. "Mama," he said, choking on his traitorous words, "she was my sister."

His mother did not verbally reflect upon the content of his words, but she continued filling the pot with water from the faucet, and when the fresh, clean mountain water stopped flowing, she spoke, her voice firm and steady as she gestured outside. "Astronomers tell us that if the sun were to stop shining suddenly, there would be eight and a half minutes left of sunlight; people would not know for those precious minutes that the sun had died." She turned and walked to the iron stove, set the pot onto the black metal holder and turned the knob, and faced her son. "Your sister is alive until I do not feel her loving warmth," and then she smiled affectionately; "I will always feel her loving warmth."

Carlos, though prepared, still wavered in his declaration. "Are you still clinging to the phone call from that madman? That was nearly a year ago..." There, he had dipped into the unspeakable topic; he had fallen into an inviolate territory and made accusing footsteps toward a sacred structure.

She looked at him as if he had punched her hard in her soft belly. "You don't know who he is," she whispered, not wanting to defend Joaquin against accusations even from her eldest child.

"Two years, Mama, two years she has been gone," he continued, emboldened by her lack of voice, as if it were a signal that she had capitulated to his accusations, as if her untenable emotions held her positions. "In child abductions, if the child is not returned within three days..." But even he could not quote the macabre statistic. "Mama," his voice was tender now, "you've got to let go; you have to start living. The police have closed the case. Last year, when three of his Gang," no one could mention the name of Slaughter in this home, "were found with this mannequin, when at first it was reported that it was a young girl..." But once again his courage lapsed as he remembered how his mother had been ill for weeks after the shock of the news, even though it was quickly discerned that a childlike doll figure that resembled Sylvia had been in the backseat of the crushed vehicle. "How much longer, Mama? How many more years until you admit..."

His mother turned around quickly, her beautiful, swarthy face illuminated by great emotion. "Forever, Carlos, until forever," she cried, "until I see her again."

He was caught up now in the emotional tumult, and his normally taut restraints were unhinged, slipping off his male ego. "And what about Beatriz and Juan? You think about Sylvia as much as you do about them; we're losing you to a lie…" There, he had breached the carefully woven bond of civility between mother and son, and he felt sick inside; but still, he had to consummate his charge, for he reasoned he could see so much clearer now than when his little sister was taken, so long ago. "Let her go, Mama. Admit that Sylvia is dead—Sylvia, my sister—I loved her too, but she is gone, and we're not."

She stared at him as if he had just confessed to a horrible crime, but then her entire being transformed, her visage adorned now with blessed hope and radiating a luminous splendor of Fidelity and Love as she whispered, defiantly, proudly, confidently, "Amongst the faithless, faithful only she," and she turned around to continue fixing the delicious supper.

And this was the Summer of the second year of the family not knowing.

Alyssa

There were always girls coming and going, some being dropped off at underground cabins and some at aboveground cabins, and some girls disappearing forever. Despite the avowed threat of death for runaways, there were always girls running away, for the girls saw it as their duty to try to escape, the same way prisoners of war attempt to flee their captors.

It was the electronic bracelets that prevented the girls from any escape of merit; any girl who left the camp was detected within one minute and could then be tracked wherever she went. It was the great stumbling block, and it kept them in line, but there were always girls who lost control of themselves and simply ran, yet they were inevitably caught and punished, or if they became a chronic problem, they were killed.

There were three girls now: Sylvia, who was nearly eleven; a girl who was almost twelve, named Margo; another girl, Alyssa, who was twelve, and who had already told the other two of her plans for escape, but for now, Sylvia had managed to dissuade her.

"But I cannot wait any longer," Alyssa said one day, wiping the sweat off her flushed face after a harsh run; "I don't want to be dropped off at a cabin." Her countenance reflected the horror of the unknown about these secretive places, which haunted the girls. Once, when they had happened upon one of these camouflaged aboveground structures, they had seen foreign-looking men driving away with a girl or two, and this had cast them into a frenzy at their fate. "I won't wait any longer," Alyssa said, her dark visage full of passion.

"But there must be a way out," Sylvia answered, narrowing her eyes. "Maybe if we could cut the bracelets off."

"Cleo did that last year, and she was beaten for it," Margo said.

They hushed themselves as two of the male adjutants came by and looked the girls up and down, smiling all the while.

"They are creepy," Alyssa said. "If my father were here…" Now all of the girls were silent, for mention of family always sent them to the blessed sanctuary of their private thoughts.

It was agreed that Alyssa should wait, but that waiting without seeking answers was useless, so the girls vowed to find a weakness in the electronic-bracelet system.

A week hence, and a palpable crack appeared that the girls sought to exploit. Sylvia had been standing near one of the younger adjutants while he was discussing a glitch in the system that would not detect a bracelet being removed. Sylvia had anxiously returned with the information, but Alyssa was incredulous.

"And you are sure he did not hear you?" she said, frowning. "As if he was testing you just so we would try to escape, and they would come after us?"

"I was behind a tree; he did not know I was even there, and then he moved away, and I waited for the longest time to be sure he was gone, and then I came back here."

"But why now? Why a problem now with the bracelets?" Alyssa asked.

"Maybe there are always problems, but we were just too afraid to try to find them," Margo said, looking for approval.

"Maybe," Alyssa responded, "but we still need something to cut them off with." Margo asked her when she would attempt her escape. "Well," she said, sitting down with the girls, as all of them picked up their textbooks for their daily studies, "they search us in the morning and before we go to bed, so it has to be right after the last bed check."

But it all seemed too impossible, and the chances so dismal that they began to forget about the plan. Days went by, and no ideas occurred to them, nor did any easy escape routes, and the girls became discouraged; but then Sylvia saw, by chance, a chain cutter in the black bag of one of the men, and the girls began to formulate a plan; and when they had devised the best one they could, they began to wonder if perhaps the error in the electronic-bracelet system had been fixed. "But we cannot worry about that now," Alyssa said. "So it is all set."

And so they simply waited for the moment, and when it did come, they hoped it would go something like this:

Margo was to wait for the signal from Sylvia, and then Margo was to tell the young adjutant that there was a snake in the bushes near her, and he would hopefully leave his tiny post and investigate, while Sylvia would lean down and pick up the chain cutter and toss it to Alyssa, who would bend down and cut her bracelet and throw the cutter back to Sylvia, who would then place it exactly in its former place in the leather bag; but this deceit had to be executed after the bed check, when the female adjutants were out making their toilet and while their captor was performing his unsavory acts, which the girls did not wish to speak of, and when the other adjutants were turned around or busy cooking food or simply occupied elsewhere. It would have to be performed in perfect synchronization, or the outcome would be a perfect physical disaster for the girls.

And then it happened; the moment came, and the girls recognized it, and Margo, having seen the snake—such snakes that were forever in the woods and bothering them—ushered the poor slithering creature near the camp, and then she stood near the bush and turned around and called to her potential hero for rescue. Of course, the young fool walked over, and upon confirming the presence of the snake he forgot about any suspicious activities of the girl and proceeded to stomp the creature to an untimely death. It was then that Sylvia, during that brief window of opportunity, reached smoothly into the bag and grabbed the metal clippers and threw them to Alyssa, who expertly caught them with her strong and sure hands and then bent down, and with one quick stroke, snapped the irksome bracelet in twain, and in another perfectly fluid motion rose up and tossed the clippers back to Sylvia, who then nervously replaced them in the exact spot of the black bag and then casually walked toward Alyssa. When the young male fool came back from his daring deed, there was no reason for him to know he had been outfoxed by three female children.

As the girls lay in their sleeping bags, they sweated the foul sweat of fear that seeps out of the trembling body and absorbs the acrid sense of terror and then seeps back in again to deliver an explosive cargo that unsettles every nerve and thought. They waited like naughty lambs that stand in disguise before the stalking wolf; they waited for their Master and captor to find them out and approach them and strike them and swear at them and threaten them with a horrible mutilation or a slow and vicious beating that would lead to a slow, crawling, agonizing death; they waited and waited, but it did not come, and so they waited some more, but when it did not come, when the riot of being found out did not arrive with sticks and rocks and the black whip upon their persons, hope dared to raise its resplendent head for a brief sojourn in the clean, crisp air; yes, hope came and settled above them like a rainbow cloud, and it covered them in a fervent optimism.

Alyssa whispered to the girls she considered her sisters, and she fought hard to repress any tears that might disassemble her courage. Her voice was low and sweet, like a warm Spring breeze that brings succor to those afflicted with disease. "I will bring back help." But the girls dared not embrace or talk too much for fear of being found out, and so Alyssa looked at them and said, with great devotion and Love, "We will always be sisters no matter where we are; where one of us goes, the other goes too."

"And my God is your God," Sylvia said, softly sobbing.

With this, Alyssa, spying the absence of movement in the camp, and seeing her path clear, took the map she had drawn of the way back to a road they had seen a week before, and then quietly and stealthily she crawled out of her sleeping bag and through the tight circle of Cedar trees and right out, right past the sleeping adjutants and clean away, clear and clean into the sweet embrace of a night-bride black as pitch with an absent moon for a husband and massive clouds covering the frustrated stars. The girls could not sleep, so excited and worried were they, but eventually they fell into a light slumber.

The light of day came adorned with a dull, gray overcast shadow that dumped gloom onto everyone and everything. The girls awoke with a start. Their captor and all of the adjutants were standing in a power circle around them, arms folded, staring with the glare of impending punishment. Sylvia instinctively looked to Alyssa's sleeping bag, and white shock ravaged her face, for in the bag was Alyssa. Sylvia looked at Margo, who was just waking, and then both of them looked at the circle of condemnation around them, and then they looked to Alyssa, and they felt the prick of terror cut into them.

They watched in horror as their captor walked up to the sleeping bag and lifted up the top cover to reveal the dead body of the girl. Sylvia and Margo shrieked and began to scream.

Slaughter spoke like a leviathan that has finally found the troublesome tick upon its great, scaly girth. "Did you think we would not know?" he began, as he stood with a giant tree limb in his hands. "Do you not know that we know everything you do and think?" He smirked. "Tell me, who was responsible for this—one or both of you?" He watched in a haughty silence. "It does not matter to me, for the most painful punishment will be meted out to both of you."

Sylvia, trembling, and still gazing in sorrow at her dead friend, abruptly rose up and stood perfectly erect before her accuser. "I did it. I planned it all! Margo didn't do any of it!"

But Margo jumped up, defiance riding her proud face. "I helped too. I helped. I did!"

Slaughter smiled widely. "Then both of you will be beaten until..."

"And so what!" Sylvia shouted. "What will you do to us, huh? Will you kill us, will you? Who would you have to torture then? I hate you. I hate you for what you did to Alyssa, and Andrea, and all of the other girls..." And she did not weep now, but stood bravely and defiantly against her jailer.

"I should make both of you sleep with her cold, dead body. I should," he said, his voice lowered into a sinister octave where it boiled and baked and hardened into a cast of malevolent promises. "I should, but I won't; not this time, not until I get more girls, so for now, for now..." And he turned around and walked to his adjutants and whispered instructions, then turned back to face the girls. "It will come, soon, and you will be provoked."

Five nights later, as the girls slept, they were awoken by loud bangs and cracks and much laughter and shouting. They looked up and realized that the day of reckoning had come, and so they scooted inside their sleeping bags and let it come, the pummeling of the rocks on their tough bodies and the leather cat-o'-nine-tails cracking and snapping and stinging their tough outer shells and the thick wooden sticks whacking them and hitting them and beating them for what seemed an eternity, but in the end was just a long, draining, and roiling minute. And then it was abruptly over, and the adjutants went back to their posts, and the girls wept and consoled each other and spoke of Alyssa and wept some more, and then the gift of golden sleep overcame them.

A few more weeks went by, and Margo was dropped off at an underground cabin, and more girls joined the sad troupe that marched and marched and toured the tangled underbelly of the green and brown forests.

On the Trail

Winter graciously gave way to Spring, and the land blossomed; it was a time when Man was not rushed in his work; he could sit down and cogitate about things, he could move freely outdoors, he could work the land in peace, or he could plan and begin anew some great monument to himself or Nature. But none of this mattered to Joaquin who, due to the intense lobbying efforts of Jacob Shipper, was now a Special Deputy United States Marshal. What he did, he did regardless of who was around him or the innate value of the weather. The trail of his quarry had grown cold, and his burden increased. On the ground, he found nothing; in the police records and contacts, he found nothing; and on his intuitive hunches, he found nothing. Slaughter had vanished, without physical trace, without even the faint smell of chaos normally left behind as he plowed his way through civilization. Joaquin knew that such a man could not move through the world without hurting part of it; such a man could not move through a town without hurting it any more than a tornado could; it was as much a part of Slaughter's nature to destroy as it is for any predatory beast. Joaquin knew this, for the Giant had told him so, when Joaquin did not know it was Slaughter the Giant spoke of.

Spring gave way to promising Summer, but Summer proved to be a cold and empty mistress, as She gave up no information regarding the enemy. When he had exhausted the resources of Summer, Autumn came in, promising much and giving very little. Winter seized power before Autumn was finished with Her special teaching song, and the trail froze.

Joaquin turned his hunt toward the east. "A predator marks its territory and remains its prisoner," he thought, walking along the path. "He will go where he has people and he can disappear into the land." He walked a little farther, and then thought, "Time to eat."

It was always time to eat, or time to prepare, or time to cook and save food. He could easily grab a handful of berries and eat them as he ran or walked. Berries were among the easiest foods to eat because he already knew about them. He had grown up in the wilderness and understood the rules of eating raw food. He knew about tasting certain parts of a plant to test for acidity or irritation to his lips. But berries were easy because of their very colors; he knew that white and yellow and green berries had a low rate of edibility, so he stayed away from them entirely; then there were red berries, with a high edibility rating, but he often picked berries as he ran and did not want to stop and examine the type of red berry bush. Aggregate berries—like raspberries and blackberries and mulberries—had a high edibility rating, so he tended to concentrate on these as he moved along.

He could not take the chance of illness on the trail, so he was very conservative with his food choices. He sometimes chewed on raw tubers, like carrots or bulbs, like wild onions or nuts, like almonds and filberts; when he cooked, he made sure the meal was gourmet, and he often made pemmican from it for later use.

When he wanted to catch fish, he would sometimes catch them barehanded in streams, or snag them using hooks and lines made from branches, or snare them in shallow water using a spear he had sharpened from wood. To cook the fish, he would first gather rocks and lay them closely together, place small pieces of twigs atop them, light the twigs with his flint rock, allow the fire to burn down to ashes, and then place the filleted fish atop the rocks. He used other methods when he was in other areas, but he was always careful to make pemmican after cooking the fish, and this is how he did it: he would take some of the fish, grind it up, mix it with natural preservatives like lime or lemon, add berries and nuts, roll it into small balls, leave it on a rock to dry, and then store it in his backpack. Cooking was a constant, and he refused to eat the food of the city.

He stayed away from cities, refusing rides in cars, refusing police transports in helicopters, and refusing the comforts of buildings and soft beds.

"How," he would often think, "will I catch these mongrels if I leave the trail? Is he not as cunning as the fox? Is he not more animal than human, living in the shadows of the forest? I must live as he lives, hunt as he hunts, and go where he goes, or I will fail."

Loneliness nibbled at him. He sometimes felt despair as he traveled for weeks without encountering or talking to people; occasionally, he would check in with Montoya or Shipper, and the few minutes on his cell phone would greatly cheer him; but as much as he wanted to talk more, he knew he could not. When the conversations ended, he would continue on his journey, feeling refreshed.

Nighttime soothed him as he lay in his sleeping bag and stared up at the tranquil stars. He knew what was to come when he fell asleep, and this was the secret of his survival in the wild. He would dream of them. Every night, every single pitch-black night, regardless of the day's events, he dreamt of his wife and daughter. In his dreams they were a family; in his dreams, they were together again; in his dreams he had what he wanted more than anything anyone could possibly imagine. He would wake up in the morning revitalized and eager to gain the hunt, yet melancholy slowly hunted him from a distance, slowly catching him throughout the day until finally ensnaring him before the embers of twilight sprinkled onto the land. But then he would cook and eat and dream, and everything would be fine, and he would wake up, and the day would start all over again. If he could not dream about his beloved family, he reasoned, he would have died.

The trail turned east, and he turned with it, crossing the Oregon border and traveling through Klamath and Lake counties, dipping into Nevada, then back again into Oregon, and over into Idaho. He came up through the Black Pine Mountains, and continued through the Snake River Plain, through the Boulder Mountains, and up to the Salmon River Mountains.

He was following a trail his foe had frequented in the past. He had no choice but to follow this now. He tried to stay off the main roads, but sometimes it was impossible. There were times when the local police would stop and question him, and he would always leave them incredulous when he offered proof that he was indeed a Federal Marshal.

When he reached the Salmon River Mountains, he stopped to camp near a pristine lake for the night. There was a cabin of a biologist who had faint but discernible ties to his foe, and this cabin was a few miles in distance. "Here," he thought, "I shall wait."

He ate well that night; he had carved a spear out of a tree limb and used it to catch fish, and then he had skewed them on wood and cooked them over a fire he had made of twigs, which was inside a semicircular wall of rock he had built to keep out the strong, swirling winds.

He slept soundly in the Spring-flavored night air, and he awoke refreshed, then ate, washed, and scouted a two-mile radius and found the anomaly he sought. There, as he stood behind a Spruce tree in his lightly colored green and brown clothes, he watched the man plodding along, and his own visage was aflame with wrath and vengeance.

"He comes for me, and yet I have come for him," he thought, "and I have found him as easily as a father finds his own infant in his own house." He watched in disgust as the armed man recklessly walked through the brush. "This man is in my house, and yet he is not even as a child of the forest, but an alien here who stumbles in the dark and disrupts the Harmony he cannot see; and I am like a father who was born and bred here, and who knows what must come and how it will be done."

Joaquin circled around the man and watched him from every angle and every point of the compass for hours, and the man never knew he was being watched, just as a baby deer would never realize the unseen presence of the king of beasts until it was firmly in the lion's jaws; and so, when Joaquin was satisfied that the man was incapable of retreat or proper defense, he said, at a safe distance and in utter anonymity, "Ho, assassin, you will surrender your arms to me, the man you seek even now."

The assassin who had approached from the east stopped abruptly in his tracks and raised his weapon on high, and his eyes searched the dense verdure before him but saw nothing. "Show yourself, lawman."

"You are ordered to surrender, assassin," Joaquin said, after altering his position. "Or you will lie down with your thieving kin, the jackal, and share his cold bed as the ants raise the alarm to come and eat your stinking carcass."

The assassin of the east scowled and shouted, "Fight me like a man."

Joaquin moved as if he were the wind, sifting unseen and untracked through the verdant kingdom of flowers and ferns, and then he sent his battle cry up into the perfumed air. "But you must be a man to fight a man, and so I say to you, surrender, jackal."

The assassin proceeded to empty his weapon into the speckled and striped shadows of his imagination.

"You will surrender your weapons now, assassin," Joaquin said, after changing his position again. "You will lay them down and remove your shirt."

The assassin of the east smiled as he should not have smiled and then returned this command with more volleys from his rifle, and then he dove to the ground.

Joaquin shot now, not at this man, but at the man who had so clumsily attempted to approach him from the west, and he dispatched him with great ease; he then turned his icy visage forward and measured the distance to the assassin from the east by assessing the assemblage of dense plant life between himself and the man, and he clearly saw the path his bullets must travel to successfully kill him; and presently, he did kill the man, and he walked up to him and removed the assassin's earphone and cell phone; and then he walked back to the other assassin and removed the man's earphone and cell phone, and then he stood with judgment scrawled across his burning countenance and said, "Had you a soul, you would not have been here; and I have done what I need to do, and better me than any other, for I will not hesitate in taking your life or others like you, but neither will I boast," and he took a long, deep breath, and he looked toward his camp, and he started back to it.

When the police came, he instructed them to inform the families that the men had died in a hunting accident.

He called Montoya and Shipper, and he prepared to leave the site, wondering why the deaths of these men were even a thought in his mind. "Why?" he wondered. "Why should it matter? They deserved death." But as much as he tried, he could not ease his conscience.

That night he dreamt of his family, and as he approached them they retreated from him in terror; he fell to his knees, trembling, his hands outstretched toward them. "What have I done?" he begged them, looking about himself. "It is I, who loves you more than his own life, and all the life on earth; all life who has lived before me or who lives now or who will ever live—I put beneath thy exalted presence."

His wife, dressed in her white Spring dress, looked at him with compassion.

"Husband, do you not see what you are becoming?" He shook his head in earnest. "Look," she said, gesturing to his hands, "and behold the testimony of those who bear witness against thee." He looked again at his hands and saw that they were covered in a dark-red blood, and he recoiled in horror against it. "Do you know why?"

"Surely, I have done nothing but avenge the wrong done to my family," he said, and he looked longingly at his daughter, who clutched her mother's dress. "I would gladly cut off my hands if they offended thee, so I might embrace both of you with my pitiful body."

"But it is not your hands you need to smite, but your emboldened heart, which even now begins to harden and turn black."

"Why? What have I done except kill those who needed to die?"

She looked at him with love. "Darling, did you hesitate to kill the men in the car?"

"No," he shouted, "they deserved to die, for the death they gave to one who was so innocent and unwilling to resist them."

"These were men who truly deserved death?"

He looked down before her, knowing her next words. "You do not think I should have killed the two men…"

"And what did you do to prevent their deaths? You knew they were coming; you allowed them entry into your trap so you might destroy them."

"Yes, I wanted to kill them; they were men of vile character; they needed to die."

She closed her eyes and turned her head and allowed it to tilt downward. "You could have captured them…"

"No," he replied anxiously, shaking his head, and then he said grievously, "yes, yes…"

She looked up again, her face awash in sorrow. "O, darling, my darling, could you not have arranged that the police find them? Could you not have wounded them?"

"Yes, I could have, but the man I track needs to know…"

"To know that the man who follows him is as ruthless as he, my love?"

He was silent, gazing at his bloodstained hands. "This is war, and in war, there are no virtues, no rules, no moral sentiment, for those who oppose you."

She retreated a step farther from him, her daughter next to her. "My love—in war, men kill each other, but if there exists no humanity, then all are guilty of murder." He stood, silent. "We will not be with you again until you understand that the need for someone to die is not determined by the law of Man, but by the law of God. The Giant taught you this; you need only to listen."

"But you cannot leave me," he said; "what am I to do without you?" And he fell to his knees, stretching out his arms to his beloved daughter, who wept for him. "What will become of me?"

"My love," she said passionately, reaching out her hands to him, "my husband…" And she vanished, as did his daughter, leaving him to weep as he fell to the moist earth, his head buried in the dirt. His dreams of them stopped that night.

And now he knew that he whom he hunted now hunted him, so he altered his course, traveling in random paths until he found evidence of his foe in a cabin deep in the southern Oregon woods. From there, he followed their path again.

The Tracker

He would not be deterred by anything or anyone in his pursuit of the enemy. He hardened his resolve to capture his foe, he hardened his heart against compassion, and he hardened against his want for inner peace; he would not stop, he would not rest, he would not relax or enjoy life or listen to any merriment or be a part of any idle chatter or allow his mind to moan for the luxuries of the sweet allure of civilization and the great treasures therein of human pipes piping and metal cars rushing and hot food simmering and his own mind becoming glazed over with longing for the gentle mercy of sleeping undisturbed in a finely built structure; this was his lot now, to be apart and away and beyond the trappings of soft Man, and he embraced it fully and unabashedly and knew it was now a part of him; he had passed the final boundaries between the family of people and the family of Nature. "I am home," he would say, looking about the splendid forest, and he wondered if he could ever go back.

He lost any sign of his quarry for a short while, but then he picked it up again.

It was now Autumn, when the warm air is still profuse with the rich nutrients to engender life; the plants proudly wore their rainbow-colored robes of perfume and velvet, their luster reaching its golden-tipped zenith, their robust existence seemingly eternal, their beauty unparalleled. Everywhere there were bright flowers, their stem-posture erect, their soft petals reaching high, their multihued petals painting awe and wonder; and everywhere there were red and pink petals and purple-speckled stems, and flowers with white and yellow elongated clusters, and purple flowers with rounded violet-blue clusters, and flowers with mellow yellow and hot mauve clusters; there were flamboyant flowers with their noble bearing and high-riding silky plumes and violet banners, and there were shy flowers with their humble shades of deep green and cool icy blue. And if one looked ever so closely into this wondrous congregation, one could see that there were silly ingenues with their powdery blue bonnets and silken purses, and proud young men with their bold breastplates of golden armor that glittered in the luminous sunlight, and little boys and girls sitting and smiling in small circles, the girls rocking to and fro in the honey-scented breezes, their rosy ringlets bouncing lightly about their radiant faces, and the boys bobbing up and down, their crimson faces grinning like carefree rascals. Islands and islands of these natural messengers of vitality and robust life adorned the forest floor, a civilization of artless creatures from the treasure trove of Nature to bring joy to the world.

And everywhere in the forest there was the breezy song of hope and promise, all along the brown trail of dirt and twig and pebble; up in the hearty, verdant trees, in the lustrous furry coat of the rabbit, in the gentle flight of the Red-tailed Hawk, it was there; it was there in the men with their strong muscles and confident gaze, and in the women with their long black tresses, as the lovers walked hand in hand along the sloping trails; and everyone who saw it recognized it and understood it and obeyed its special language to enjoy this sweet nectar of life now, to live and enjoy every moment now, to embrace it and be happy, now.

But this could not be for one man who ran past it all, past all this sublime glory—instead it filled his mind with a higher purpose; yes, he recognized it all, but he saw it in its individual parts and not as a whole, lest he be swept away into the land of contentment.

When he saw the spreading ocean of rich foliage and crystal-shining streams before him, and the scurrying animals with their cinnamon-colored ears and sleek brown coats, with their plush white furs and black tails, with their quick hops and bold jumps and squiggling movements, he looked deeper; when he saw the insects with their sulfur-yellow wings and greenish bodies, with their smoky-gray feathers and burnt-brown bellies, with their perpetually moving, slender antennae and furtive steps and nervous digs, he looked deeper; when he saw those lone monoliths, the steadfast sentinels of the forest, the mighty trees, with their shallow fissures in their thick coats and their crooked branches spreading out far and wide with their dark green needles, with their red-brown cones and heart-shaped blue-green, orange, and red leaves and small, precious fruit the color of the deep azure sky, he looked deeper; when he saw the delicate flowers, he looked deeper; when he saw the black, fertile soil and the rich mulch and the prismatic, translucent minerals with their radiating aggregates and infinite forms, he looked deeper; and when he looked deeper he saw the sacrosanct soul of Nature, a logical, harmonious, symmetrical manuscript that emanated in every variety of life. In this holy writ, as he lay or sat upon the good green earth, he absorbed the raw energy of linear life; he saw, he felt any irregularity, any indentation, any disturbance, any coerced movement, any litter discarded by sloppy, careless, lazy Man; so any smashed debris or crushed life, any crumbled, shredded, infected life or dirt or mineral, he found it and inhaled its mauled scent and felt its broken skeleton. He felt the ruptured burrows of insects and animals, saw the shattered, fragile web of the tiny spider, heard the mournful cry of the bird whose nest is touched by unclean hands, listened to the plaintive wail of the animal whose private sanctuary has been breached by a wayward interloper, and smelled the offense of cigarette smoke clinging to outraged leaves and the slightest odor of gasoline fumes that hung like a funeral wreath on tender bark.

And when he did happen to come across the tracks of his quarry, he could see the damage done in the land as clearly as an ordinary city man sees the carnage done by a plane crash to a neighborhood full of houses.

Any unnatural action in Nature leaves a palpable scar on the busy culture of flora and fauna.

Joaquin, the custodian of Nature, would find minute scratches on the surface of boulders, and he would see the compressed dirt and dust and sand marked by shoes; and he would follow these markers to the dirt and then measure the footprints—their depth and width and height—and as he already knew the weight and height and gait of those whom he hunted, he knew if these were the right tracks.

He would follow the trail of his quarry, which crossed a path that worms traveled, and as he knew that worms ventured forth in the early morning and left tiny mud pebbles behind, if the footprints had crushed the worm cast, then his game had come late in the morning; but he knew that if the worm cast lay undisturbed in the footprints, then his game had gone by late at night.

He would find broken leaves, broken twigs, and broken spider webs, and upon inspecting them, he knew that if these leaves were still green and not brown, then he was only a few days behind; if the twigs had a lighter color and still showed their fibers, he was only days behind; and he knew that if the footprints were beside a fresh spider web that was spun at night, it meant that his quarry had passed before late night.

And there were times when he found that his quarry split up, and he was not deterred; and there were times when his quarry exchanged shoes, and he was not deterred; and there were times when his quarry employed elusive skills, and he was not deterred; he was not shaken when his game split up because he could read pressure releases, which were like personal identification cards, in their footprints, and as he already knew the unique signature card of each member of his quarry, he was never fooled into following a group that did not contain Sylvia; the transferring of shoes did not fool him because it was the height and weight and gait and personal habits of the quarry that identified itself to the Tracker; and as for his quarry attempting to lose him, he was not fooled, for he knew that in deceptive techniques like walking backward, the footprints are wider apart, shorter, and the sand and soil and the grass inside the prints are still swept along in a forward movement.

So, he saw it all and knew it all because he had already seen it all and done it all and he was not fooled and could not be deterred nor shaken or broken or perplexed, and thus he moved onward and upward and crept closer and closer to sighting his quarry.

And then Winter came, and with it great power and fury, burying the land in its titanic desire for grandiloquent expression. And Joaquin was not deterred.

Up the Crystal Cathedral

He was far north now, and he had on his white camouflage polar clothes. He changed his clothes with the seasons and the region. He wore green and brown clothes for forest and woods, white for snow country, black always for night. His shape and shadow had to be indistinguishable from his surroundings, his silhouette and the surface of his skin and clothes had to effortlessly fall into the natural energy flow of Nature; and his physical movements had to be fluid, his placement amongst Nature's children had to be part of a logical, symmetrical posture, or he would be seen as an artificial insert and be spotted by his quarry. He moved now with the fineness and sleekness of a snow-dwelling creature, gliding smoothly along the crumbly snow.

He was immersed in damp snow now, and the fluctuating temperature allowed the snow to thaw and refreeze.

He found six tracks he determined were not more than six days old. He rechecked the equipment he had recently purchased along the way. All was in readiness as he continued traveling north into the heart of Montana.

And then it happened. He came across a large Search and Rescue Team which, he soon found out, was looking for two lost children. At first, they were suspicious of him, but once he displayed credentials that the police officers in the group verified by phone at their headquarters, the Team turned to him for aid.

But he was not interested; instead, he asked them about the possible whereabouts of those he pursued, but as he gained no good information from them, he moved on.

"You're a tracker," one of the men from the Team cried. Joaquin turned around. "You're a Deputy Marshal sworn to protect us from harm, and you won't stop and help us now?"

Joaquin was loath to explain himself for any reason, so he merely stood and stared at his accuser.

"These are my children," the man said, "for the sake of God, please stop and help us." But he saw that his passionate words were without sufficient force to unfurl the rigid oath that the man had recently taken, and his words fell into a frustrated pleading. "How long have you tracked the people you seek?"

Joaquin hesitated, and then he said, thinking that perhaps the people still might help him, "Over two years."

"Two years?" the mother of the children cried, exasperated. "My little boy and girl have been gone for twenty-four hours in this awful weather, and they'll be dead soon if we don't find them. Two years?" she lamented, holding her head as if it were about to burst. "And you cannot add one day?"

"No," the Tracker replied, without any hesitation at all, and then, turning around, he moved on.

"I can't stop now, not for them, not for anybody, not for any reason," he thought, attempting to assuage the pangs of guilt that bore up in him. "I have been sworn to serve and protect..." But he stopped in his very tracks, and for a moment, he found himself as the father pleading for the life of his own children. "I cannot let sentiment," he grunted, moving on, "obscure my mission; I cannot lose them now, not when I am so close..."

And then he stopped again, frozen, his thoughts obliterated as his naked heart examined this dilemma from every conceivable angle. "And if they were my children," he heard the gentle voice of his wife say, "and you had the chance to save them, and the girl, later; if you even had a chance, with all of your great knowledge, darling, you might save them all." And then he heard his little girl whisper, "Daddy, you know the right thing to do." And he heard Sylvia say, "I will wait for you..."

He was shocked that when he regained clarity, his feet were slightly cold; he checked his watch. He had stood immobile for nearly ten minutes, much too long in this harsh Winter weather. He immediately began to walk about and shake his arms vigorously to bring circulation into his limbs, thinking of his family and Sylvia, and then of the lost children.

The Search and Rescue Team was walking down a snow-white slope, looking for signs, when they turned around and found the Tracker upon them.

"Tell me everything," he said urgently; "now," he commanded. He quickly determined that the Team was going the wrong way.

He explained to them about the problem with damp snow and how the sun ages footprints and the shade keeps them fresh. The Team begged him to show them how he prevailed against this. He bent down and placed his gloved finger into the rear of the small tracks before them. "If it breaks up easily, it means that the tracks are fresh; if not, it means the tracks are older; but if the snow is turned into an icy gray, it means the tracks are older. See, here, these tracks are fresh." The visages of the Team were illuminated with a fantastic awe and hope, as if a supernatural force for good had come down from the heavens to bring succor.

But it was twilight now, and the Team was fraught with panic, for they had neither the equipment nor the special knowledge to track people at night; they looked to the lone monolith before them, and they laid their trust in his hands, and they bowed before his expertise like children before their omnipotent father.

The Tracker bent down and took out his infrared-vision goggles and began to inspect faded footprints; he then took out his flashlight that emitted blue light and shone it on the footprint, revealing two slight, small tracks. He measured them and then measured the gait and determined that they belonged to the two lost children. He moved swiftly now, stopping often to inspect the prints, to measure the gaits, which were becoming shorter and irregular, a sure sign that the children were weakening.

The men and women of the Team silently followed him like a faithful flock, ever confident, ever silent, ever hopeful.

And then, just as the great, black, bleak mountain of space above them relented, and the ice diamonds so expertly set inside them receded away, just as the first sprays of argent light stretched across the crystal, rosy dawn, the Tracker fell upon a fresher set of tracks; and then, with great expedition, he led the Team toward a group of snow-covered, tall trees. Therein, huddled together, and having smartly dug a small igloo-like structure, were the two Innocents, alive and soon to be completely healthy again.

There was much hugging and laughing and kissing and crying and diverse kinds of emotions flooding the happy scene, but when the Father and Mother turned to embrace and thank the Tracker, he instinctively backed away from them, feigning excuses and appointments to be kept. They stared at him in bewilderment but expressed their explicit gratitude for his kindness. He acknowledged all of it with a slight nod and moved on back toward his own trail. He could not, would not, must not feel the warmth and ease and joy of human Love—not now, not yet, lest it weaken his resolve and bury his iron will to win.

When he was far away from them, he took to beating himself about the head, and he cowered inside of himself and shrank down and knelt to the ground and stared at the lifeless snow. "O, Anna and Maria, I have done the right thing—now," he whispered, and he let his head fall against his chest as he wept. And then he stood up, renewed, and once more he pledged his life and liberty to finding Sylvia.

The wind was blowing harder now. He soon regained the tracks of his quarry and so resumed the hunt. His resolve strengthened. "I am a better man—now," he thought, "because of what I have just done; I must help people; it is who I am, it is who we are; this much I do know, the Giant taught me so," and he paused, his face wearing an expression of shock and wonder, "and Anna told me so, so long ago..."

He was approaching a region rife with high, rising mountains and frozen streams and ponds and waterfalls. He moved on toward an enormous rock wall that loomed large before him some three miles in the distance; darkness had once more descended upon him as he examined footprints that seemed fresh, and he hesitated, and he looked up at the rising mountain of gray-black rock, and he took out his infrared binoculars and scanned the cliffs. He changed into his black clothes now, as was his ritual at night. He pressed on.

He stood at the base of the rock mountain that extended for miles on either side of him and admired the elegance of the frozen waterfall in front of him and stooped down to examine footprints, pondering their existence. "It is a curious thing to walk right up to the base," he thought. "Why would they..." And then his movements halted when he heard a slight rustling sound above him. He took out his small parabolic listening device and put it to his ear and aimed it on high.

"We have already checked the perimeter, and he hasn't come around, so we will wait until he does come."

"How long, do you think?"

"Don't know, but the boss man says maybe in one day; but we have orders and we wait to do the job, no matter. Now fan out; all of you should be about fifty meters apart, and no more talking until he is dead."

He couldn't be certain but he ascertained, based on the isolated movements and hushed whispers, that there were five men, each perched on the edge of the precipice. He knew each man would be equipped with infrared technology and the finest weaponry.

One step on either side of the waterfall, and the men above him would surely see him; for now, lying flat against the mushroomlike base of the frozen white wonder gave him complete anonymity; and then he took out his cell phone to call for backup but discovered that the signal was gone, and so he took out the other cell phone that used another company for its signal, and it too was useless. He checked his GPS device and saw that there was nothing but mountains and snow for miles around him. He could not leave now or in the morning. And then an idea struck him as he looked straight up the slender body of the frozen waterfall. "Therein shall I climb," he thought, and then he watched the only men he could see, how they nervously crawled along the top barrier, looking to the left and right of the waterfall and beyond it and never at it or down its length. "They do not expect the unexpected; this is good, they are ordinary men; and so up this frozen ladder I shall crawl," he thought, and he slowly bent down and with great circumspection took out his white camouflage polar clothes and exchanged them for his black clothes and then checked his rifle and knife and assorted weapons, and then he carefully and slowly took out of his backpack the metal crampons. These particular crampons were clamp-ons, and they were specially designed for steep ice climbing; they were rigid, allowing the climber's feet not to tire on the climb up, and they were equipped with antiballing plates, so snow would not ball up on any of the twelve steel points that dug into the snow for traction.

He then took out his two white steel ice axes, the kind with the pick on one side and the adze, for chopping holes, on the other, and he slipped his white polar gloves into the nylon straps and looked upward at the tremendous vertical angle. He put on his white plastic helmet.

He would not use the ice screws or the rope or the belays, no; he would instead use the axes and crampons and his raw human strength to navigate successfully to the top; he would just dig the front points of the crampons into the soft ice and swing each ax above his head and step up with both feet and then swing each ax again and step up again. He would not use the ropes as backup because if he fell along the way, it did not matter if the belays saved him, he would be found out, and he would be dead with a fair amount of bullets in him; no, he would not use the ropes because he had no time now. He simply had to get to the top before the first innocent bright rays of dawn rained down on him and painted him all too clearly to his enemy. But he did attach two ice screws to a long piece of white string and then wrapped the string around his neck so that the screws hung down over his chest; now he was ready. Yes, he would go up slowly and surely and silently, just like a stalking tiger.

He had climbed many ice mountains and frozen waterfalls while in the Special Forces, so he had the knowledge and experience; he had climbed rock mountains and snow mountains and grass hills with every conceivable angle these last few years on the trail, so his hands were strong, and his grip was sure.

Yes, he would glide up this frozen chandelier like a silent army that was driven by Justice and Freedom.

The wind was blowing fiercely now, and he hoped it would carry away the small noise generated by his diggings. Thus, it began.

He raised his left foot and carefully dug the sharp metal points into the ice flow, and then he dug in his right foot, and then he carefully lifted up the first ax and dug it into the soft ice, and then the second ax; he looked up and saw that the men had heard nothing. He lifted his feet.

The ice had formed when the weather was just below freezing, and it adhered nicely to the stone mountain, and as it was somewhat soft he did not have to dig the ax in too deep, nor did he have to kick too many times with the crampons to find a solid hold; this was crucial, for he did not wish to make too much noise. He was thinking now about how fortunate he was to have the soft snow and the howling wind, and the fact that he had discovered the men above him while he was standing against the waterfall; and he could not help but feel he was protected, and that he only had to serve Justice and Goodness in order to succeed. He began to think of what the Giant had told him those few months in the wood; but he could not think about all of it now, so he called it away into another region of his mind, and he thought only of the climb.

He was climbing a frozen mass of hanging, dripping icicles that were wedged in between the folds of jagged gray stone. At the tail of the silent white sculpture there were clusters of cauliflower formations, and these he climbed easily, and then he reached the point of the waterfall where it was straight up. He kept his body in a tight triangle shape, his legs spread wide, his pick directly above his head. He crept slowly and carefully up the pockmarked, ridged, hanging sculptures. He would lift one ax and then the other up and above his head and quickly drive them into the frozen water, then climb up, then wait and listen with the mini parabolic, which was still attached to his ear, for movement on high; and when no sound was transmitted down to him, he continued onward, slowly, methodically, cautiously. He could hear tiny streams of water flowing in a bubbly melody over the rock that was beneath him.

When he was halfway up the solid pillar, he slipped when he had only one ax securely in the ice, and his feet came out from under him, and he hung precariously, dangling to the side and feeling his strength seep out of him and into the laughing icicles. He urged his strength on, and he pushed himself back and swung the ax up and found a good hold and then dug in his feet and rested for a moment, listening anxiously to any excitement from above. He heard great commotion on top, and he did not move; he could hear them talking anxiously and moving about and shifting their positions and discussing urgently the landscape before them, but they would not leave; he heard them speculating and slowly assuaging their anxiety about this disturbance, but still they would not leave; and his muscles were becoming weary maintaining this position, and his body became colder as it pressed stagnant against the mass of ice crystals. When they did leave, he continued the climb, more carefully now.

The frozen waterfall was some three hundred feet high. His great strength began to wane because of the slow and agonizing technique he was using to ensure that the men above him heard nothing. He did not know what time it was or whether the light was coming soon, but it began not to matter, for his hands were beginning to freeze; he would have to hang one arm low and shake it hard, and then raise it up and take hold of the ax by the strap and then let the other arm down and shake it hard, too. Pain from the cold began to drill its weary self into his fingers and hands and plant its malevolent self into his very bone; his shoulders ached, and his back throbbed with agony, and his legs were like lead, and his arms shook in violent spasms. But none of this mattered because he could not go down or go around the stone mountain, so he was here, here to stay, and he had to go on, to force himself up, up, up to the top before he was betrayed by the virgin droplets of gauzy sunlight assembling its golden robe over him.

It would have been better to have done this with the belays and the ice screws and the rope, he thought, and then he cursed himself for beginning to have doubts about what he had to do, and he knew this would weaken him; so, he cleared his mind of such clutter and concentrated once more only on the climb.

Shreds of icicles crashed down on his helmet, and fear seized him as he stopped and listened in panic. Nothing came from above. He tried to move on, but his fingers were now becoming so cold that even his constant shaking of them had little effect. The top of the ridge seemed to recede far away into the endless black firmament. And then horror grabbed him and impaled him against the side of the ice palace. The first rays of dawn had crept over the top of the mountain. He could not understand how it had all happened so quickly; how his hands had frozen too quickly and how the sun had come up too quickly and how his quest might now end; but he could not stop now, must not stop now, had no earthly right to stop now, so he continued on, somehow, throwing up the axes and kicking in the crampons and not worrying about the noise or his dead fingers or the cramping and tiring of his muscles or the innocent rays of light fastening themselves to his white cloak.

He was edging closer to the top, and he felt so close that he tried to imagine himself already there, but his arms and back and shoulders were so laden with pain and exhaustion, and the air was so burdened with the powerful wind, and his body was so desperate because it was operating on spent fuel that he simply could not; and so the inevitable happened just as he was about to launch the axes into the coarse ice, the violent wind swept up to him and spun around him a weighty shield, which caught his weakened body and propelled him backward, suspending his body in midair as he tried to balance himself; he felt his feet slipping out of the crampon grip, and so instinctively he let go of the axes to adjust his position; there, he righted himself and leaned back into the wall of ice and clung to it like it was his nurturing mother. He listened for any movement above, but nothing occurred, and he could feel the sheer magnitude of the freezing ice tear into his thin membrane of defense and impale his waning strength. He felt for the two ice screws and put one in each hand and looked up and then put in the first screw and drove it slowly into the ice, and then he drove the other screw in and then propelled himself upward. Every pull now felt like his muscles were shredding and detaching inside his trembling body.

He was near the top, and he could not feel his fingers, but it did not matter, he pressed on toward the mark, digging in with the ice screws and digging in with the crampons and sliding in physical torment over the striated snow stream. He could hear the men talking and laughing and slurping drinks, and he abandoned all caution and summoned up every bit of his strength into reaching the top so he could simply lie and not hang by his muscle-weary, muscle-cramped, muscle-starved-for-oxygen arms and legs. He made it, but just barely; right at the top he managed to grab hold of a jutting piece of rock, and then he laid his exhausted body on top of it and nearly fainted; but he could not faint, he told himself, Sylvia needed him, Sylvia waited for him. "Sylvia, Sylvia," he heard echoing in his fading consciousness. "She waits for me, so I must not fail, because if I fail she will die, and only I can find her; so, I must live, I must live, I must live..."

He awoke and found himself at the top of a frozen stack of fused-together structures, and he was still miraculously embedded in the white veil of the white snow. He was secretly glad he had become one with the ice temple, and he imagined that it was impressed with his courage and had rewarded him by taking him into its white bosom and protecting him from the enemies of Nature. But it was time to act, and as he tried to reach into his backpack he found he could not feel his hands nor control their movement, and he watched helplessly as his right hand wavered around the white backpack, struggling to reach in and unwrap the magical presents he had brought for his tormentors. He knew exactly what to give them to settle them down for a long Winter's nap, but his fingers could not grip the cover and pull it up to reveal the contents therein; he was watching and listening to the men on the right side of him, watching them drink their hot coffee and laughing. He saw their idiot faces reflecting the false belief that everything was fine, and then, turning his head, he saw the men on his left side drinking their hot coffee and laughing and assuming everything was fine, all the while his numb fingers were fumbling near the release latch of his white backpack. His body was still hung halfway over the edge of the rock mountain, and he knew that he still must have presented a good camouflage to the men around him. But then he thought he released the latch, and so he dug his hands in, and as he looked back to the men, one of them on his extreme right happened to look up and frown and cock his head, as if he was not sure of what he was seeing. Joaquin felt two cylindrical metal objects, and he thought he grabbed them and activated them, and it was then that the man began to say something and then stood up and reached for his gun. Joaquin flung his arms out on either side of him, hoping that his hands opened and that the correct objects were in them, and then he closed his eyes and quickly felt inside the backpack for the two black Taurus pistols.

The stun grenades exploded, and the men, in their deadly blindness, were shouting now and shooting their weapons everywhere at everything, and Joaquin was shooting low on both sides of himself. It was a terrific eruption of human sound and noise and firearms explosion for a seeming eternity; and then the clamor abated, and the smoke cleared, and the bodies were counted, and only one still survived.

Joaquin opened his eyes, and he surveyed the carnage. All of the men were dead. He hoisted himself up onto the cliff with all of his might and then fainted dead away.

He lay for some time in a mild delirium, and then he awoke and coerced himself into crawling over to the men to make sure they were dead, and then he searched their equipment. He checked his cell phones, but he did not even curse when they were still without a signal. He came up on his knees and shook his head and arms and then propped himself up on one leg and then the other, and he began the tortuous walk back to town. "I must report this. I cannot leave them here," he said to himself. "Even I cannot do such a thing." And so he began to stagger back toward the town he had passed hours ago.

At the hospital, where the two children who were rescued from the snow had been taken, the parents of the boy and girl stood outside in the lobby amongst their family and friends. It was getting dark now, and in their warm halo of Love and solicitude the Mother and Father could not fully celebrate the well-being of their precious children.

"And what of him?" the Mother said to the Father. "The man who saved them; what of him?"

But the Father had no reply, for he was thinking about the sort of man they had encountered.

A great eruption of noise occurred, and they could plainly hear the excited nurses and doctors talking of the five dead men who had been found at the top of a mountain bluff. The Father and Mother knew.

"How can he do these things?" she said again, looking out through the large double-glass doors and into the cold, bleak night. "How can he live out there and not want what we all have?" She groaned, remembering what the officers had told them about the Tracker. Her husband held her tight as he too gazed into the murky darkness.

And then a distant figure appeared, but they could not discern its identity as it approached the hospital; presently they could plainly see that it was a hooded man who was limping and slapping his arms about his body. The Mother became chilled to the bone, and she sought to break from the warm embrace of her husband and run toward him.

"No," he said, watching the man staggering along toward the hospital, "wait."

And they both waited and watched as the man began to stand up more erect and to jump up and down and move his arms up and about and shake his head to and fro; and then the man stopped and seemed to take in the entire scene, looking this way and that and up and down and then raised his arms on high and stooped down and jumped up high and landed solidly on his feet, and then he hesitated and stood totally erect; and then slowly, uneasily, he turned away and walked back into the black pitch of a frozen tide of nightfall.

The woman began to cry as she reached out her arms toward the fading image of the man. "What kind of man is he?" she sobbed, thinking of her life and love and family. "How can he—how can he live like that?"

Her husband held her and stroked her warm head and brown hair and kissed her and then said, not wanting to weep, "I do not know; I do not, but I tell you this." He began to feel warm tears well up in his eyes. "I do not know, but I do know this," he whispered, passionately, as if what he was about to say had already happened. "If our children were kidnapped and taken away into the night," and now he wept like a father who knows his children have escaped the icy sepulcher and now reside in the house of warmth and sanctuary, "I would want him to search for them."

And they watched the lone figure disappear into an unknown world that had been sculpted and lived in by ancient men who had taken a vow of Chivalry and Righteousness in their eternal fight against the tyranny of injustice.

Jenny Pitcher

Inside the Houses of Slaughter there was always something for the hostage children to do; there were many aboveground and subterranean houses in many remote locations around the country, where these children languished, sometimes for years. First and foremost the children were educated so they would make adequate mates for Slaughter's highest-ranking male foreign and domestic business associates. There were books to read and movies to watch and poetry to memorize and political and economic and philosophical theories to learn; there were long and dreary essays to write and ancient speeches of dead philosophers and kings to devour and limitless newspapers and magazines to peruse so as to gain a proper understanding of the culture they had been sequestered from and the one they were going to.

But this was not all that was available for the girls; they were also taught proper poise and posture, elegant walking and feminine talking, and the proper application of makeup to highlight their best features and hide their worst; there were lessons on fashion, lessons on manners, lessons on interaction between man and woman, owner and slave, parent and child; the girls were schooled from sunup to sundown, and after that, they were allowed to relax in their small, iron-barred rooms and listen to music or read books. There were no toys or games or any other item that might encourage the girls to remember their delicate age.

The Houses of Slaughter were like factory outlet stores that sold the Slaughter brand of terror to industrious criminals, franchises overseen by the Master himself when he came around every few months to check on the progress of his pupils and the manufacturing of various kinds of weapons of mass destruction.

And in each of these entrenched safe houses there was a failsafe mechanism that was activated either by a watcher or by a sophisticated perimeter-detection system; the manual written by Slaughter demanded that the system be switched on if it was found that the authorities were stalking the house. The members of the Slaughter organization were reassured that once this system was operating, a rescue beacon would be sent to Slaughter, and then their imminent rescue would be at hand. And underneath and around each and every house there lay, just like a coiled cobra ready to strike, a sizable amount of explosives that would be detonated approximately two minutes after the system was hot. This was why, in the manual, it was stated emphatically that the people inside the house had to be absolutely certain that the threat was genuine.

In the last six months, three of these safe houses had been blown to hot cinders and black ash by the inhabitants therein, and to the chagrin of their Master, two of them seem to have been blown for no apparent reason.

Slaughter never rested too long at his own domiciles because he knew that a stationary target is easier to catch than a mobile one. But for now, he had landed at one of his wooded enclaves for a visit and a final assessment of his pressing plans.

Sylvia was in her room, kneeling at her bed, praying as she did every night and every day. Her long, thick black hair hung around her supple shoulders; her powerful legs were tucked underneath her strong body; and her brown, slender hands were tucked under her chin. A knock came on the door, and the door opened.

"Hello," a voice said sweetly, "I'm Jenny," and the youth walked a few steps and extended her hand, but she found no outstretched hand in return. Sylvia merely stared at her from the safety of her bed. Jenny sat down on a green wooden chair next to her. She held up her slender hand with the diamond bracelet and then put her index finger to her closed mouth. She pulled out a small, yellow plastic box and waved it around the room, and then she came back to her chair. "We can talk now, Sylvia," she said, smiling, "the bugs are asleep for the night." But Sylvia would have none of this conversation, and still kneeling, she commenced her silent communion with God. Jenny nodded her pretty head. "I understand completely," she began, "and it is a good thing that you do not trust me, for who am I to you but another one of his attendants?" She appeared, as judged by her bearing and poise, to be near the age of twenty. "Look, I am sorry for interrupting your little prayer-fest, but I was sent here to prepare you for Monsieur Beauregard, your future fiancé, and we haven't a lot of time for frivolities." Upon seeing no response from Sylvia, she sat on the bed next to her and looked at her full in the face. "Look, Sylvia, I have been well versed on your whole history and the whole savior-saint-Tracker-myth who you think is coming for you, but I have to tell you, it isn't going to be; it just isn't, don't you see? The only god around here is that big man in the next room," and she nodded toward the room without ever taking her eyes off her audience. "He is the only one we are allowed to pray to, and the sooner you get used to that, the better for you and everyone else." But when she still did not receive the expected response, she merely, and casually, extended her hand and slapped it quickly and hard against the face of her silent partner.

Sylvia could feel the perfume from her attacker engulf her. She looked over to her attacker, and she turned her face toward her, and bowed her head again, and so again, her face was slapped.

"Look, little girl, do you think I care about your sad offer to allow someone to slap you even once? Being weak around here will only get you killed; you must know that by now. I have been sent here to ready you for your man, and that is what I am going to do, whether or not I have to beat you senseless to listen to reason."

Sylvia looked up, her face full of calm. "I will pray for you too, Jenny, as I pray for all those whom he has hurt; my mother taught me this much, to pray for those who willfully despise you, and for those who are despised, as you are."

Jenny slapped her again, and then frowned in regret, but refused to acknowledge it verbally. "Look, do you even know what you are babbling about, with all that noble drivel? It is just something your mommy taught you, and so you held onto it like some kind of lost dolly. Well, you need to grow up fast, and even faster around her, because this is your life now."

"You mean this is your life now."

"What?" She nearly laughed, incredulous. "How long have you been with him, almost three years? What isn't getting through that round head of yours? No one leaves him unless he lets them leave, and we both know how he does that."

"You have accepted your fate, but not me; I know I will be rescued."

She laughed heartily. "I have told you your little savior isn't coming for you, not now, not ever; five more men were sent after him, and we received confirmation that he is dead." She extended her lips in mockery. "Sorry, honey, but he was just another mortal man who came up against the wrong person."

Sylvia commenced praying once more, but this time, aloud. "God, I pray that You protect him whom You sent to rescue us, and I pray for all of those girls who have been taken from their homes, and their families too; but tonight, I especially pray for Jenny," and she bent down and laid her head nearly against the ground, murmuring imperceptible prayers.

Jenny sat, transfixed, staring, bewildered at the pious girl before her. She lit up a cigarette and flicked her fingernails while she smoked and stared at the anomaly before her. When Sylvia finally got up and sat on her bed, Jenny put out her cigarette and then said, her face adorned with genuine curiosity, "So who else did you pray for?"

"I prayed for him and all of his friends to stop doing these bad things."

Jenny cursed. "You are pathetic! How did you last this long with him? I know he has kept you on the road longer than any other girl. I thought it was because your Tracker-saint had found some of the safe houses you were at, and the boss did not want more houses compromised, but really," she said, and she leaned forward, "I think it is his pride, that if your savior found you, it would make him seem less than superhuman." She smiled in satisfaction at this revelation. "You know you are being groomed for his number two in command, right? That is about a year away, and this is just the beginning of your lessons. That is reality, and that is where we are right now, and so I really need you to cooperate and listen up to the ways I can help you survive the relationship."

Sylvia simply smiled. "That will never be, because he is coming for me," and she shut her eyes. "I know he is. I can feel it; I know it because I can still feel my family praying for me: my mother, my two brothers, and my sister," she said, and she nearly wept. "My mother would never forget me, and she would never give up on me; my family prays for me, and God has not forgotten me or you." She opened her eyes and looked to Jenny. "Don't you see that there are good people in the world who want to help us?"

Jenny sat still, her face frozen by despair. "No, I don't."

Sylvia was aghast. "Don't you even want to be rescued?"

And from a cold, dark grave already dug and lived in came a cold, dark voice already worn out and accepting of death. "No."

Sylvia stared at the comely girl before her, at the fancy dress and the silken, curly chestnut-brown hair and her soft, china-blue eyes and her thin lips and her arched eyebrows and thick brown eyelashes and her small, svelte figure, and even though the picture painted was that of a woman, there were fragments of betrayal in the face that once gathered together, for even a moment, spoke of secret places. "How old are you, Jenny?"

Jenny did not respond immediately, as she was still contemplating the unselfish act of someone caring for her, and then she said, without emotion, "Fourteen."

Sylvia shook her head. "I am nearly twelve…"

The two diverging worlds of flesh and blood and bone stared at each other, and their souls gasped at the large emotional chasm that separated them.

"How long have you been here, in this terrible place?"

Jenny looked around the room as if she were remembering events she no longer thought about. "I don't remember."

"But this isn't where you should be; you should be…"

"That is enough, brat," Jenny shouted, slapping the bed. "You are talking about things that will never be! Your family can pray for you all day and night, and that won't free you from who you are going to be, and do you know what that is?" She then explained, in a narrative uncensored and entirely brutal and honest in its pictorial description of the job therein, about the immediate future for Sylvia, who now wept. "See, see! You know it is true, you are here to serve these men, and the other girls have other men come for them, and that is who they are, and this is who you are now, and the sooner you quit thinking about the past and let this present become a reality, you will survive." She was proud of her handiwork, that her graphic depiction of a girl's life in the Houses of Slaughter and beyond had sobered her defiant pupil. Her voice was softer now. "The sooner you accept it, the better; we need to cover quite a bit," and she looked at her diamond-studded watch. "And we have only twelve hours before he moves on again. So let us begin, yes?" And she touched the girl on her head as if to signal her sympathy.

Sylvia looked up at her. "But I am not weeping for me," she said, shaking her head, "I am weeping for you."

She cursed again and stood up and paced around the room in her four-inch spiked black leather pumps. She lit another cigarette. "Do you think you are the first little idiot to have fantasies about being rescued—do you? Haven't you seen enough girls lost to the hungry wolves and freezing snow and boiling sun because of their foolishness to try to escape?" She stood fully erect now with one hand on her slender waist, the other holding her white cigarette, her face screwed up in a fury as she turned to look at Sylvia. "I have seen dozens of little girls come through here, whining and hoping and praying that one day some hero would come crashing through these walls to save them," she gushed, but then shook her head as she quickly walked toward her. "But it just doesn't happen. He is too well organized, too well financed; don't you understand? There are too many of the bad guys," and she pointed to the house itself, "and not enough of the good guys," and she pointed out toward civilization, "looking for you, and how many did you have looking for you? One man?" She laughed. "One man against an army?"

"You don't know him; he is not an ordinary man," she began, looking in earnest at Jenny. "I remember my mother talking about what he could do..."

"Oh, please, I heard his biography; he was the town fool! You had some homeless man wandering the country looking for you!"

"Have… I have a man looking for me."

She threw up her hands. "I don't believe you! You are going to get me demerits, and your stupid little naive self killed; and to tell you the truth, I don't care what happens to you, but I have to live here after he shoots you and drops your body off a cliff somewhere."

Sylvia was unperturbed. "Do you expect me to be afraid? I have been with him for nearly…" But she would not say it, as if the saying of it gave power to her captor. "So now, what else can I do but pray?" she said, and she commenced praying in silence, in her kneeling posture, against the small cot.

Jenny collapsed into the chair and buried her head in her hands. "You are impossible," she moaned, her crossed legs bobbing up and down in a steady, nervous rhythm. "I don't know what to do with you, I really don't," she whispered, shaking her head and massaging her face. She sat thusly for a fair amount of time, pondering her situation.

A giant roar assembled itself in the next room, and vague screams became organized words. "Jenny" smashed right through the thick walls, and the mistress of this House of Slaughter vacated the room and ran to her grand Master.

There was much shouting and violent cursing and objects thrown and more shouting and fists pounded and walls shaken, and then an eerie silence landed with a desperate thud. Sylvia listened and recognized the power tantrum of her captor, and she slid closer to the beige cot when she reasoned the second part of the barbed rant was to come. And then it did come, the slow opening of the door and the urgent pleas and the final desperate act, the awful truth of the gunshot battering the brief silence into submission and then hanging its wicked sword in the night air. She knew what had happened; she knew that the failure of one of the adjutants had once again been rewarded with those steel projectiles that find their way through a hot tubular tunnel and then lodge unceremoniously into the flesh of a human target. She clasped her hands harder and bowed her head, and she thought of her family and of Joaquin, and she prayed for Jenny and all the captive girls, and for the wicked men and women of this criminal family to repent. There was nothing else she could do, but to her, it was the only thing she wanted to do; it was what her mother had taught her, so long ago, in their cozy, warm house in the town of Redwood, where she would play with her brothers and sister and listen to her mother tell stories of her noble father and how he had died and how his killer had been brought to Justice by the great soldier and officer Joaquin Bridger; during these times when she yearned for her family, she would shut her eyes and dream herself there with her family, imagining life the way it would be if she were there with them, sitting by the red-brick hearth and drinking hot chocolate and reading books and listening to sweet music and looking outside to see the lovely white snowflakes falling gently through the cold air.

An hour expired, and the door opened, and Jenny came in, but she looked different. Sylvia sniffed the air and could smell the strong, musty scent of her captor fouling the place. She peered into the penetrating and now incandescent cobalt eyes of the girl, and she saw the horror within that was hidden by the expertly woven mask without. During these last few years she had seen optimistic, strong girls with the resilience of wild animals too often snared and beaten and every ounce of their enthusiasm squeezed out of them and returned as feebleness and subservience; and she saw this now, she saw the drooping posture and the hollowed look of defeat hovering like a suffocating aura around Jenny. She knew what had happened between the obedient servant girl and her Master, who proudly wore the black-death head about his hulking, hairy body, and she bled empathy for her. She did not care if Jenny refused her offer of solicitude. She rose and put her arms around the hunched-over girl. No resistance occurred. In a moment, Jenny laid her head on the shoulders of Sylvia and then wept in a controlled, low sobbing.

But it did not last long, no, for Jenny soon held up her head and affixed a hard gaze onto her face that dried up the tears as if they had been scorched in a furnace. "We need to get to work," she said. "You need to learn much before the dawn." She pulled away from her human comforter and stood up, lit a cigarette, and began to nervously walk around the room.

Sylvia sat in amazement, staring at this youth who had the worn exterior of an older woman and yet had the decaying interior of a little girl. She did not understand all of it, but she knew that it was wrong, and she would not relent in her belief that if she just prayed and did what was right, all would be well again. "But I do not believe as you do," she said softly. "I do not believe I will be here too much longer."

Jenny shook her head, and then she laughed, tears streaming down her heavily painted face that now looked on high. "I used to think…" She shook her head and shut her eyes. "I used to think that he used you as a shield against your man, to be safe, to be sure," she said, and then she let her head fall, and she opened her eyes, and her face became hard as stone. "But now I know he is afraid of your man—afraid, him, the big man himself; afraid of one man he can't seem to kill…"

Sylvia leapt up, excitement in her voice. "He is alive, isn't he?"

"Yes, he is. He killed the last five men; killed them dead, every one of them," she returned, without looking at her. "And you knew it, didn't you? You knew he would keep coming," she said, and now she looked at her. "But how? Why him? Why won't he die like other men before him have died? I have seen a hundred men die, and heard about the deaths of hundreds more, and yet he lives; so why—why him and not all of the others?"

Sylvia did not have to ponder this for long. Her voice was full of certitude, like the captive soldier who hears his troops bugle in the near distance, and it was full of calm, like the captive soldier who never feared he would not be rescued. "Faith," she said. "Faith in God, the one thing he cannot control about us."

Jenny looked to her and nodded her head. "I believe you." She smiled. "I believe you believe it, but I cannot; I have seen too many girls die here who had great faith in being rescued."

"But I don't know about them; I know about me," she answered. "And I know that good girls die every day in the world; but I do know this, Jenny, that whatever happens, I will have my faith whether I live or die, and he will not take that from me."

Jenny turned around and wept again, her mind raging against such a bizarre philosophy. She dropped the cigarette and stepped on it lightly. "Tell me more."

Sylvia walked to the bed and reached down and lifted up the mattresses and took out a small, black book; she turned around and sat down.

Jenny turned and saw the forbidden object. "He would cut off your hands if he found that on you; you know that."

"Sit with me," she replied, "we have only until the dawn."

And they did sit and talk until the dawn of many things Jenny had never heard but had hoped and wished and prayed for, and when the morning did come, she found it too difficult to bid her new friend farewell. There was so much she wanted to tell her but would not. However, she would protect her now as she felt she must, for she felt as if she were an older sister to her now, and it was her first and last obligation to allow Sylvia to leave this house without further woe. The two embraced, and then Sylvia was summoned, and she departed with her captor and his men in their black SUVs.

The rest of the day Jenny contemplated all that Sylvia had taught her, and she thought of her misbegotten life and where she was going and how much longer she might be there; she thought about the other two little girls in this House of Slaughter, and she thought of the two men who were left in charge to carry out the Master's orders.

He had spoken freely to his subordinates around her, for there was no reason to do otherwise, as she had never given him pause to doubt her loyalty. He had told his two men that the Tracker was still coming, and that this man had already caused too much damage to his organization, and that he must be killed, killed now, killed the very next night. He told them that the Tracker was aware of the explosives around the perimeter and that his scrutiny would begin at a designated distance. So it was decided that the explosives would be put out much farther and that these two men must activate the system and promptly leave once the intruder was sighted. The Master did not divulge his own latest path to even his men, as was his practice.

Jenny had heard all of it, and she had already gained an opinion on the subject. It was eight o'clock in the p.m. when she surreptitiously slipped the two little girls out from the door in the back of the cabin, and with a kiss of Fidelity, she ushered them toward a safe route; she knew the girls would never find escape unless her plan came to fruition. It was 8:15 p.m. when she passed by Monsieur Beauregard, and she secretly sneered and then passed by his adjutant, and she secretly scowled; she gained access to the control room with the key and opened the door and sat down at the electronic panels. It was all too easy, she thought; after all, she was the mistress of this house, and she knew where everything was, and she had been trusted explicitly.

And of course she knew the codes for the explosives; of course she did, she was a natural-born eavesdropper, as all children are, and she was still a child; and now she had the access codes and the key, and as she sat there and listened to the men make their idiot preparations for what they thought was a clean departure, she set the codes. She thought of what Sylvia had said and had taught her, and so she took out the small, black book and began to read it and shut her eyes and imagined Sylvia back home—back home with her family, and happy and laughing—and then thought about where she, Jenny, was supposed to be, in the blessed arms of love and the good life, doing what she was supposed to be doing, growing up as a young girl in the world and liking boys and listening to loud music and being silly and not having to worry about guns and men and shouting and gruesome deaths and untoward things happening to her. She then heard the two men pounding on the steel doors and screaming and demanding to be let in, and knew that they had been alerted to her deception by the electronic devices attached to their key rings, which she had not been able to get away from them, but she did not care anymore, and so blocked the clamor from her mind and let her thoughts drift away to where she wanted to be. She thought about it all and then read some more and then shut her eyes and heard the first explosions, and smiled as she had not smiled in such a long time and imagined what life might have been like had she lived.

Aftermath

When Joaquin came to the demolished safe house, he beheld the local authorities searching through the smoke and ash and debris. It was the fourth house he had found like this, two of which had been blown up because of his approaching presence. He proffered his credentials to the men in charge and briefly related his search to them, and he was told that two little girls had been found wandering the hills not far from this place. He walked over to the girls, both of whom were wrapped in brown woolen blankets, and he stood before them. They were young, just babies, he thought, perhaps eight or nine, shaking and frightened, their faces still stained from the tears of their escape.

"I am a police officer, girls," he began. "Do you know what happened here?"

The oldest girl spoke, her hands still clutching tightly the thick blanket. "Jenny let us go; she let us escape." He asked her about any other girls in the cabin. "We think a girl came in about two nights ago; we are never let out of our room when guests arrive." But she began to sob.

He looked to the other little girl. "Who was in the house—do you know? It is important. I am here to find John Slaughter." The little girl stumbled backward and began to sob, and she ran back toward the police officer who had found her. He looked to the other girl, and he said softly, "I am sorry; I am," and he remembered his own little girl, and so he bent down on one knee and addressed her in tenderness. "It is important, very important that you remember, anything, anything at all. I want to help rescue all the little girls like you..." He would not say anything more, for fear of further upsetting her.

The little girl stopped her sobbing, and when she moved toward him, he abruptly stood up and took a step backward; he felt a cold dagger dig deeper into his heart. "Tell me," he said, "tell me anything else you know that might help me."

The female officer who had found them came for the little girl and stood there as if to guard her from this severe man, this wayward maverick, this ancient warrior who did not make sense to any stranger who beheld him. The officer put her arms around the girl and began to escort her away, but then the little girl turned around and stopped and stared at him. "Her name was Jenny Pitcher; that was her name, Jenny. And she was my friend; she was mean sometimes and sometimes nice, but she protected us and watched out for us." The Tracker said nothing and simply gazed in wonder at the courage of the child. "Last night, Jenny took us and told us she was setting us free, but we knew that we couldn't get away because other girls had tried and always got caught because of the cameras and ankle bracelets; but Jenny smiled and took off our bracelets and said that the cameras would be asleep tonight and that we shouldn't worry about it, and she had written us a map; and, oh, yes, she wrote something else on it about a girl." Joaquin wanted to speak, but he relented. "But I lost the paper, I did, I don't know where it is."

He could not keep silent any longer. "Do you remember what it said? Please, it is very important." But the female officer insisted that the girls go with her now, and she turned and walked away with them. Joaquin stood in agony, his heart dying for any small fragment of information, and then his heart shouted out, without his mind even knowing it. "He killed my little girl; he killed her, and he killed my wife, too." The female officer stopped dead in her tracks. "He killed my little girl when she was just about your age, and he took a girl—just about your age—and I am following them, and I want to find him and stop him so he will never do that again." And there he stood, baring his soul to the world, and he waited for the tiniest slip of news so he might gain something, anything, anything at all.

And the little girl stopped sobbing, and her eyes looked him up and down, and then she frowned and thought and thought and pursed her lips, and then she looked back to him. "I remember—I remember I read it, and it said that Jenny was going to make sure that he had the chance to rescue her; but I cannot remember the name on the paper, I'm sorry."

"Don't be sorry," he said, nodding his head, "you've done great," and he watched as the two little girls walked away with the officer.

He talked some more with the officers and discovered that the explosives had been set on a perimeter that was much farther out than those of the surrounding cabins already destroyed. He sifted through the debris for clues and walked the entire perimeter, thinking—thinking about what the little girl had said—thinking about what was on the note about someone receiving another chance; and when all of the authorities were gone, and he was sitting on a large boulder and pondering all of it, he thought of who Jenny must have been. "If," he thought, "if Sylvia had come and met Jenny, and Jenny, Jenny; yes, Jenny," and he stared at the sooty black ash and debris of the cabin, "she met Sylvia, and they talked, and Jenny heard her story; yes, she would have found out about me, or perhaps had already known about me, and heard." He stood up, looking about the perimeter. "She heard that Slaughter was going to sabotage the perimeter with more explosives to finally stop me, and so she swept up the two little girls in her arms, and she wrote that note." He felt the awe of inviolate Love sweep over him as he walked over to what he imagined was the control room, "and she opened the door," and he put out his hand, "and went inside," and he stepped through, "and she sat down and set the access codes—somehow she got the codes, but she would, being a survivor—she would have gained them long ago, and then she must have sat down and waited; yes, she waited for the explosives, knowing she would..." He put his hands through his thick black hair and then down his thick-bearded face. "She sacrificed herself to give life to the two little girls, and to Sylvia," he said, and he fell back. "And for me; she sacrificed herself for me." He knelt down in the smoking wreckage and pondered the bravery of those in battle. "And her name I will remember forever," he said, sobbing now. "I will remember you forever, Jenny Pitcher, and I will one day find your family and tell them of your glorious gift, this gift you freely gave us." He sank completely to the ground, and his head touched the burnt chunks of wood and twisted metal. "And what greater gift than this, that she laid down her life for a friend," he heard the Giant whispering to him, and so great was his sorrow and hurt that he lay there for a great duration.

He awoke as the last streaks of blackest night veiled themselves into the celestial firmament. He raised himself up, covered in layers of delicate, crystalline flakes, and inhaled deeply the rich aroma of the wilderness around him, and then he checked his equipment and walked over to the tracks that had been made the night before. He inspected them and knew they were of his quarry, and he stood up again and looked toward the budding diamond dawn that sparkled and shone like a new Creation. "I must not fail; I must not," he thought, moving slowly on; "not now, not after so much; I must not fail, not now, after so many have given so much for so few; but is this not the way of the world—that we leave the easy company of a hundred to look for that one who has wandered astray."

And then he slowly vanished into the velvet white curtain of a gently falling snow.

Rendezvous

The man, covered in thick deerskin clothes, wearing deerskin moccasins, his brown backpack on his back, his rifle tucked neatly inside, came to the edge of the northwestern forest. There was a winding road that swept around it and down into the small town below. He stroked his thick black beard and then ran his dark fingers through his long black hair, and he walked easily down the steep hill, as easily as if he were part of the earth, moving in unison with the soil and flora and fauna, in Harmony with all of it. He never wavered, never fell too far forward or stumbled too far backward, gliding through the gray pebbles and green and brown brush with great elegance. He came to rest upon the black concrete–paved road, and he frowned, as he had lately begun to grow weary of artificial structures in the midst of Nature.

"Deer crossing," he whispered, reading the yellow sign that had a White-tailed Deer drawn in black on it; "is that for the drivers or the hunters?" A full-grown adult female deer and her two fawns came cautiously out of the bushes just slightly down the road from him, and upon seeing him, they froze, staring at his noble stature; yes, he was Man, enemy and merciless hunter, but this man stood unlike any man the mother deer had smelled and seen.

The man emitted sounds, low, braying noises, and the deer stood rapt in attention, ears pricked, head up high, wet black nose twitching as she sniffed the fragrant air; then the man quietly and gently, as if he were indeed a deer and not a savage man at all, walked up to them, and the deer did not fear him. As he held out his callused, rough hands to caress the brown and black coat of the mother and the red coats of her two beautiful daughters, they felt a strange peace over them for what would come one day.

A car came swiftly along the road, too fast to allow for adequate braking, so the driver, at once incensed that deer were on his road to town and that a man was standing with them, swerved around them, honking his horn and shouting.

The deer, startled, awoke from their communion with Man, and they scampered away into the brush, and the man, dismayed, continued down the road.

He did not travel far until he reached a bend in the road that wound around several loops, where it eventually deposited travelers into the heart of town, and it was here that he came upon a slowly approaching black and white sheriff's patrol car with two officers inside its black-leather and wire-cage womb.

The man had come to abhor the city and pity its indigenous people, who had altered their innate instincts to conform to artificial laws to suit interaction in an environment that bred chaos. "They cannot understand me, but I understand them; thus, I will never explain myself to city brutes," he thought, thinking of the man who had honked his horn and sped away. "Every noise doesn't have to mean something," he whispered, smiling as he thought of the Giant. "He was my teacher," he thought, and he felt pathos choke him, "and my friend."

"Hey, buddy," the officer of higher rank began in an authoritarian tone, "where are you headed?"

The man decided to abide by the law, and he turned his head toward the driver who was the owner of the burly voice. "Anywhere I choose," he replied, looking at the man as if the black-uniformed officer were nothing more than a Boy Scout on neighborhood watch.

To reply in such a fashion did not digest well in the thin palate of the officer, who was used to enthusiastic groveling from the citizenry. "Well, you're not headed into our town now," he said. His voice became a caustic warning. "Turn around."

The man, thinking of all the towns he had traveled through, and how most of them had not accosted him, shook his head. "I have business in town," he said casually, walking at a slow pace, and no longer looking at his protagonist.

"Who with?" the subservient officer said, and promptly received a harsh rebuke from his partner.

"United States Marshal Jacob Shipper."

Silence smacked the officers down like they were straw men in a hurricane. There was activity in their car, furtive calls to their headquarters, hushed talk, and quiet panic; but it was a contaminated thread that wove its juvenile self through their ideas that compelled them on, a prevailing idea that spoke of peeling the tough bark of this defiant drifter from his muscular, hard flesh; O, the boundless joy that erupted in their reptilian brains when word arrived that their superior officer was absent; they quickly jumped into their primordial stirrups and fastened on their savage exteriors. "He ain't in," said the officer in charge, a malicious grin smeared across his face like a dust storm, and then looking at his suspect, "and you're out." He pulled the car in front of the stranger as his companion asked for backup units. The man simply walked around them. "Halt," the officer in charge cried, opening his door and drawing his gun, his red, coarse face growing the heavy fibers of wrath as he witnessed the stranger walking on down the road.

A few moments passed until the next black and white patrol car came screaming up, its signature yellow lights flashing. Two more men deposited themselves and their car in front of the amused stranger.

"Crossing guard must have shown up, I gather," the stranger said, crossing his arms, standing in a relaxed pose, with no residue of anxiety upon his relaxed face at all.

"Hands up," the officer in charge commanded.

"No," the stranger returned, inhaling deeply, "actually, I have authority to tell all of you to put your hands down." The officer repeated his order. "I am a Special Deputy United States Marshal," the stranger replied casually; "cease your childish behavior." It was frightening for them to behold the absolute certitude that roared across his placid face, as if it dwelled there without any worry or fear of antagonists.

The entire situation was wrong, and the officers sensed it. "Prove it," the rookie officer cried, as if crying such a command gave weight to his words. His immediate ranking officer glared at him, for no veteran officer ever gives an uncooperative suspect a chance to explain himself until the suspect has been subdued. The request was withdrawn.

"Down on your stomach, now," the commanding officer yelled.

The stranger, arms outstretched, his feet set apart in a strategic stance, said in earnest, "You do it."

Adrenaline surged through the officers like the elixir of life. Two of the senior officers approached the suspect with extreme circumspection, and they reached out to grab his arms.

It was, as the officers later recalled, like trying to pull down the gnarled, heavy limbs of a young and mighty Oak tree, so fierce was the resistance in the arms covered in deerskin; they then tugged at his wide-apart legs, but it felt as if the sturdy limbs were rooted deep into mother earth.

"Just like having children at your feet, isn't it, Joaquin?" a voice said, and the officers jumped out of their crinkling, crackling wits.

"Afternoon, Jacob," Joaquin said, watching the men slowly back away from him. "Don't have their training wheels off yet?"

The immense respect in the voice of a superior officer toward the stranger cowed the men, and their instinct to serve and protect fled like a whimpering dog.

The two friends shook hands.

"I received your message that you would be arriving soon," Shipper said, waving off the men with a lacerating stare, but looking to his friend, he said, striking the man's stout shoulder, "How is life on the trail? Ready for a hot meal?"

Joaquin smiled. "Is Ricardo here?"

"Yes," Jacob Shipper replied, expelling a short laugh, "he arrived this morning." He had, for a moment, forgotten that he was talking to a man who was too far removed from the delicacies and refinements of modern times. Jacob walked back to his car, watching Joaquin begin his run to town, leaving the other officers entombed in a kind of goo that hung shamefully from their impotent faces.

Joaquin did not enter the office of Jacob Shipper, for this was an alien thing for him to do now, just as a soft bed seemed wrong, just as forced heat and air-conditioning and processed, prepackaged food seemed wrong; now that he had assimilated back into the authentic embrace of Nature, such things in his mind would weaken him and dull his senses. Nature, he knew, would not reveal her secrets to a man who shielded Her from himself at every convenience. He needed to feel extreme heat and cold, to feel the soft pearls of rain fall upon him, to bathe his tired and stinking body in amniotic fluid—in the placenta of the earth—a sparkling, clean, and cool refreshing lake of calm; he needed to feel the divine texture of soil and twig and rock and leaf beneath his bare feet, and only then could he listen and follow where his instinct traveled; he needed to eat food in its raw, unnatural state, drink water without chemical masks and filters, breathe pure, oxygen-rich air into his lungs, and in this way, could he keep Nature within him and about him, and recognize Her and be with Her.

"We have leads on Slaughter now," Ricardo said, and then he smiled at his much-absent friend. "It is so very good to see you, Joaquin," and he slapped him on his shoulder.

Joaquin could not, would not celebrate nonessentials, nor the niceties of life, the unnecessary events, the frivolous matters, lest such soft, civilized ingredients take seed within him and corrupt him; for then would he be on the outside looking in, an unnatural man unable to recognize the subtleties and harmonies of Nature, a man no longer willing to sleep in snow blizzards and gladly wear hoar frost upon his wrinkling face. No, he must resist all invitations to subvert what he had become so that he would find Sylvia.

He clutched the Winnie the Pooh doll tucked safely inside his waistband, and his resolve hardened. "He is headed north," he said, his unwavering, hard visage deflecting the oscillating tones of friendship's embracing bond.

Ricardo smiled still, knowing Joaquin had spun an icy, rough, dark nest to reside in until the quest was over. "We know he is up to something; we have found dead bodies, who when they were identified, turned out to live in other regions."

"The man is a cult leader," Jacob said, frowning, leaning against his desk and crossing his long arms, which were covered by his brown and tan uniform.

"He is an architect of tragic, unreasonable irony," Joaquin began, his face like granite that burned hot from his anger; "he is drawn to it, as is every conqueror." He thought of his days past, those five long years where he stumbled about aimlessly, and he felt great shame that someone like Slaughter could get the better of him. "He believes in his own immortality, as if he were appointed by God to rule, an heir to a timeless kingdom, but such a kingdom occupied by past and future conquerors." He had cogitated every day on the subject of his foe's character and designs, graphically mapping each known move his enemy made, using his computer to read more about the history of Slaughter. "To simply conquer ordinary people is nothing to him; to conquer against ordinary odds, to conquer ordinarily, is as wrong to him as it is for a caged lion to eat cooked meat. No, gentlemen, his life's blood comes from the red marrow of ironic, epic, exalted fate, commissioned by the authentic tongue of history to smite the unenlightened."

Ricardo and Jacob knew this narrator, but surely, this did not stop them from sensing a stabbing, haunting dread that he was unlike any man they had known, a man with smoldering black eyes who carried the silver sword of eternal vigilance against injustice.

Indeed, Joaquin had come to believe that in Nature there exists a balance, where Harmony and Goodness reign; but if chaos and wickedness were to prevail, all of Nature would be unbalanced. "Some must rise as others fall," Joaquin had long ago decided, "to right the wrongs, to stop tyranny; it has always been, and always shall be. I have been chosen by the eternal breath and rhythms of the earth, the very blood pulse of life itself, to protect those innocent." He had smiled then, for then he had thought of God, whom he had recently begun to consider as the author of the universe. "If there rises a tyrant who dedicates himself solely to wickedness, and ordinary man falls prey to its awful power, then there must concurrently rise someone who is dedicated solely to destroying that tyrant; there must be balance, and so for every agent of darkness, there must be a reciprocal agent of light; and it doesn't matter how long it takes, or how much you must give up, it must be done."

"Do you have any idea where he is headed?" Jacob asked.

Joaquin walked over to the map of California that sat atop the patrol car. "Here," he said, dragging his fingers along the deep forest ridge, "living in the dark shadows of infamy, plotting his revenge against Mankind. It is there I will meet him."

Ricardo's face screwed up in astonishment as he gazed at the map. "But that must be a two-hundred-mile swath."

"I will be there," Joaquin said, and he pointed to Redwood, "in five days."

"Ha!" Jacob burst out, laughing, "forty miles a day? And I do believe you can do it too, Joaquin Bridger!" He slapped his friend's hard, broad shoulders. "You know we will offer any help we can, but I know how you feel about helicopters and planes scaring off the enemy…" He stood, rubbing his chin as he stared hard at the map, then looked to Ricardo. "Still, don't you think we could set up covert checkpoints on auxiliary roads? Here," and he pointed to several places on the map around Redwood.

"Meet me in Fallbrook," Joaquin said. "Anything more and he'll sense a trap; the only way," his voice grew icy cold, as if he were gazing at his foe now, "to catch this snake is by cutting off its head."

Silence subdued his friends' faces, and then both of them laughed heartily.

That night, Joaquin bade his friends goodbye, and equipped with the newest-generation tracking equipment, he started off on his journey along the coast.

The Woodsman

An hour into his journey, he found a small, silvery pool with heavy gray mists hovering over it, and he decided to wipe off the artificial stench of the town that clung to his skin and clothes like black rain. "How can I be part of the earth when I am infected with the cysts and boils of Man's easy comforts?" he mused, while shaking his clothes and pounding them on rocks; and then he slid into the quiescent water and sat inside it and immersed himself in it, and upon lifting his head above the water, he felt as if he had lost more than just the ordinary dirt and extraordinary contamination from Man's incestuous relationship with technology; he felt as if he were flushing his mind from the ambitious sounds and fused tensions of civilization; as if he were cleansing his heart from the irony and moral pollution that reeks out of the stagnant pit into which Man casts his encroaching will; as if he were purging the last vestiges of Man's corrupting influence upon him from his soul; and as he sat there and stared about this peaceful temple, as he breathed in the rarefied elements and gazed upon the silent green and brown foliage dressed in its royal finery, he felt his mind become uncluttered and his heart become unburdened and his soul become purer; and he felt freer, as if he had been enchained by the daily machinations of Man's duplicity and fooled by Man's burnt offering to its gods, mammon and power; and he stayed in this sultry bath until he felt as if he owned himself and answered to no man or no thing; and then he slowly rose from the scented water and put on his clothes again.

Soon, he was back on the trail that was one mile east of the shoreline. These days, he could pace himself at a steady, rhythmic run for many hours, drinking water along the way; when he grew fatigued, he would rest against the base of a large tree trunk and munch on pemmican, the food of the ancients, the nourishment of the arctic explorers, and this time a delicacy of tough jerky that he made from wild venison, mixed with animal fat and finely chopped fruits and nuts, and molded into small balls. He had no time to cook now, only time to run and nap and give minimal attention to the functions of his body.

There was an urgency in him now, as if he and his nemesis were compelled beyond human ability to meet and determine a victor in this eternal quest for power, a battle both men yearned for; in war, there can be only one victor.

It was high Summer, when life in the forest blooms without restraint, and all is robust and full of vibrant color and emitting sweet scents; the Pine trees were green and full of juicy, sugary sap, and the Redwood trees, the monoliths of the forest, sprouted their thick limbs with layered needles far and wide; shrubs of all kinds flourished and eagerly grew toward the warmth of the sun, and there were blue elderberries, with their evergreen leaves and brown, furrowed bark, and their loyal messengers, the honeybees, buzzing around their cluster of delicate white blossoms; and California Sagebrush, with its greenish, grayish leaves and its spicy fragrance; there were California Poppy flowers with their deeply orange, deeply lush, saucer-shaped petals that sometimes wore splashes of yellow like a new Spring dress, and the Seaside Daisy, with its yellow sun emitting pink or lavender rays. Everywhere there were symmetrical, ornamental flowers, sometimes translucent, often creamy, always colored in the most handsome tones, sometimes glowing pink or shining green, sometimes speckled or branched, clustered or hanging. There were flowers that were aromatic or pungent, stinking and sticky, prickly and velvet soft; it was life flowing in its ebullient abundance, washing the sleep of Winter from its stiff cellulose vines, a celebration of untrammeled, upward climbing and radiating a flux of streaming energy, infusing its potent elixir of life into every waking organism.

Joaquin rode the wave of this beam of effusive power as he ran under a cloudless sky, running with ease alongside the drifting, warm currents of air; he was a species of the forest now, just as the frontiersmen before him had been, as the native Indians had been, and as the Giant had been.

A male Bobcat appeared from behind a Cottonwood tree after clawing it, and its tufted ears pricked forward at the agile human intruder, its white-whiskered, black-lined face held high at attention, its brown-and-black-spotted fur on end, its back arched as it observed its visitor running by; once the danger passed, it fell back to clawing the striated brown bark. Three male Purple Finches, oblivious to their guest runner, flew above him on their route to the exclusive enclave of a single, waiting female, their musical notes splashing the air with joy, as if to say, "What do we care about the world above or below us? We are off to the world of love."

He, the male human being, wearing a light brown leather deerskin and deerskin moccasins, was now as much an integral part of Nature as the sinewy trees and robust flowers and creeping insects and leaping, crawling, flying animals; they simply moved one way, and he moved another; they merely found nourishment in one manner, and he in another; he did not disrupt or maim or judge or contain, change, destroy or steal; he became one more thriving species that fit into the intricate Harmony of the forest, which flowed in a perfect, circulating, seamless pattern. They could not betray his presence to those foreign entities, who came in sterilized, polluted garments and vehicles to hurt and wound and alter and annihilate, any more than a giant Cypress could betray a Red-Breasted Sapsucker for pounding acorns into its bark so the wily bird could eat the insects that came to eat the tasty yellow nut. All of it simply was, in total and simple symbiosis, and if one neighbor species was evicted from this humming, peeping, twittering wonderland, one small brown shrub or one tiny yellow insect or purple flower or one hairy, neurotic rodent, the whole delicate ecosystem would collapse. So no species was saboteur, egregious informant, or revolutionary bent on cataclysmic change; this, they would leave to ignorant, avaricious Man. Joaquin, they now knew, was no mere man; he was simply one of them, having transformed beyond the hysteria and laziness of the barrier of weak flesh to become a brother and protector of the forest.

Spotting clumsy, recent human movement throughout the forest was as easy for Joaquin as tracking footprints in the freshly fallen snow is for a trained Ranger. Does not the deer, with its keen sense of smell, know whither comes a team of human hunters, and does not the eagle, with its extraordinary eyesight, see an awkward plane in its path? Everywhere there were broken twigs made by disorganized union, smashed plants made by a lack of economy of forward motion, artificial debris made only by selfish, thoughtless, heartless Man. Joaquin followed these aberrations as if they were glowing white pebbles laid in full view in sooty darkness.

Occasionally, he stopped to refresh himself with cool water from a pristine spring, or to munch on pemmican or root tubers or berries, and when he did, he kept watch on the trail, gleaning from the polluted, scarred forest floor deeper evidence of insidious human trespass.

"They seek to cover their tracks," he thought, amused. "But they are like pigs wallowing in manure and not aware of their awful stench." He stood up, fully erect, head held on high, sniffing the air. "After all, how can they be anything except what they are? If they do not know differently, how can they know otherwise?"

He began to run again.

It had been lucid in his mind, in vivid detail, that he had already moved across an artificial barrier into a land rarely inhabited by human beings. "He lived there, but I could not see him, not really," he thought, remembering the Giant, as he jumped over a small Manzanita bush. "How could I? It is like explaining love to someone who has never experienced it; but nor could I recognize him because I was on the outside looking in; and now I have been in both worlds, and this one I prefer. People are corrupted as easily as a baby offered sweets." He ran for some five miles, reflecting upon days past, the waste of his five years of existence apart from living and contributing and experiencing change and emotional treasures with loved ones. "I ceased to exist, when I should have sought to overcome grief with purpose; now that I have purpose, I am; and because I live in the community of people, I share their humanity again; yet, I am still not part of what I was before, and I do not know if I can go back home again." He mused upon life with his family, and although it had seemed idyllic then, he could not conceive of such an existence now. "I have crossed a bridge that I destroyed with every step I took to this world I now inhabit." He no longer lost control of his waking moments, no longer wept uncontrollably, no longer fell prey to emotional tumult. "I have sealed each wound with mortar and brick; and like bone, I am stronger once broken and healed."

He had not thought about his life after finding and returning the girl, for he had banished the idea of it from his mind.

The present was now and every moment until he completed his quest; the future was sealed in another time-space continuum, unattainable; and the past was a distant dream, a memory of another life: a different era, another man, irretrievable. He often thought, "Now is now, and I live to serve what is before me, not what is behind me or too far ahead and away from me." Thus, this was how he lived, in the now, allowing nothing past or future to trouble him.

He had run effortlessly for an hour, his mind affixed in a steady, flowing tide of welling, radiant energy that cuddled him to its inner, warm fire, which was a constant nourishment for his body. He ran as if one connected to the rich, fertile soil, as if his cells electrically bonded to the very electromagnetic pulse and hot, molten blood and sinewy tissue of the earth itself, feeding off its raw, dynamic power to propel his miniscule body, as if the earth were unconscious of the mortal boundaries of human limitations.

He ran with herds of male deer and past curious Red Foxes who peeped out of their burrowed dens; he ran near the Spotted Owl, the Winter Wren, the Red-Tailed Hawk; and he was a member of their nuclear family, and they merely looked up with a relaxed visage, as if to say, "Oh, it's just him." And some of the older ones, gossips really, seemed to say, "Hasn't he a mate yet? Doesn't he know it's the thing to do? Maybe then he will settle down."

Occasionally, he crossed paths with human beings, and when this occurred, they often asked themselves what year it was, or if they were educated and prone to whimsy, they asked if perhaps a time-space variance or a black hole had admitted this stranger from another epoch—and if so, could they go with him? But then this infinitesimal moment would dissipate, and they would conclude, rather quickly and efficiently, that the leather skin–wearing aberration before them was simply a man cut loose from the constrictive bonds of the state's nearest mental health institution.

He was as much a frontiersman as those of days past, but the frontier he had entered was not made of earth and dirt and wood, but of a long-forgotten vision of what people once were, why they were, how they were meant to survive; such men are alone, even amongst people, because they are a breed of a singular element not found on any scientific chart. They are the composite elements of Sun and Earth and Water and Fire.

As he ran, he was conjoined with his fertile environs at a cellular level, and he glided on inextinguishable fuel from fresh, clean, fragrant air that sent scintillating molecular bubbles of an effervescent joy throughout his robust lungs and into his hearty red blood stream. Oxygen throttled him with a dynamic infusion of raw, unlimited power.

He slept on a bed of dry leaves four hours each day, from midnight to four o'clock in the morning, at which time he arose, ate sparingly, obeyed the gentle murmuring of Nature to cleanse his system, washed and scrubbed and brushed, drank cool water, and continued on his journey.

On the third day of his journey, he found evidence that compelled him to pause, consider his position, use the ESN system through his handheld computer, and contact Shipper and Montoya.

He squatted down, his black-bearded face taut with curiosity as his dark eyes scrutinized the object before him. "The man has no shame," he decided, looking at the adult male human corpse that he recognized from the files as one of his foe's companions. "He believes himself invincible; well," he whispered, and a magnificent, curved scowl crossed the rough regions of his face as he stood up and looked northward, his head held high; he began to boast, but suddenly checked himself, and his face became grim, "talking isn't doing," he whispered, hard and mean like the mighty bear that stalks the prey that killed its young; and closing his eyes he saw himself already there amongst his foes, combating them, and he was pleased, and then he smiled and said, as if to contradict himself, "I have seen the future; now just live it."

And so he began the last part of his epic journey.

The Trail of Tears

On the fourth day of his journey, Joaquin began to sense, in his mind's eye, in this profound eye with a lens once encrusted by civilization but now crystalline transparent, unnatural movement in the ebb and flow of the forest, in the steady stream of life forces, in the lifting and gently swaying motion of the flora, in the diffuse light and soft waves of darkness, in the cooing and purring, in the tender, sweet murmuring of the fauna; those things behind and beyond him, those things above and below him, all of the life-forms seemed affected by some synthetic disturbance. He saw it in the path of the falling brown and orange leaves, leaves not ready to fall, ripe, healthy leaves disturbed from their hatchery by tense birds; he saw insects and animals on the ground in disarray, in altered poses, in wrong habitats, chasing the wrong quarry, insects and animals that had been displaced by something alien to their home; yet, the signal had been sent from far away, but not too far distant. An ordinary citizen of the city would have seen nothing, but for Joaquin, it was as easy as witnessing people scurrying about in a crowded city after an earthquake.

He looked down and saw a small cluster of speckled green leaves; he bent down, and upon further inspection, he noticed the dark bruises in them that had caused the speckling. He turned over one leaf and saw sand dug into its underbelly. "Shoes," he thought, "crushing the leaves into the ground; yes," and he looked in the direction of more leaves that had been knocked off their mother branch, and he looked ahead.

He carefully walked up to a stream and bent down and saw that there were plants disturbed along the shore, and there were rocks that had been stained from splashing. He moved in closer and saw the tiny pebbles that, when disturbed, are moved about and throw off sediment, and he saw their shameful nakedness, and he also saw many pebbles that were lighter in color next to their brother and sister pebbles, and he knew that these were pebbles that had had their dark sides flipped over. He nodded his head.

Thus, he pressed ahead at a quicker pace, and then, after finding the answer, he hastened back and traced his path beyond his stopping point, and once again, satisfied with an answer, he pressed ahead again until he found a place to rest his weary self and wait for the answers to come to him.

He was sitting in a leisurely pose, in a relaxed, passive posture, his back resting against a tall Redwood tree as he munched on some chewy, flavorful pemmican. His eyes were closed the way a man would close his eyes as he rested in the warm, tranquil safety of his home.

Presently, inhaling deeply and sniffing the air, he recognized a malodorous smell, and his keen ears heard a disquieting roar in the complex and frail landscape about him; it was the dragging, heavy, stale odor of ignorant Man stumbling about in the wilderness, and he closed his eyes and listened to the mutation approaching; and just as black smoke from a chemical fire stinks up its environs, he felt this fouled air increase in density.

"Now," he abruptly called out, after he had traced the burgeoning stench of Man to his flaring nostrils, "you will stop where you are, assassin, and we will talk," but it was issued curiously, as a stern rebuke. "I could have killed you at the spring as you filled your green canteen; come, let us parlay like proper warriors."

Silence churned in the rarefied air for a few bleeding seconds, then movement occurred some forty meters north of Joaquin, and it abated and stopped again, the same sound a prairie dog makes when he is digging his burrow and then hears a sound, pauses to locate the noise, and once satisfied there is no danger, continues to dig. The face of Joaquin was as flaccid as cream on milk. "I allowed you to live to allow you to live," he said, eyes still shut. "You need to learn to listen," and he cocked his head. "Soon, your Southern twin comes—listen."

"Riddles," the man replied, looking about desperately but seeing no one, "from a court jester without a king."

"Did you think," Joaquin replied, still sitting behind the massive tree, his back toward the assassin, "he would trust you to kill me by yourself? Ask your associate, when he arrives, how tasty the blueberries were as he sat on the boulder that was covered with green moss." His bare hands were folded neatly upon his lap, done so to bring about passivity and encourage calm. Several tense minutes transpired, steeped in want and woe for the assassin, and then Joaquin spoke again, once more as peacefully as if he were amongst friends. "Your accomplice stands some sixty meters back; call to him and identify yourself."

"How do I know he isn't one of yours?"

Joaquin, eyes still closed, merely expelled a long breath of patience. "Remember the spring, pilgrim."

A swirling wind swept around and about and in between the two players, picking up red- and green-colored leaves and brown twigs and fluffy, winged creatures. A Blue Jay squawked about her mate being late for feeding time, a mate killed, on a fancy, by the Southernmost assassin. Joaquin heard the deep moans of the female. "Greetings, bird killer," he said in earnest.

"Who are you?" a voice hollered from behind them.

"Tell him who you are, or you'll soon be spending eternity mounted on a hunter's wall, watching your murderers play billiards with goose eggs," Joaquin said.

The Northernmost assassin, his ebony face split into opposing camps of disbelief and acceptance, finally spoke. "I suppose it doesn't matter if I name the man who hired me, since all of you will be dead soon—Slaughter," he said, still holding a fierce grip on his McMillan M-87 sniper rifle as he gestured toward where Joaquin was hidden.

It was, quite simply, the pause that exhilarates those forsaken, for it was the pause formed by creeping, nebulous doubt. "Liar," exclaimed the Southernmost assassin.

The assassin of the north proceeded to describe the orders from his employer, and soon, albeit reluctantly, the assassin of the South was coerced to agree that Slaughter had contracted for two killers. "So, let's do our job and get out of here; we get paid regardless," he said, gripping his Stoner SR sniper rifle.

"Did you kill the Blue Jay?" the Northernmost assassin asked. "Did you?"

The other assassin frowned. "I stuck him with my knife; target practice on animals keeps me awake." And then frowning, he said, "How'd you know?"

The Northernmost assassin pointed his gun toward the bunch of trees he thought Joaquin was behind. "He knew; he also knew I stopped at a spring for water, and he knew the color of my canteen, and you," he pointed to his counterpart, who fell back in alarm, "he said you ate blueberries while sitting on a rock covered with green moss."

The other assassin, his white face steaming crimson outrage, cursed. "What is he, psychic?" Upon receiving a glaring rebuke from the other assassin, he frowned. "So, he know'd things about us; so what that got to do with us killing this here hog?"

"If he knew what you were doing, and what I was doing, and when we were coming, then why didn't he kill us?"

Both of the assassins, attired in clothes conducive to camouflage, looked toward where they supposed their target was, and then at each other, and they agreed to meet.

Joaquin opened his eyes; he looked long and hard toward the two gunmen, wisdom perched comfortably atop his tranquil face. "Why would a man hire two men and not tell both men about each other? You act as foil for me, so the true assassin may earn his bread." Now he would sit and let this tasty morsel thrown from his masterful menu digest like a sour ball in their churning guts, but a sour ball, once dissolved, that would taste like the most bitter gall and vinegar. Such a planting device had the effect of tickling the supposed doubt the two assassins had harbored about their temporary employer; and so he continued on, just as a man does who pounds even harder as the nails he drives into a wooden coffin sinks even lower. "Don't bother checking the company directory for your retirement benefits." There, he was finished with the last acrimonious offerings, which began to dig into the thick skins of the two killers.

"Good," he mused, scrutinizing their disturbed countenances. "You think about it." He expelled a long, slow breath that was residue from paltry incertitude. "I will kill only that which needs killing, and nothing more." He thought of the Giant. "The rest I will leave up to God."

"Why did you let us live if you knew we were sent to kill you?" the assassin of the north asked, after explaining what "foil" meant to his compatriot.

"You are men, and thus, you can be bargained with; he who comes after you has no soul, and thus he must be destroyed."

"Oh, I don't trust this sly dog," the assassin from the South said, spitting off to the side. "He don't talk straight." And then looking to his antagonist again, he said, "Now here, I got a question for you, Einstein; why don't you just kill all three of us bad guys?" And he spat again, his head turned tilted toward the ground, and he said, "Even if I do believe this nonsense about a third assassin, which I do not!"

"If two of you," Joaquin said simply, "then why not three?" He let the challenge of his logic haunt their minds for a moment. "I give you life, and you give me life; I need to be free of the Third Killer; he has no blood in his veins, no conscience in his reptilian mind; he kills the same way a wolf kills a sheep, and that is out of compulsion."

"Oh, now I get it; he's afraid," the Southern assassin said, smiling arrogantly.

"No, I don't think so," the other assassin replied, staring intensely at Joaquin. "It's something else, something far more complicated, right?"

"Live right now, and both of you will die; if you agree to listen to me, I will tell you how to kill the Beast from the East."

"Beast from the East; shoot, you ain't doing nothing but stalling for time," the red-haired, leather-hatted Southern assassin drawled.

"Go ahead," the other assassin imposed, without protestations from his fellow, "and tell us why this other one wasn't hired to kill only you."

"Outstanding observations," Joaquin cried, "because, you see, he is a finisher; he doesn't begin things, he ends them; he is paid a great deal of money to contain a spreading disaster and to defeat that which seems undefeatable."

"Makes sense," the Northern assassin said, rubbing his bare chin, "and we were paid in person."

"Now tell us how to kill the beast," the other assassin said coolly.

"Sit," Joaquin commanded, as he continued to sit cross-legged under the same Redwood tree, "and place your weapons aside; I will not talk to faithless men."

After some time and much deliberation on the subject of trust and honor, the two killers reluctantly agreed to forsake their weapons, leaving their rifles leaning against their respective trees, as Joaquin, without his weapon, now approached from behind his tree.

"Go ahead now, and this had better be good," the Southern assassin said, "and I'm getting the creeps just thinking he's coming this way; shoot, I'm beginning to think he's the boogie man." He attempted to assuage his trepidation with a laugh, but he failed.

"He is," the Northern assassin said, looking to Joaquin for answers. "So when will he come?"

"Too soon," Joaquin said, settling down under a tree and leaning against the striated, thick brown bark. "He knows men such as you are not vigilant after a killing; he will attack when you are well on your way home, when you have begun to think of other things. Now, how to kill this Thing." And as he began his narration, his two listeners were mesmerized by their host's command of the secrets of Man's nature.

"You speak as if you know him," the Northernmost assassin said, after hearing a brief psychological profile of the Thing to come.

"No," Joaquin replied. "I know men." He looked at both of the killers, and then he watched as the orange sun lost its lofty throne in the high heavens and dipped below the horizon. "I have seen the light and dark of Man; I have seen Man from every height and depth and breadth, from inside his wicked skull to the blessed light shimmering from his wife's inviolate Love for him; yes, I have seen Man, and I know he is not God." His voice was terrible, and full of premonition. "I know that he is capable of every sinful deed."

"What!" the Southern assassin exclaimed, as if he had been punched in the gut. "I ain't good? I pay my taxes. I pay for my kid's schooling and braces; it ain't like I'm out stealing money from charity cans."

"A Rockwell painting come to life," the Northern assassin said, amused, looking at his associate; and then to Joaquin, he said, "Go on."

"The Thing is a predator from birth, and he knows nothing else except to conquer and destroy; it is his compulsion, the same way a salmon travels upstream to mate. When this killer kills, he kills for nourishment, for bliss, for Harmony, for breath and motivation and purpose of life; and when he comes, you must not risk a trap, as he will smell it as surely as the leopard smells the salty scent of stalking Man."

"Then how are we going to catch this monster," the Southern man asked, irritated, "if we don't sit and wait?"

"You don't sit and wait; you go on as if you had completed your task, and you simply go on as you would have; only then, when he thinks you are at ease, will he strike; even the lion has the sense to stalk those unaware."

"But how can we kill him if he comes after one of us? We can't kill him alone," the Northern assassin bemoaned.

Joaquin looked to him. "We must make him believe that one of you is injured. In that scenario, who would be followed?"

"The wounded one," the Southern assassin said excitedly, instinctively raising his hand as if indeed he were in school again.

"No," Joaquin said as he looked to the other assassin, his face signaling his want of an answer.

The big eyes of the Northern assassin narrowed as he looked about the shadowy forest, seeing the last streaming, glittering rays of burnished silver twilight falling through the leafy branches. "The healthy one; yes, the healthy one, because he knows the other one will be slowed down, and he can easily catch up and kill him." He looked to his teacher for approval. "Isn't that right?"

Joaquin, aware of the other assassin's need for inclusion, looked to him. "Is it?"

"Yeah, I guess so," he said, rubbing his stubbled, red-whiskered chin. "This fellow doesn't take chances."

"Exactly," Joaquin said quickly, to cut him off so the assassin would say nothing foolish. And so to solidify this successful endeavor, he altered his course: "So who wants to be shot?" Both of the killers reached for their weapons. Joaquin laughed heartily. "He won't believe it if we use animal blood; it has to be the genuine blood of Man—and not from a knife wound: he might have a blood analyzer to test for bullet fragments. Don't worry, it doesn't have to be serious, just messy." He waited till both of them were sitting again. "You must understand this man has no soul, and you must think of it this way; if you find a Diamond-Backed Rattlesnake in the room of your child, will you consider it a duty or a choice to kill it?"

"Duty," both men said, and they gingerly slapped each other's hand on high.

"Volunteers," Joaquin said, pounding the tree, and in so doing, dislodged his carefully hidden rifle, which fell cleanly into his waiting hands. He smiled mischievously and said, "Just in case you thought I had invented this third man," and then he put aside the rifle as his astonished audience breathed easier. "It would be best if we enact a struggle so he can see the marks. So," he said, vigorously rubbing his hands together, "who will it be?"

"Why do I get the feeling you're lookin' forward to this?" the Southern assassin said, still eyeing Joaquin's rifle with some suspicion.

After some fierce debate, it was decided that the Southern assassin, being the least senior of the trio, should receive the flesh wound. "My wife don't like blood on the carpet," he whined, standing erect as he faced Joaquin.

"Tell her it's modern art; maybe you'll have a new career," the Northern assassin said, smiling slyly.

"How come," the Southern assassin replied, looking at his fellow, "I get the feeling you is making fun of me without me knowin' it?"

"Say, how do we kill this snake?" the Northern assassin asked. "And what about the body?"

"You must be exact in your procedures this time," Joaquin began, and as he narrated how the deed was to be done, he was careful to lead the men down a bleak path that would puncture their tenuous equilibrium and cause them to ponder an unknown future.

The Northern assassin, while he listened, grew pensive and anxious, and he said, when his host had finished the instructions, "And what about when it is all over—what about us?"

The countenance of the Southern assassin grew grave.

Joaquin stared at the men, but he said nothing for a long time; and then finally, he spoke in a low, harsh whisper, so that the men were coerced to lean toward him, "You are murderers of men."

The Southern assassin threw up his hands. "So we ain't Boy Scouts, but what happens to us? Ain't we helping you—ain't that worth something?"

Joaquin, his face calm, spoke in a tone bereft of emotion, "Every member of the Slaughter Gang will be taken into custody; and everyone associated with the Gang will be arrested."

"What—us too?" the Southern assassin responded, clearly outraged.

"There are no favorites in this operation," the Northern assassin said to his colleague, and then looking at Joaquin, he said, "Isn't that right, lawman? We get no merit badges for helping you."

Joaquin said nothing, and his face said nothing, and this nothing was worse than something to these two men, now.

"But what about us, huh?" the Southern assassin whined. "What about it? What do we get out of all this? Ain't we risking our necks to kill this murderer of murderers, as you call him?"

Joaquin spoke easily and quickly. "You will live another day."

"That ain't right, no sir, that ain't right, a'tall," the Southern assassin cried. "We help the law, and we go to jail—now, that ain't kosher."

The Northern assassin, who had been studying Joaquin, looked to his brother again, and then he said, with a sly smile, "We're criminals, friend, and criminals go to jail for their crimes." And then he looked at Joaquin. "Isn't that right, holder of the eternal flame of Justice?" He knew no reply would come, and then he said, his voice somber now, "What about leniency?"

Joaquin stared at him. "What about it? It is as if you say—I am merely a lawman; I have no authority here."

"But you can make recommendations."

"Yes."

"Well, after we do our part—you can make them."

Joaquin said nothing, and his face said nothing, but this was something now, and the men accepted it.

Joaquin departed to continue his journey to the north, leaving the two assassins to contemplate the plausibility of the deed and another alternative plan.

The Southern assassin, with a fresh gunshot wound to his side, hoisted up the Northern assassin as if, in fact, he was hoisting up his dead prey, and then proceeded, by sheer will and brawn, to carry his amused fellow some distance, and without abatement, to the rocky shore, whereupon he deposited, with great relief, his laughing freeloader onto a misshapen boulder of smoky black and gray that was smooth as glass. Next, he sat down and stuffed a ripe smack of zesty chewing tobacco into his mouth to celebrate his long, arduous walk.

"Now I know why that scoundrel Slaughter didn't want us going back by the sea," the Southern assassin said, spitting dark juice on a slimy, moss-covered rock near his fellow, "and to meet his man with the rest of the money in the woods."

The Northern assassin, pondering his own fate, said, "So what does your family think you do for a living, assassin?"

"Sales," he said honestly, and this solicited laughs from both of them after it was revealed that his fellow used the same story to explain his absences. It was good to laugh too, for it flushed away the crisis in their heads about the dreaded third assassin.

"Think there really is another assassin?"

"Maybe," the Northern assassin replied. "Makes sense."

"Do you think we'll really get leniency?"

"Don't know."

"Will we even take it?"

The Northern assassin was quiet.

"We going to kill that feller if his story is a lie?"

"Maybe," the Northern assassin said in a harsh whisper as he rubbed his chin.

"We going to kill that feller if his story isn't a lie?"

The Northern assassin raised his head and listened to the whispering wind through the winsome trees.

The black ocean of night ebbed as red dawn sprang up and spread its luminous wings over the cool land, awakening Man and beast from their warm nests.

Joaquin had not slept, kept wide awake and tense by the possibility of his plan exploding. "If there were a third man, I would be..." But he refused to bargain with an easy fate, as he knew the malevolent, pragmatic mind of his nemesis; and so he pressed on toward his destination, ever vigilant for foreign smells and sounds. "It has been too long," he whispered, running now, feeling the Winnie the Pooh doll. "There must be an end."

He did rest several times to savor the rich offerings of potent aromas around him, and he slowly chewed his flavorful pemmican and drank pure water from his leather-covered steel canteen. "I need to give them time for the other plan," he mused. "But not too much time."

There were more clues on the trail, more than thirty miles behind his prey, clues no citizen whose life was indigenous to the city would ever hope to spot; but to a tracker, especially one who lived in the wild, the clues were as easy to notice as they would be for a city dweller who follows the long, black marks of a skidding car. "He is careless now, in a hurry, unafraid," he mused, on his hands and knees as he observed footprints in the tall green grass, and then looking closer, he saw a fragment of a sunflower seed shell. "Good," he said and smiled upon standing, "he won't be expecting me."

"You're right." A voice cleft the morning air with its sudden impact and vile colorings. "He won't ever see you; now turn around slowly, hands up, and say, 'Cheese.'"

Joaquin obeyed the intruder, and when he had done so, he knew he was staring into the soulless face of the third assassin.

Boasting

John Slaughter was walking at a brisk pace in front of twelve of his disciples, four bodyguards, and one child, lecturing on the precise character traits of men biologically suited to lead the common rabble. "Do you know why," he was spouting, picking up a loose stone and throwing it at, but narrowly missing, a scurrying Deer Mouse, "great men are great? I shall, of course, tell you." He gestured behind himself. "I walk point, hither," he said, and he squatted down and slapped the dewy forest floor, and he sprang up to walk again. "Just as all great men do, I stick out my neck," and he did so, "because I bring change, and the great horde of imbecilic, DNA-altered world trash doesn't like change because it might compel them to get out of their soft skin and suffer." He turned his head to see if his flock of obedient birds was still in its wing pattern. "Did you see that yonder squirrel—how he so adroitly avoided my deft missile? 'Greatness' must be like the animal in the woods—alert at all times, ready for any attack, never at rest, ready for change, innovative, ruthless, willing to do anything for survival. Yes," he suddenly shouted, hands held on high, "disciplined instinct with purpose, design, articulation—such as our march, here, now, seeming madness to the common fleas who see life through their weak flesh while riding the backs of dogs. Great men are chameleons—to survive, they do the unexpected, they transform themselves—we transgress one level to the next, attaining great sagacity with every silver cumulus cloud we ascend, until at last, we reach Olympus and kneel in prayer with the gods immortal themselves! Ah, life, I love it so!" But then he looked behind himself and said disgustedly, "If only I didn't have to share it with people!" He looked up to the heavens. "How could you send them to vex me? Ah, a burden I shall overcome!"

He broke into a sudden run for a mile, never once looking back at his struggling entourage and assorted guests; and when he did, he smiled that dangerous smile of want of destruction. His voice was foreboding, yet curiously cheerful. "I will wager no small sum that all of you remember Professor Bergson, he who failed to keep up with our power runs; I admonished him about too many donuts, but he, mistaking his three PhDs for a sign of intelligence, shrugged me off." His thick lips pursed, his face wistful, as he watched those around him panting heavily and then said mockingly, "And now, Professor Bergson is so much fodder for the very plants and insects he once was a pioneer in studying, tsk, tsk." And without any forewarning, he took to a run again, but this time he could only manage a half mile, and he feigned to quit because of his lazy crew. "I can't kill all of you at once. Who would do the laundry?

"Thinning the herd, as all of you know," Slaughter began again, after his pulse had lessened; but his cell phone rang, and as he listened to the caller, he continued to speak. "Better to find out now who was meant for the salt mines and who was destined to own the salt mines and the slaves. And who," he shouted to no one in particular as the group passed a small, serpentine stream in the midst of a field of yellow daisies, "would have thought we would travel thusly? Those fools, those perverters of natural science—the authorities—seek me everywhere, but not here! Do the unexpected, and you will be triumphant!" He abated his stampeding pace and turned to glare at his adjutants. "Comments from the aflatoxin-ridden peanut gallery, eh? Mutated DNA got your shriveled tongue? Well, speak, you lapdogs, you human retrievers; we are nearly at the termination of our glorious march." He turned his attention to the caller on the cell phone, issued a few abrupt orders and walked on.

A little while later, a small yet profoundly strong voice rose up like the warm plumes of purple smoke from cannon fire. "Was it the soon-to-be-terminated 'Terminal Assassin'?"

"Eh, what's that? Mocking my strategic plans…oh, it's you, is it?" Slaughter smiled, yet once more, it was not one derived from the kind of joy people experience, but a paralyzed breed of irony. "Poor girl." He never addressed captives by their given names, for he sought to strip them of their past. "Your rescuer is not to be."

Sylvia marched up to him, unafraid. "Your words are not deeds; you need three to kill him," and she turned her head this way and that. "You have sent seven before that, who failed, and your trap at the cabin did not work; oh, yes, I know of that too." And then she thought of Jenny. "Where is Greatness in that?" There were pious tears assembled, eager to generously flow down her sullen cheeks.

He laughed uproariously and said, "You have learned to speak freely at times and to carefully choose your words; good, you are learning; now," and his voice grew mean and heartless without a transitional period, "get back in line."

Sylvia threw back her head, her thick black hair falling upon her shoulders. "I challenge all of you; I say that Greatness comes from the pure of heart; I challenge all of you to a race, and the last person..."

"Too many books read," he said, frowning, "and noble ideas are for slaves," and signaled to his men to violently remove her from his exalted presence, but his cellular phone rang. "Saved by the ring," he said, he grunted, and lifted up the phone, set it to speaker, and turned up the volume.

"I have your prize," the voice cooed. "Listen to him being freed from the sufferings of this accursed Age." After gunshots rang out, the connection was severed.

"Ha! Nirvana achieved! The little nuisance cleared! Now back in line, you little rascal," he said and nearly smiled, beaming with pride as he watched the men take Sylvia back to her place in the pack. "We have a date in Redwood." He clapped his hands to his mouth and said, in a great whisper, "I just love irony! The whole town goes tonight!" He carefully took out the brown wooden box and raised it on high, as an offering to unseen supernatural forces. "After we are done, no one will get near that genetically modified strain of a bloated carcass for a millennium." And then his voice changed, not merely in tone and volume, but in its very form and nature, as if it had been constructed by something dark and frightening that yearned to escape from his mortal body. "Would that my words of judgment could dig a fiery pit and bury them alive; yea, even my thoughts transmuted into physical reality—and therein would I dwell in the home of the gods."

"Evil of great magnitude may only be checked by Goodness of greater magnitude," Sylvia thought, remembering what Jenny had said long ago, and although she was not sure of the exact meaning, she knew it had to do with her rescuer. As she looked around at the group and pondered the fate of her rescuer, she did the only thing she could, and that was to pray.

Opposing Forces

The third assassin walked a full circle around his prisoner, holding a gun in his right hand, smiling all the while, nodding his large head, his ruddy face animated by intense pleasure. "I've heard a great deal about you, I must say, and I must give credit where credit is due; you have been an elusive target for my employer; but then, that is why I am here." He leaned his jutting jaw forward to whisper, "There always must be one who succeeds, you know, and there is always someone who is better." He stood fully erect, admiring his captive as if he were a fisherman admiring a bounty of glittering, silvery fish in his net, and he said, "I do admire your work with those two second-stringers back there," and then he cupped his left hand to his mouth and whispered, "both of whom I will shortly kill, and with great pleasure, I assure you; if it's one thing I can't stand, it's a black mark on my professional business." He nodded his head as he paced back and forth. "You must have paid them off handsomely to betray their craft, and to go along with such a seemingly elaborate but oh-so-stupefyingly foolish plan. Now," he shouted, his free hand held out, "credit where credit is due, but your ruse—I can imagine it now: take his body to the shore, double back, he'll follow the strong one; how quaint! And to gamble on me following them first; how perfectly daring! Well," and he rubbed his clean-shaven white chin, "did you want me to kill them, perhaps? Were they supposed to kill me, perhaps? Oh," he smiled, throwing his hand out again, in a foppish manner, "the drama, the possibilities! Just wait until I get home and tell the missus about this sad, sordid tale! Why, she won't sleep for weeks, the dear!" He laughed out of sheer derision or sheer pleasure—it was impossible to detect by his captive. "But you do know your mistake, don't you?" The silent response of his audience disturbed him. "Come, come now, you've lost the game. Don't be such a spoilsport; let us exchange notions, you and I, before I kill you. What is the point in pouting, eh? Now, the mistake, any guesses?"

"The footprints," Joaquin said, nearly inaudibly.

"Very good, bravo! And even though you switched shoes with the other assassin, you were betrayed by those importune pressure points, now weren't you? Oh, isn't that just so exasperating—no matter what you do, and no matter how much planning and effort you put into a project, there always seems to be some slight hitch—oh," and he threw his free hand about as if he were at a social gathering, with a mischievous smile upon his ruddy face, "such as you not figuring on me being one of the finest pressure-point interpreters in the entire world, who can tell the difference between a hundred-and-eighty-pound man and a hundred-and-seventy-nine-pound man as easily as a commoner differentiates between the footprint of Bigfoot and a Gambian Sun Squirrel—now," and he smiled and lifted up his chin, "be honest," and he smiled more widely. "Come now, did you consider such a possibility?"

"No."

He laughed and applauded the air with his empty hand, and then he began shaking his head, and he said, "Tsk, tsk, but aren't we being a bit disingenuous? Is that the only mistake you made? Come, come now, you mustn't depart this world with a lie burdening your savage heart, must you?"

"I did not believe in you."

He threw out his free hand in a fast fury. "Yes, I knew it! You never did believe there was another coming for you, or you would have made better provisions for me; that is why people like you only start the race but never finish." He smiled and shook his round head. "You didn't believe in me, but I believed in you, the same way I believe in the tooth fairy and Santa Claus." He smiled again in his pure merriment. "You've just got to believe in the absolute impossible so you can be ready for anything, or you get caught in reality, and that hurts." He pointed his index finger of his free hand at his quarry and pulled it back. "Ouch." He laughed like the little boy who has won all the purie and steely marbles once again.

"Oh, drat, don't you just hate that? Two small mistakes and it costs you your life! No second chances in our game—high stakes, high yield." He cupped his left hand around his mouth and whispered, "I used to be a stockbroker," but he shook his head. "Too risky." He let out a hearty "Ha!" in approval. "But, oh, what a letdown for you! Oh well, but this is why I am simply the best in the business, and you are simply a distant second place, and second place is the first loser. You know," he smiled crookedly, "competing against men such as you makes me sharper; you know the old saying, 'iron sharpens iron,' and all that; actually, I want to thank you; thank you," he said, gleefully, nodding his head toward his prey, "for not being mediocre; killing you is like killing a big, brown, brawny stag." He issued a few internal "harrumphs" and then easily pulled out his cellular phone. "Business part of it, you know, has to be done; and by the way, I do appreciate how wonderfully cooperative you've been; very professional of you—no begging, no silly escape attempts—simply a practical acceptance of your fate; well, first you and then those two other junior-varsity benchwarmers, and I'll be home in time for the evening business report." He dialed and then held the black phone to his ear and said, calmly, "I have your prize; listen to him being freed from the sufferings of this accursed Age."

Two bullets ripped into the assassin's body, and he fell, plop, like a downed lion that was stalking a wild stag, but a lion shot not by the hunter, but by the stags. Joaquin shut off the cellular phone.

"Alternative plans are always better than first ones, don't you think?" the assassin of the North said, smirking as he took a bite out of a ripe, delicious red apple he had carried for the celebration of the kill, his other hand holding his rifle.

"So, that's the big man," replied the assassin of the South, rifle in hand. "Ain't so big on the ground, is he? Ain't we bigger now?"

The Northern assassin looked at Joaquin. "We agreed to kill him at the same time—ego thing," he said, slapping his fellow's hand. "Well," he continued, stepping over the dead man, "he fell for the footprint decoy, as you predicted, and came right for you."

"You know," the assassin of the South said, staring at the dead man, "when you first told us about the plan, that you wanted to make this louse think that we had met and killed you, and that one of us had taken your body to the sea while the other went home, and to make this scum want to come for the assassin going home first and then come back for the one carrying the body, to tell you the truth, I thought you was crazy; but then you said that he would see through this and notice the different footprints, and he would think it was all a plan, and he would come after you." He spat on the corpse. "And to think he was going to kill us, after all; now who is the betrayer, you rat scum!" He delivered a vicious kick to the dead man.

"We owe you," the Northern assassin said to Joaquin, "and you owe us."

"Promises to keep," Joaquin replied softly. And after telling them of a safe house where they could await the authorities, he shifted his stance and cocked his head, and he said, "There is one more thing you can do, not for me, but for you." He inhaled deeply and exhaled slowly as the two assassins stared at him with utter attention. "You walked into a fire when you became what you are, and you have been there for so long now that you no longer feel the heat from the flames; you walked into the fire, and you have lived there for so long that your soul has shriveled to a lump of black coal; so now, you must walk out, clear out of the fire, and back into the land of the living, but you cannot be what you once were, for you will only fail, so you must be as you were when you were innocent." The visages of the men became quizzical. "There was a man, a giant of a man," he continued, "I shall tell you of him, and his philosophies." And he did, for a long while, as the three men sat down and Joaquin spoke of the passions and Truths of the Giant; and when he was through, the assassins, who had been silent throughout the testimony, nodded their heads.

"Remember what the Giant believed," Joaquin said finally. "By what a man is overcome, by this he is enslaved."

"By what a man is overcome, by this he is enslaved," the assassins recited faithfully, as if their hearts had, for the first time, heard such a grand vision for living.

"We'll be going, then," the Northern assassin said, genuinely smiling, shaking Joaquin's hand. "You have them now, just as you wanted it." He yearned to ask him why, but he could not.

"Yeah," his fellow interjected. "They think you're dead," and he too strongly shook Joaquin's hand, and then the men exchanged shoes again. He wanted to ask him why—why risk your life to pursue a man for someone or something—but he could not.

Joaquin watched the two men disappear into the thicket of the forest and then closed his eyes and listened to the vagaries of Nature filter through his searching mind. He then turned his attention to the dead man at his feet. "You were right; there is always someone who is better," he whispered, and then he grabbed hold of the two pistols he had tucked between his belt and the front of his pants; and keeping them near his body, he turned around and fell to the ground as shots exploded over his head, and then fired twenty consecutive bullets in a sweeping pattern into the thicket; and now there was only silence, a dreaded silence he knew had to be as he walked over to the two bodies, which were lying some twenty meters apart; he stooped down and verified that the Southern assassin was dead, while keeping his guns drawn on the other man, and then he walked over to the Northern assassin and found him still alive.

The man smiled faintly, gasping for air as Joaquin held his hand, and then he gulped, and his body rose up and issued a painful spasm; when the agony subsided for a brief moment, he whispered, his countenance yielding sorrow and emptiness, "You did not mean anything you said to us..."

Joaquin's face had no trace of guile at all when he said, "I meant all of it." He cradled the man closer to his own body.

A smile of fondness appeared through the mosaic of pain on the assassin's tortured countenance, and then he said, with great pathos, as if he desired that his words do more than simply express the philosophy of his heart, "It is hard to kill a good man." A profound sadness appeared upon his face. "But we have to be who we are," and now his eyes were wandering past the face before him, and a mist of regret formed in his darkening eyes, and his grip strengthened for a moment as he shouted, "Could you ever believe in men such as we..."

And then Joaquin said, with a great passion for Justice, "I wanted to..." But the man died, and Joaquin sighed and felt his heart grieve as he laid the man to rest; and then he gazed upon the fallen man, and he issued forth words with such great pathos that it seemed he desired that they do more than express the philosophy of his heart. "I wanted to believe that the Truth is there for all men, no matter where they are or what they believe in, and that all can be saved." He shook his head as he stood up and looked again to both men. "Is there no hope for them, Anna? Must all of them die with bloodied souls..."

He walked back and picked up the third assassin's cellular phone and called Shipper and Montoya at their respective checkpoints. "He used this cell phone, and he called this number," he said to Shipper, who was some twenty miles away, and then he relayed to Montoya, who was some ten miles away, the same information. "I need higher ground," he thought, and then he set out for it, purposely leaving behind the bad business of those things that sometimes must be done despite our greatest desires.

He changed his course to due northeast and soon came upon a mammoth construction of stone and bush, replete with manmade rock steps winding up the curving, sloping mountain. He leapt up to the first step and began his ascension with the agility of a wild mountain goat, his footing sure, his balance maintained, his ability to shift placement of boot to safer choices instantaneous; he had adapted to this hard climb as he did for traveling across soft or hard snow, for crossing rushing streams or for running down steep, pebble-streamed hillsides, his chance for misstep the same as any wildlife in the region.

In twenty minutes he had delivered himself into a wide stretch on the stone mountain, where artificial steps abated, signaling an end to human adventure for the common man; but he, with unbroken rhythm, leapt to a free-standing, giant gray boulder, and from that one to another, and then he leapt up to a steep chasm.

A nearly vertical face of the mountain met him now, punctuated with cracks and fissures and jutting rock shelves and green shrubs and bush growing out of its splintered side. Joaquin never hesitated, never cogitated upon the idea of retreating, and after mentally ascending the arduous stone face looming large before him, he simply leapt up to the first available ledge, grabbed a jutting piece of rock, and began to climb.

His fingers were like flexible stone, long and lean and able to hold fast with a steel-like grip to allow their master to hang for the longest duration. He had learned balanced climbing as a child, improved upon it while in the Special Forces, and had become expert at it the last three years—so to keep the weight over the feet and keep the hands for balance was second nature to him. Now, as he climbed, he performed the layback, where the climber leans against an offset crack, and where the feet push and the hands pull against the offset side, thus allowing the climber to move more adroitly up the rock face at a steady pace, like a professional; and he did push holds, where one pushes hard against a small portion of rock; and he did pinch holds and jam holds, and cold-pressure holds and friction holds, and this hold and that hold, and this push, and that pull, and he did it all with the ease and agility of a youngster rising up through a grand tree in his own backyard in pursuance of utter freedom and joy.

Nothing could stop him now as he soared up the rock face; no earthly form of radical prejudice, no deformed mass of upheaval from Nature, no river broad and deep, no hot desert long and wide, nothing so treacherous, nothing so low or high, nothing so steep down or steep up, nothing so hot or cold could contain him.

For every environ he encountered, he shifted his abilities to adapt and conquer. This is the mark of the true warrior and woodsman.

In an hour he was at the top of the rock precipice, his miniature binoculars out as he munched on pemmican and drank fresh water from his canteen. He saw nothing, and then he checked the ESN system and found movement some two miles north of his position.

He ran swiftly along the plateau, calling in his position and that of his suspects to his comrades, and once this was accomplished, he unleashed the full fury of his speed along the sloping summit.

There is a bleak boundary between what is attainable and unreachable to a man, a destitute region that is filled with doubts and fears created by Man, a dark geography insurmountable unless the man can release inhibition and incertitude within himself that preclude his victory. To achieve such a lofty goal, a man cannot labor for his own selfish benefit, for such triumphs are vacuous and ephemeral, as they add nothing to the clarity and Harmony of the world; but to seek the elusive treasure for a noble purpose that is felt in the heart of men everywhere is what propels a man to greater power.

Joaquin skipped over deep splinters in the plateau with the elegance and ease of a bird flying around a Cedar tree; he avoided small rocks, soared over bushes, and ducked under jagged precipices as if he had run this twisting vein of rock a thousand times, for when one is born and bred in the wild, such formations are encountered daily, be they gnarled tree trunks to climb or overhanging fat limbs to avoid, or clumps of Manzanita or clusters of cacti or thick tangles of brush to run over or around. Nature leaves a blueprint for Man to decode, and once it is mastered, he can run effortlessly in Her invisible footprints.

And then the moment came when he caught sight of the Slaughter Gang standing about at a secluded site, seven black SUVs parked next to them. "Not this time," screamed in his thoughts as he poured on the heavy steam to propel himself at a greater speed along the rocky ridge.

But he then stopped, dead in his tracks, unable to move, his mind adrift, his quarry in his sight.

Does the cheetah, whose stomach grumbles for want of food, cease his charge against the stupid zebra? Does the cobra, as it lunges at its rodent prey, stop and merely sit, paralyzed with indecision? No, and yet Joaquin, as much a predator as the beasts of the field, could not physically go any farther.

He stood, feet weighted as if in cement to the gray stone floor, his face stricken with sorrow as he felt his mind drifting away as it once had, when he would lie for hours mumbling about the memory of his family, when he was the prisoner of shame and guilt—its cell mate, its fool—when there was nothing he could do to prevent it, but this time, as he was swept into this standing coma, he began to think, and he held on to this one particular thought, as does the soldier who thinks of the one precious thing in his life before he is swept into the terrible cyclone of battle. The steel trapdoor within Joaquin's mind shut as he fell into it, and he was its prisoner once more.

Joaquin stood in plain sight on the plateau, a clear target for his enemies.

He was where he had always been in days past, when his mind had to seal out those outside forces it could not control.

"My love," his wife, Anna, said. "I did not expect you back again."

He took her slender hand as they walked in a field of golden lilies, while their daughter, Maria, played around them. "But this is where I belong," he said, kissing her.

"Do you know why you came here, Joaquin?"

"To be with my family, whom I love above all things," he said, smiling, gazing into her luminous eyes.

"And I love you," Anna said.

"I love you, Daddy," his precious daughter said, as she knelt in the plush field of aromatic flowers, and presently she leapt up into his arms and kissed him.

"It is easy to love us, is it not, my husband?" Anna said, watching their daughter run about again. "But to love others whom you do not love or have a reason to love, this is hard for Man."

"I do not hate other men," he said, frowning; "only those men who seek to harm Innocents."

"There will always be such men, my darling, and will your heart always be filled with such hate?"

"But how can I love such men who do grievous harm?"

"Thou must love them because thou were first loved by God."

"The Giant said as much," Joaquin said, and then his voice became wistful. "Yes, he spoke of other fantastic things."

"Do you remember, Joaquin?"

His face burned bright with the clarity of remembrance. "Forgiveness," he said slowly. And he grew pensive, and then he said, "But how can I forgive those whom I hate, even as I do battle with them?"

"It is a hard thing for Man to do; this is so, my husband, for to do this seems contrary to his natural impulses; yet to hate your enemy brings sorrow and sin to you. It devours your soul."

"The Giant," he said, his countenance pained now, "when he lay dying, he spoke of such things; my love, how could he not hate such men who did great violence to him?"

"O, Joaquin," she said, caressing his thick, wavy black hair, as she stared into his fiery black eyes. "He saw what happened to himself when he let hatred seek its natural course."

He began to weep. "Yes, I remember."

"It is the same path for thee, my love, my wonderful and brave husband."

"But the assassins—I gave them the chance to go…"

"Yes, you did; you thought of their lives, but you used them to do your bidding too. This is the empire of sin growing in your heart; it hungers for new territory, using any excuse for nourishment."

"To kill these men today..." he whispered, staring into her beauteous face.

"In battle, to kill the enemy is necessary; it is killing, if the battle is necessary; if the battle is fought by an aggressor for his own malevolent purpose, then it is murder."

"But these men must die," he protested, looking at his daughter frolicking about and smelling the golden and violet flowers, "for the crimes they committed; it is the law of God and Man."

"Men die for their crimes; they may pay with their body and soul, but thee, my husband, must not pay with thy body and soul to avenge wrongdoing." She took his hand as they walked toward an effulgent white light that seemed to warm his face and bring Peace to his heart. "You have traveled a long and weary road to come here, and we have spoken of many things, but all of it was to lead you to what you have been searching for."

He stared at her in wonderment. "Forgiveness," he whispered, weeping again. "I must not hate them, but I must do battle with them. I must not, in killing the enemy, murder my own soul."

"Thou art a soldier of God now," she whispered, watching her daughter come between them and take both of their hands. A loud explosion echoed in his ears. "Even now they seek to do thee harm; go now, my love."

"Go, Father," his daughter said, so pretty in her white Spring dress. "I love you."

He picked her up and kissed her tenderly on her cheek and held her fast as another loud explosion ripped near him. "I feel as if," he murmured, looking at her, "I will not see you again."

"You will, Daddy, in your dreams, as it should be; there, we will be with you always," and she kissed him tenderly on his cheek.

He kissed his wife. "I love you so much."

"I love you," she said, wiping away his pious tears. "Now go, and do what must be done," and she smiled as she recited one of his favorite expressions. "And do it famously."

He was standing still upon a flat field of gray- and amber-colored chipped stone, and bullets, much like angry bees, were buzzing around his body, when he suddenly acknowledged his current whereabouts. Immediately, he dashed to the safety of a rising column of rock that shielded him from his shooters, who were a mile from him. "I order you," he shouted, hearing his powerful voice echo in the canyon below, "in the name of the law, to lay down your weapons and surrender." But his last words were drowned out by more paid gunfire. "It's like trying to hit the moon with a rock," he thought, thinking about his opponents' chances of striking him as he pulled out his rifle and readied his extra clips. He could hear car engines starting. "No," he said in a guttural roar, "not this time; it all ends here," and he went around the rock shield and began to run, "today," he shouted, rifle on the ready as he spied his entrance down into the valley of tall trees.

As he ran along the ridge, the eight bodyguards who were north of his position were discharging their weapons at him, but if he stopped to battle them, his quarry, in a black SUV heading east, would once more escape. "I will have to rely on Montoya and Shipper," he decided, as he found his quick exit down to the plains. There, to his immediate right, was a long series of boulders of all sizes and shapes, some together, some apart, some smooth, some jagged, yet all of them forming a long but disjointed, crooked line to the ground below; but it was clear that he, in order to navigate such a hazardous terrain, had to wager his life on his talent for balance and agility and strength. A misstep meant for him perhaps a broken limb or fractured skull, but such a state would not last long as the eight bodyguards would soon come and execute him.

Joaquin never hesitated, and after securing his rifle on his back, he veered sharply to his right, seeing the SUVs on the dirt road that wound toward the stone mountain, and he plunged, with great force, over the steep side.

It was necessary to land with both feet on the first giant boulder, because the drop had been so precipitous it had created too steep an angle to do otherwise; as it was, he landed squarely on his two feet. He took two quick, short steps and jumped to the next boulder, which was nearly at the same level as the first, and landed on his left foot, and then with his right leg, he swung his body out and to the next boulder, which was slightly below the previous one. Bullets swept by him like importunate flies, but he could not think of them now, they meant nothing to him, for it was the treachery of the elliptical, vertical and horizontal, upside-down, right-side-up, curved, misshapen rocks that attracted every ounce of his attention.

His right foot came down smoothly and perfectly upon the glossy, sloping surface of the next boulder, and thus this sequence was initiated and interpolated into his brain, hardwired now into an unbroken rhythm where the body attained perfect symmetry between space and rock and terrain. He popped down and off the boulders with the facile agility of a brawny Bighorn Sheep.

He saw only the boulders, no separate road below, no canopy sky above, although both figures were spliced into the intricate maze inside his mind; and as he sought each proper place to step, whether to place both feet or one, when to take a step, when to merely push off with the foot that had just landed, he still heard no shots in the far distance but just the bullets that sang their wicked song about him. Soon, he had disappeared from the marksmen's sight, and they were forced to get into their cars and drive toward him.

His feet hit the sweet, flat, dirt ground, and he began to run due east to catch a small mound that would allow him to see the seven black SUVs driving swiftly along the winding road. He heard gunfire from both sides of himself, but it was exchanges of gunfire, and he reasoned that Montoya and Shipper had moved in from both sides; but it did not matter now, as he knew what must be done. He unsheathed his rifle.

There, sandwiched in between two big all-wheel drives, behind two more and ahead of another, was Slaughter, in the backseat with a gun to the temple of his small hostage. He only walked point when the danger perceived was minimal; such is the epitaph of all cowards.

Joaquin peeled off the SUV blocking his view of Slaughter by putting two bullets, in quick succession, into its two side passenger tires.

This section of the valley, with its cluster of Redwood trees and Coast Live Oaks and dirt paths, was lit up by the tremendous clamor of battle as both sides fired upon one another. Montoya and Shipper had instructed their men not to fire upon the enemy with hostages; still, this accounted for only one SUV and each remaining one had armed men who were feeling the full firepower of the law.

Joaquin grabbed the bullet that hung around his neck, the very same bullet that had hung around the neck of the Giant but that he had specially reformed into a 7.62 mm cartridge that would fit into his own rifle, and he placed it into the chamber.

In his mind, Joaquin began to strip away every peripheral, nonessential figure from this chaotic scene so that he might focus on the one vehicle now within his grasp; slowly, everything began to dissolve and melt away into the nebulous outer ring of a bright nucleus he had created and where now were fixed two people. He aimed his rifle and poured the great depth of knowledge into what he would see, and once again he saw a man with a gun who was obscured by a coat over his head and that of his victim. Joaquin's body froze and went numb as his loitering memories of anguish rose up to challenge him.

Inside the SUV, Slaughter, peering through an opening in his coat, saw a division of officers in the near distance, approaching his vehicle. "Irony," he said and chuckled, and pointing his gun at his driver, just as the Jeep turned a sharp corner, shot and killed him.

When Joaquin saw the 4 x 4 begin to tumble, he cried from the deepest depths of his being, "No," and time itself seemed to heed his passionate plea. Everything about him except the car and the two passengers inside crystallized into the focal point of his heart and soul and mind; he felt weightless, bodiless, as the SUV turned one rotation, and he saw the tumbling bodies inside, and he saw the jacket loosen from Slaughter, and he saw the clothed shoulder of the girl, and then he raised his Accuracy International sniper rifle. He placed the black hairs of the PM6x42 telescopic sight into the dark confines of the swirling car, and felt as if he were inside it with the moving bodies, as if he could hear their bodies hitting the sides of the vehicle, as if he could hear their desperate cries. He instantly absorbed their rocking motion, adjusting to their tumbling, bumping, banging movement, feeling the flurry of their circular world until his mind stepped into a crystal-clear, fluid stream of images that emitted a constant pattern. Every moment a slightly altered image of the two bouncing bodies appeared to him: a strand of her black hair, a piece of his fleshy earlobe, her nose, his neck—the jacket was dislodged a bit—her forehead, her left arm and right arm and left eyes—the jacket was dislodged more—his right eyes and left ear and nose, until finally, in one vivid, transparent, effulgent blaze of revelation, Joaquin was able to project exactly where the two bodies would be in the next instant.

He stood, in synchronization with the riotous storm within the vehicle, poised to take the shot, and he said, clearly in his mind, even as his crosshairs focused on the rolling figure, his heart a fountain of Truth, "God be with me," and then he squeezed the trigger.

It was a single bullet he sent from his rifle, but then the lucid picture inside the rotating Jeep sank into the debris of disjointed pictures, and the vision was lost; and so he began to run toward the Jeep, which continued to roll over the small clumps of grass and smooth dirt.

He ran, rifle in his right hand, with apprehension of such great proportions that horrors indescribable visited his mind as he crossed the open field of tall green grass. Fear swallowed him whole, and all events great and small, all faces, all emotions, every blink and breath from his personal apocalypse to the gentle Giant to his endless searching to leads and false leads to remembering the horrors of it, all was a swiftly moving kaleidoscope in his mind's eye.

The black Jeep came to rest on its metallic black back, and Joaquin, his face drenched in sweat and agony, ran up to it, rifle out, unable to speak or think or plan. There was now either victory or defeat.

He saw movement under the cover of the green jacket, and at that moment, nothing mattered anymore, for if he had failed, he deserved to die; if she lived, the world was alive again; and thus, this sole idea passed into his mind as he sheathed his rifle. The rest of the battle raging about him did not matter.

A hand wriggled free of the cloak.

Joaquin fell to the brown dirt upon his knees and reached in to take the two reaching hands of Sylvia—Sylvia alive and well, Sylvia who was pulled over the dead body of John Slaughter and into the waiting arms of her rescuer. "Forgiveness," he whispered, weeping, as he held her. A small brown box, which lay at the feet of the dead man, was slightly open, and inside of it were several small vials that contained a red, clear liquid.

"I knew you would come," Sylvia said, as she too wept, her chin upon his sturdy shoulders. She pulled her head back to look at him. "I prayed every night as Mama taught me; I prayed to God to rescue us," but her tears increased, and she could barely speak. "And you did," she said, and her sobs flooded her voice, and she fell back into his strong arms, afraid no more. "I knew you would come," she whispered again, full of pride at her great faith.

He stood up. No more shots were heard.

Shipper and Montoya came running up from opposite directions, their men in tow.

"It's all over," Shipper said, rifle in hand, looking with joy at Joaquin and Sylvia.

"Yes, all of it," Montoya said, rifle in hand, smiling as he looked at the Man and Child.

Joaquin put out his hand and shook the hands of his friends. "Thank you," he said, weeping no longer.

Sylvia whispered in Joaquin's ear, and he let her down. She walked over to Shipper and embraced him, thanked him, and kissed him on his cheek, and she walked over to Montoya, embraced him, thanked him, and kissed him on his cheek. "Thank all of your men for me," she said, smiling, weeping no longer. She turned to look at Joaquin.

He knelt down in front of her, reached into his waistband, retrieved the Winnie the Pooh doll, and handed it to her.

She wept anew as she took it and embraced him once more, and whispered to him, "I love you."

There was one more act to be done, and he knew the route. And then, as if she intuitively knew, she put out her little hand, a gesture of affection, and he took it, and both of them began the walk toward her home.

Ricardo and Jacob began to weep as they watched, in silence, as the two freed prisoners disappeared into the now-safe terrain.

Police business with the Man and Child would simply have to wait.

Promises to Keep

Juanita Chavez walked out of Sylvia's room and stood in front of the red-brick hearth, staring at the brown mantel that held pictures of her four children and her long-dead husband. Any picture of herself she had removed. She moved slowly across the family room and opened the door, looked out at the wispy fog, sighed heavily, and shut it.

"Mama," Carlos said, his lips pursed with anger. "Every day you do the same thing. She is not there, so why do you look?" She merely looked at him as if she were wounded. "Why can't you let go? Why? It has been nearly three years, and nothing, nothing at all. Why, Mama? Why do you kill yourself waiting?" He had decided long ago that by lacerating her with unbridled honesty, she would desist in her false hopes.

She simply stared at him as if she had never heard such abrasive, traitorous talk. "Faith," she whispered.

"Oh, faith," he cried, exasperated, slapping the open palm of his hand against his brown forehead, "and what about the millions of people who die every year? Where is the faith of their family? Do only the 'bad' people die? Many children die every day—innocent children—and their parents have to accept it." He took a step toward her, but he kept a physically safe distance because his volatile words ignited an emotional bonfire between them. His voice became gentler, though still coarse. "You must be strong; you must be strong and accept it. It has been too long; you must let go now, for yourself, for all of us, so that we can live again."

She was a helpless creature now, unable to defend herself, and she could only moan deep inside as she felt the deep, bitter inconsolable hurt of her loss.

Carlos, not able to gain a verbal response from his mother, felt remorse, and he sought to touch her, but to be the one who inflicts the wound and then brings solace painted a distasteful picture inside his heart, and so he stood still.

She looked feeble, worn down, ready to collapse physically and mentally; every day she prayed for the safe return of her daughter, and every day she fought the impulses inside of herself—and the strong pulse of society and its history and logic in such circumstances—that said her beautiful daughter was dead, long dead and buried, and that she, Juanita, was weak and destructive and a bad mother to her living children. She read such pronouncements on the furtive glances of the people in town, and on their collective faces she saw a blistering portrait of accusation against her. "But for what?" she would scream in her mind. "For loving my daughter, for never giving up, for having faith in miracles?"

His voice was softer now, just as a once-sharp steel sword, struck constantly against a boulder, grows weaker. "Mama, I want to believe too; she is my sister." His hands were held out in a supplicating gesture, as if he meant to massage his fervent words into her. "I love her too, but we have to be realistic. Life goes on. She is dead." He had not meant to say it.

"Dead," Juanita echoed, staring still at the majestic fir trees across the road. "Dead." She turned around, her pale face fading. "She is dead to you," she said, and she clutched her chest. "But not to me." Her visage flamed crimson. "She lives," she shouted, "until I know she is dead; yes, yes, Carlos, other innocent children die every day. I know that; do you think I am a fool? I know," she cried, her black eyes narrowed with fury, her face animated with wrath, as she bent over as if in pain, but still looking at her eldest son. "I know your father is dead, but Sylvia…" she said in a guttural tone, standing erect. "They'll have to show me her dead; do you hear me! She lives in my heart; she lives in my dreams, in my thoughts, in my prayers. How can I give up on her?"

Carlos, feeling attacked, ran to the door and opened it wide, showing the slowly lifting fog. "You go ahead and wait, Mama," he shouted. "You run to the door every day and open the door to see if Sylvia is there and waste your life. But for the living," and he pointed to himself and toward the rooms of his brother and sister, "we have to live, now! Living is living, not dying; Mama, please, you're dying! Come back to us now before it is too late." He slammed the door shut.

Juanita walked slowly to the hearth and lovingly gazed at the pictures there. Her voice lost its warmth and embraced rapture. "Do you know why I believe, Carlos? Do you? It is not just because I am a mother; no, this is not the only reason. It is my faith in God, and because He has sent someone to find her and bring her back."

"Oh, Mama, not him again, please! Not that madman who wandered the town for years! He's insane; everybody knows it!"

"You don't know," she shouted, incensed that he would slander the name of the man upon whom her earthly hopes rested. "You don't know him."

"One phone call in all this time from him; one call about a girl in a helicopter, something the police could not even verify! The police have never even said she is still alive! They don't know, Mama, and if they don't know…"

"Stop it," she cried; "just stop it, Carlos." Her face was flushed with agony. "He promised me," she cried, nearly weeping. "He said he would find her," she exclaimed, nearly pleading. "And one day he will come back, and both of them will…"

And then, at that precise moment, her entire body fused into an electrifying receptor that sensed a sole beacon of energy pulsing into her heart. She stood as if one in shock, but in truth, she was embracing the special song of a golden beam of invisible emotion, inhaling the exhilarating fragrance of it, and then, without hesitation, without words, she dashed to the door and opened it to reveal a clear, bright, sunshiny day.

And behold, there stood Sylvia and Joaquin.

"Sylvia," she cried, and she ran out and fell upon her knees and embraced her daughter, kissing her, and weeping.

Carlos and Beatriz and Juan came running out and knelt down around their sister, hugging and kissing her as they too wept.

Joaquin stood on the white cement porch, full of joy, clutching his rifle, admiring the joy of this family; but he felt an intruder now, thinking his job was done, and thus, he turned to leave.

An unmarked car, which had been parked on the opposite side of the street, had two silently weeping men in it who had closely watched this wondrous scene. It began to move.

Juanita, unable to speak, sobbing still as she knelt and embraced her daughter, reached out her hand to touch the arm of Joaquin.

He sought to speak, but could not, such was his surprise. He simply stood there, his mind adrift. He was free, and yet he was not.

Carlos stood up, tears in his eyes, and he held out his hand, whereupon he shook the hand of the man who had delivered his sister from destruction; and then, in perhaps the most sophisticated and mature act of his young life, he put out his hands to take the nylon backpack from the rescuer.

The car halted.

Joaquin looked at the joyous family before him, and behold, Sylvia stood up, in the midst of this inviolate Love, and held out her hand to him. He put out his right hand without any hesitation or thought at all, and he lightly grasped hers. And what would be the fate of the rifle? Carlos reached for it, and he received it and the Allen keys easily.

Juanita and Beatriz and Juan stood up, and then all of them walked to the door; and Joaquin, who was not thinking of anything at all, his mind having been absolved of those things that had consumed him, felt all of it; he felt clean and good and alive, as if he were reborn, as if he was as he once had been so long ago, a state of feeling he had long since forgotten.

Carlos, walking behind them, gazed at the rifle, nodded his head, and placed the Allen keys into the screws.

The car with the two men began once more to drive and slowly disappeared around the corner.

The entire family entered the house, Juan and Beatriz with their arms around their mother and Sylvia, and Sylvia with her hand clutched to the hand of Joaquin, and Carlos slowly dismantling the rifle.

They were a family once more, and Joaquin found what he had been searching for.

The Beginning

www.ingramcontent.com/pod-product-compliance
Lightning Source LLC
LaVergne TN
LVHW091048080826
845145LV00002B/666

* 9 7 8 0 9 8 8 8 1 7 7 3 9 *